THE SPIRIT MOVES

Also by Carol J. Perry

Haunted Haven Mysteries
Be My Ghost
High Spirits
Haunting License
The Spirit Moves

Witch City Mysteries
Caught Dead Handed
Tails, You Lose
Look Both Ways
Murder Go Round
Grave Errors
It Takes a Coven
Bells, Spells, and Murders
Final Exam
Late Checkout
Murder, Take Two
See Something
'Til Death
Now You See It
Death Scene

Anthologies
Halloween Cupcake Murder

THE SPIRIT MOVES

CAROL J. PERRY

Kensington Publishing Corp.
kensingtonbooks.com

KENSINGTON BOOKS are published by

Kensington Publishing Corp.
900 Third Avenue
New York, NY 10022

ISBN: 978-1-4967-4363-3 (ebook)
ISBN: 978-1-4967-4362-6

First Kensington Trade Paperback Printing: June 2025

10 9 8 7 6 5 4 3 2 1

Printed in the United States of America

The authorized representative in the EU for product safety and compliance is eucomply OU, Parnu mnt 139b-14, Apt 123
Tallinn, Berlin 11317, hello@eucompliancepartner.com

For Dan, my husband and best friend

What we place most hope upon, generally proves most fatal.

—Oliver Goldsmith

Note to Readers

The ideas and words in this novel were generated entirely by the author without use of any AI application.

Carol J. Perry is also the author of the Witch City Mystery Series, featuring TV personality Lee Barrett along with some interesting friends and family—including O'Ryan, a clairvoyant gentleman cat; Pete Mondello, police detective and main man; River North, tarot reader and practicing witch; and librarian and techie Aunt Ibby. Their adventures play out in the fascinating old city of Salem, Massachusetts—known the world over as the Witch City.

Carol loves hearing from readers and can be reached at cperry3042@verizon.net, or at facebook.com/caroljperryauthor. Carol's website is at www.caroljperry.com, where you can sign up for her newsletter!

Chapter 1

"Say, Maureen, the couple in the Joe DiMaggio suite—Mr. and Mrs. McKenna—called me again about the perfume smell in the bedroom." Hilda, nighttime desk manager, greeted her boss, Maureen Doherty, the owner/manager of Haven, Florida's historic Haven House Inn, with the first-thing-in-the-morning guest complaint. "They say Mrs. McKenna is allergic and that their labradoodle Snicker won't even go into the bedroom. I've spoken to both housekeepers, and neither Gert nor Molly wears any kind of fragrance when they're working."

"Chanel Number Five again, I suppose." Maureen had heard the perfume smell complaint from that suite before, although not recently. The suite had obtained its name because, according to an old guest register, Joltin' Joe had spent a weekend there back in March of 1961, and it was always one of the most popular suites in Haven House. All of the larger suites bore the famous names of guests who'd once stayed there—including Babe Ruth, Jimmy Stewart, Burt Reynolds, Arthur Godfrey, and Dawn Wells.

The two women, along with Maureen's golden retriever Finn, were alone in the reception area, but still, Hilda looked from side to side and lowered her voice. "None of the newspaper reports said that Marilyn Monroe was with DiMaggio when he stayed here."

Maureen shrugged. "I know. But so many people have smelled her perfume, it kind of makes you wonder, doesn't it?"

Hilda put a finger to her lips. "Yeah, but I'll never tell."

Maureen laughed. "I won't if you won't."

"Woof," Finn agreed.

The possible presence of a long-dead movie star in one of the Haven House Inn's most requested suites was something neither Maureen nor Hilda would discuss in public.

One of the not so well-known features of their charming little city, with its quaint shops, mellow brick-paved sidewalks, and sugar-soft sandy beaches—off the well-beaten path of Florida's giant Orlando attractions—and one carefully guarded by most residents, is the fact that Haven is haunted. Not just a little bit haunted, but unequivocally, indisputably full-on, house-by-house, haunted. Almost every structure in Haven has one or more resident otherworldly beings.

The secret is remarkably well kept. No one in Haven wants the ghost hunters, the big TV shows with all their crazy gadgets—voice recorders, night-vision cameras, along with the mediums and psychics running around town, attracting all kinds of snoops and weirdos to the quiet, peaceful place Haven appears to be.

"What do you say we offer to move them to another suite until we can get theirs properly aired out," Maureen suggested.

"Or until Marilyn decides to move out." Hilda tried to muffle a snicker with her hand. "Let's offer them the Jimmy Stewart suite. It's on the same floor and just as nice."

"Good idea," Maureen agreed. "According to the 1954 guest register, James Stewart stayed here when they were shooting *Strategic Air Command*. He played a third baseman for the St. Louis Cardinals, and they shot a lot of the scenes at Al Lang Field over in St. Petersburg."

"They're obviously baseball fans," Hilda said. "That's why they asked for the DiMaggio suite. They'll love the Cardinals connection."

"I hope so. Maybe we can arrange a trip over to Al Lang Field for them," Maureen suggested, "and we can get them a copy of *Strategic Air Command,* no problem. Aster, down at the bookshop, keeps old Florida movies in stock all the time. On the way back from my beach run, I'll stop and get it for them."

"They've left a wake-up call for six. They're looking forward to trying Ted's Cream Cheese and Strawberry Stuffed French Toast Casserole for breakfast. I'll tell them about the Jimmy Stewart suite. Is Ted running with you this morning?" Hilda managed a casual tone.

"Yes." Maureen's reply was equally casual.

"Woof," offered Finn, straining at his leash as Ted appeared from the nearby dining area.

Maureen and Haven House's handsome executive chef, Ted Carr, along with Finn, often ran together along the nearby beach in the early morning hours. Maureen and Ted each tried hard, but not always successfully, to make it perfectly clear to the Haven House staff that the friendship—including the beach runs—was purely platonic. Of course, that wasn't entirely true. Maureen knew that the bond between them was a strong one, and seemed to grow stronger all the time. There'd even been veiled hints of "marriage someday" and a recent question from Ted about her ring size. Still, the idea of "the boss" being romantically involved with an employee was, to her mind, "inappropriate." Besides that, she wasn't sure what Ted thought about ghosts. It was a taboo subject around Haven, and she surely didn't want to scare him away at this point by telling him that she shared her suite with a particularly lively one.

Ted bent, scratched Finn behind the ears, and greeted the women with a "Good morning," casting an approving glance toward Maureen's matching pink shorts and shirt—part of the wardrobe she'd assembled during her ten-year career as a sportswear buyer in the now-closed Bartlett's of Boston department store. Actually, the ownership of Haven House Inn had come as a total surprise to Maureen when the lawyer's letter had arrived, informing her that she'd inherited the property from the late Penelope Josephine Gray. She'd never heard of Ms. Gray, and had no idea why this had happened, but sure enough, she owned the place—lock, stock, and—ghosts. It had taken a while for Maureen to accept the fact that she was suddenly a property owner. It had taken a little longer to accept the part about the ghosts. She'd never before been a believer in spirits or specters or apparitions or ghosts by any other name.

She'd become a believer, and she also believed in the warm and wonderful feelings that had grown between the handsome cook and herself. Maureen often wondered how Ted unfailingly managed to come directly from the warm, busy, crowded kitchen where he'd just supervised the creation of one of the Haven House's justly famous breakfasts, into the adjoining dining room looking cool, unruffled, and immaculate in shorts and white T-shirt. "Let's go work up an appetite for that special French toast," she said.

"Finn and I will race you to the fishing pier sign," he said, taking the dog's leash.

"You're on," Maureen said. "Hilda, Shelly will be here in a few minutes to relieve you. See you tonight."

"No hurry," Hilda said. "I love my job."

"I love mine too." Ted held the green door open, and Maureen stepped out onto the inn's broad front porch. Even at this early hour, she wasn't surprised to see four of the inn's year-round residents seated in their accustomed rocking chairs at the head of the stairway. Senior citizens George and Sam, Gert and Molly had, more or less, come with the inn. They, along with Ted, had lived there in exchange for work, meals, and a small salary by arrangement with Penelope Josephine. George and Sam worked as handymen and Gert and Molly as housekeepers. Ted was a bartender before Maureen had promoted him to chef. The live-in team had worked out so well that Maureen saw no reason to upset the convivial applecart.

Finn, tail wagging joyously, greeted the foursome—one at a time, with doggy licks and an occasional excited "woof," receiving in exchange loving words, welcome head-scratches, and some hugs and kisses.

"You'd better give this boy a good run," George said. "He's looking a little chubby lately."

Finn shook his head and gave a low "woof."

Maureen frowned. "Do you think so, Ted? Has he been begging for scraps in the kitchen?"

"Most of the staff know better than to feed him anything," Ted promised, "but the new pastry girl, Joyce Beacome, has a hard time resisting his 'starving puppy' face. I'll speak to her about it again." He patted Finn's head. "And no, I don't think he looks chubby."

Gert gave George a playful punch on the arm. "Put your glasses on, old man. You're probably looking down at your own round belly."

"Pastry girl, huh?" Sam rocked forward. "Any specialties?"

"She makes a mean key lime pie," Ted promised, "and she seems to be pretty talented around food in general. I think she's going to be a real asset. Anyway, you'll get to sample the pie later this week." Finn's tug on the leash was more insistent. "Let's go, Maureen." The two followed Finn down the stairs and onto the sidewalk. They began an easy jog toward the beach at the end of the Beach Boulevard, then picked up the pace as they moved onto the hard-packed sand at the water's edge, with the leashed dog in the lead.

Maureen looked up and down the early morning, nearly deserted beach. "Are we still on for that race to the fishing pier sign?"

"Absolutely." Ted grinned. "Ready, Finn?"

"Woof."

She was sure Ted would win the race, but the exertion would be fun anyway. She began with a fast sprint, pink-sneakered feet pounding on white sand. She arrived, out of breath, at the weather-beaten sign advertising Haven's fleet of fishing charter boats. As she'd expected, Ted was already there, leaning against the sign as though he'd been there for hours. Finn, tongue out and panting happily, sat at his feet.

That old sign held special meaning for Maureen. Her parents had taken a picture of her standing in front of it when she was twelve, proudly holding a fish she'd caught. They'd had that fish for dinner, prepared at a nearby restaurant. Oddly enough, Maureen had discovered a print of that same picture in a small gold frame in Penelope Josephine Gray's office. Odder still, Ted had told her that his mother had owned a small restaurant just across from the pier, and that as a youngster, he'd helped with the cooking there. Had Ted cooked that long-ago fish? Strange.

Maureen no longer pondered very much over strange events happening in Haven. The entire journey, from the moment back in Massachusetts when she'd received the lawyer's letter telling her about her inheritance, had been pretty much a series of strange events. She was almost getting used to it.

Chapter 2

The pair ended their run with a few stretches beside the large white building at the head of the boulevard known as the Haven Casino—often the site of trade shows, baby showers, lectures, and other community events.

"You go on ahead, Ted." Maureen reached for Finn's leash. "I know you have a kitchen to oversee. I'm going to stop at the bookshop to pick up an old movie."

"Okay." He handed her the leash, his hand grasping hers for a few extra seconds. "See you at breakfast?"

"I wouldn't miss it." Watching as he jogged easily toward the inn, she headed for the bookshop. Erle Stanley Gardner, the bookshop cat, looked up from where he was snoozing on the round wooden cable reel that served as a table in front of the store. Erle Stanley, who has no fear of dogs, greeted Finn with a pink-tongued lick on the nose. Maureen sat in one of the yellow-painted Adirondack chairs, looped Finn's leash over the arm of the chair, while Aster Patterson waved from the doorway.

"Good morning, Maureen," Aster called. "I've just brewed a pot of that English tea that you like, and I have fresh-baked shortbread cookies too. I'll be out in a jiffy." Aster's gray hair was tucked up under a Guy Harvey visor, and she wore a vintage Tampa Bay Lightning Lecavalier number four jersey with plaid

Bermuda shorts. Aster baked those shortbread cookies every day. Hers was one of the very few un-haunted structures in Haven. The cookies had been the favorites of her late husband, Peter Patterson, and she harbored a sincere hope that they'd guide his spirit home. Carrying a tray with a flower-sprigged china teapot, two cups and saucers, silver-plated sugar bowl and cream pitcher, and a platter of the promised cookies, Aster shooed Erle Stanley off the table and joined Maureen.

"How's business at the inn?" Aster poured tea into flower-sprigged cup, added one lump of sugar with silver tongs, and handed it to Maureen. "It's been a little slow here. I'm looking for some new kinds of sales promotion. I know you're good at that sort of thing because of your work in that big department store up in Boston."

"I'd say the inn business is about normal for this time of year." Maureen accepted the tea and reached for a cookie. *Just one cookie,* she told herself. *I need to leave room for Ted's French toast.* "The book department at Bartlett's of Boston used to run quite a few author book signings that always drew a crowd," she said. "There are a lot of authors in the Boston area, and we used to get some down from New York sometimes too."

Aster pulled an envelope from under a fish-shaped brass paperweight. "Here's a coincidence. This is from a small book publisher about a how-to author named Terry Holiday. He's in Tampa now, and he'll come to Haven if we invite him. He offered to do a signing, and he'll bring his own books."

"That's worth a try for sure," Maureen said. "It won't cost you anything. You might contact some of the local writers' associations too. They'll be happy to find you some authors from around here."

"I'm going to call that publisher today, and sign that guy up," Aster declared. "Besides that, one of those book groups meets here once a week." She glanced at her pink Power Rangers watch. "They'll be here at ten today. They're all mystery writers. They call themselves Murder Incorporated."

"No kidding. Do you sell their books here?"

"Sure."

"There you go. They'd probably love to do a group signing."

"Really? Say, Maureen, do me a favor and drop in on the meeting. See what you think of them. I'd trust your judgment."

"At ten? It sounds interesting. I'll drop Finn off, change clothes, have breakfast, and get things started at Haven House. If there's time, I'll be here," Maureen promised. "But what I came in for is a copy of *Strategic Air Command.* Got one?"

"Sure thing. A good old Jimmy Stewart movie. No problem. You just relax and finish your tea while I ring it up. I'll throw in a bag of shortbread cookies for your front porch crew, okay?"

"More than okay. They'll be thrilled." Maureen stood, paid her bill, picked up Finn's leash, and, carrying two blue Haven Bookshop bags, started down the boulevard toward her inn. The front porch crew were, as expected, happy with the gift of cookies. Molly took charge and divided the round treats into four separate piles, quickly tossing the one leftover cookie into her mouth before anyone could object.

Shelly reported from the reception desk that the folks in the DiMaggio suite had happily agreed to the room swap and were already at breakfast, and that she'd checked in one new guest. "Single fellow," she offered. "One suitcase and a laptop. I put him in the Arthur Godfrey Suite. He says he'll be here for a week or so." She turned the guest book in Maureen's direction. "Nice handwriting." Maureen glanced at the name, agreeing that Carleton Fretham did indeed have a fine hand, and undoubtedly an excellent pen.

"He's already having breakfast too. He's real good-looking. Want to take a look?" Shelly inclined her head toward the dining room entrance.

Maureen laughed. "I'm not in the market, but I'll check him out later." She and Finn climbed two flights of stairs, and Finn gave an excited "woof" and ran, leash dragging behind him, toward what the housekeeping team called "the penthouse"—the only suite at the top of the building. The dog's welcoming "woof" told Maureen that she could expect company behind her door.

The rooms had once been home to Penelope Josephine Gray, and had come not only with some wonderful mid-century modern furniture, but with a pair of senior cats named Bogie and Bacall. Bogie was a big striped tiger cat who looked as if he'd had a tough life before Penelope Josephine had rescued him, with one ear that looked like it was half bitten off. Bacall, on the other hand, was a big cat too, but she was clearly a princess. A registered French Chartreux, she was silvery gray with copper-colored eyes. The suite also came with a resident ghost named Lorna DuBois.

Sure enough, Lorna's shimmering form sat on the long aqua couch. Lorna, in life, had been what was known in the 1930s as a movie starlet, and her glamorous ghost always appeared in black and white, just as she'd appeared in her numerous films. She hugged Finn, then stood and did a model-like turn. "I borrowed this from your closet. Like it?" She wore a black-and-white version of the Hawaiian print tunic Maureen had planned to wear with white pants for the rest of the day.

"Sure. Help yourself. I got it from our new gift shop. I'm going to wear it to a mystery writers' meeting after breakfast." Maureen was accustomed to Lorna's "borrowing." Lorna simply borrowed what she called "the essence" of the item while the real outfit remained in the owner's closet—or maybe in Nordstrom's or Tiffany's window.

"Are you thinking of writing a mystery?" Lorna wanted to know.

"Good heavens, no. I have enough to do already. Aster is thinking about having some writers do book signings at the shop to increase business. She thought I might like to meet some of the local authors. They call themselves Murder Incorporated."

"Murder, huh? That doesn't sound like much fun to me. I'm wearing mine tonight to the Polynesian Fire Luau in Orlando. See you later. Bye, Finn." She began to shimmer away then for an instant, then popped right back. "I don't think you should go. Bad karma."

Chapter 3

Maureen showered and changed into slim white pants and the colorful tunic. Then, carrying the blue bag containing the movie for the McKennas with her, she headed for the dining room and Ted's French toast.

By the time 9:45 rolled around, she'd already approved the day's menus, supervised the room swap, and arranged for George to give the relocated couple the movie, a tour of Al Lang Field with a side trip to Tropicana Field thrown in, agreed that changing Gert's young kitten Jo's name to Joe was a good idea since he'd been assigned the wrong gender at birth, and ordered aerial photos of the inn property for new postcards. She left the inn by the side door and arrived early for the meeting of Murder Incorporated at the bookshop.

The murder mystery group was composed of two men and three women. She recognized several of them as occasional dining customers. Seated at the back of the bookshop's "function room," which was actually Aster's long, comfortably furnished living room, Maureen prepared to take notes of the meeting. Walter Griffith, who was apparently the group's president, announced a critiquing session in which each member would read from a work-in-progress for eight minutes, then listen as the others commented on the story.

After a few readings, Maureen realized that these authors were seriously into the many and varied methods of murdering—and each one of them so far had been extremely detailed in the description of exactly how to do it. *Talk about how-to books,* she thought. *This could be a master class on murder.* After the final reading, president Walter asked if she had any questions.

Maureen thanked them for allowing her to sit in on the meeting, then asked how they'd feel about getting together with Aster to plan a group book signing. The answers were all positive. "Aster plans to invite a nonfiction writer too," Maureen told them. "He writes how-to books. It'll be a nice change-up from the mysteries."

"Terry Holiday," a youngish blonde spoke up. "We know all about him."

"We sure do, Lynn Ellen." A chorus of negative words and a few unpleasant sounds followed.

"That hack!"

"A self-promoting clown!"

"He has to beg for invitations!"

"All of his books have been big flops!"

Maureen held up both hands. "Slow down! How bad can he be?"

"The last one was *One Hundred Ways to Bathe without Leaving a Ring around the Bathtub*. Three hundred pages." The speaker, an attractive, tall, model-slim woman with short, dark hair, scoffed. "Absolutely awful."

"You've got that right, Elaine," said a tanned man with tattooed, muscular arms. "The one before that was *How to Teach Your Wife the Proper Way to Do Everything*. You can imagine how well received that was!"

Maureen smothered a laugh and consulted her notes again. "The title of the new one is *How to Make Your City Famous and Attract Big Spenders*. I guess you'd all recommend that he shouldn't be invited to Haven."

"I think he should be shot."

"No, he should be poisoned!"

"He needs to be strangled."

"String him up!"

Chilling suggestions were delivered rapid-fire from virtually all of the members of the group. Even more chilling in Maureen's mind was the fact that none of them was smiling. She attempted to lighten the mood by promising that she'd be at their first signing and that she'd advertise the event to the inn's guests.

She stopped on the way out to thank Aster for inviting her to the meeting. "They're an interesting group," she said—honestly. "They're all looking forward to doing a book signing together."

"So is Mr. Terry Holiday!" Aster was all smiles. "I called to invite him, and he agreed right away to come next Friday. I've met him before. He comes into the shop fairly often, and he's been known to peek in the window when the mystery writers have their meetings. I'd barely hung up when his representative arrived with a dozen of his books." She pointed to an open box. "Mr. Holiday even promised to stop by later today to sign them!" She held up a book with a bright yellow cover. "Want to buy one? You can bring it to the signing next Friday for his autograph—or maybe come back later after he's signed these."

The book club members had followed her from the living room into the shop. "I'll take one of those," one of them announced. "I don't need his autograph. I just want to post the usual one-star review."

"I'll have one too," said another of the Murder Incorporated group. Before long, all five of the group members had bought the book, proving "verified purchases" for premier review sites. It appeared to Maureen that Terry Holiday was about to experience several unpleasant early reviews.

"How bad can it be?" Maureen thought as she reached for her wallet. "I guess I'll have one too, Aster," she said. "Maybe you'll have a best-seller!"

"I know," Aster said. "I even had a couple of walk-ins who bought them right after I opened the box. The bright yellow cover must attract them."

"Or the title," Maureen offered. "Making your city famous and attracting big spenders is an idea that has a lot of appeal too."

"Whatever it is, I like it," Aster declared. "Thanks for the idea, Maureen. My business has picked up already—and I can hardly wait for next Friday."

Maureen said goodbye to the lingering mystery writers, inviting them to visit the inn's dining room and gift shop soon, and with her purchase in the bookshop's trademark blue bag under her arm, she paused to say hello to Erle Stanley, snoozing in the morning sunshine on the table in front of the shop. She stepped onto the brick sidewalk, just as the 1998 Ford Crown Victoria pulled to a stop beside her.

"You thinking of taking up murder mystery writing, Ms. Doherty?" called a familiar voice.

"Good morning, Officer Hubbard." Maureen smiled and shook her head. "Not me. I'm not a writer. Just visiting."

Frank Hubbard, Haven's top cop, leaned from the window of the vintage police car. "That's good. I like to keep an eye on any group that calls themselves Murder Incorporated. It sounds subversive to me. Glad you're not a part of it." He dropped his voice, leaning closer. "Have you got any feelings about that bunch?"

Maureen had become acquainted with Hubbard because she'd—quite coincidentally—been connected to a few suspicious deaths within the small community, and he'd become convinced that because she'd been helpful to him in solving the crimes, she had some sort of special "feelings" about such things.

"No feelings," she insisted. "They sure write some creepy stuff, though."

He pointed to the blue bag. "So did you buy one of their books?"

"No." She slid the top of the bright yellow book from the bag. "It's a how-to book. Strictly nonfiction."

"Oh. Well, have a nice day, Ms. Doherty." He sounded disappointed as he pulled away from the curb.

"Good day to you too, Officer." She waved in his direction and continued along the boulevard, quickening her pace as she concentrated on her "things to do" list for the rest of the day. First of all, she'd have George hook up the ozone machine in the DiMaggio suite. She'd purchased the odor-eliminating generator as soon as she'd learned that not every guest—nor even every ghost—obeyed the strict No Smoking rule. Not every guest was bothered by Chanel No. 5 either, but it seemed prudent to eliminate the problem whenever it occurred. Next on the list was a project she'd been putting off for a while. Among the possessions Maureen had inherited with the inn was a large trunkful of memorabilia assembled by her benefactor, Penelope Josephine Gray. Ms. Gray had apparently been a saver of everything. She'd been a downright, out-and-out, absolute hoarder—and Maureen had inherited not just a vintage inn, but a king-sized storage locker full of things the old woman had deemed "too good to throw away." Ms. Gray had, according to the director of the Haven Museum, intended to use the materials in the trunk to write a book. This would be a good time, Maureen felt, to begin to catalog the contents. Maybe there actually was enough material in the trunk to inspire a book about Haven. She'd already discovered several topics of historical interest in it, and she'd barely disturbed the very top layer of packed papers. "Maybe," Maureen thought, "just maybe, I could be the one to put together Penelope Josephine's story. It would be a way of expressing my thanks to her for the gift of my wonderful inn."

She recalled the recent brief conversation with Frank Hubbard about her "taking up writing." *It most definitely won't be a murder mystery.*

That "things to do" list didn't leave her a lot of extra time, but after lunch, she allowed herself half an hour in her office—with the door open so that she could keep an eye on the reception desk—to open the aged steamer trunk for another look at the contents of Penelope Josephine's trunk.

She reached into the bottom drawer of her desk, pulling out the jangling ring of keys that had come with the inn. She searched for the small, squatty key marked with the number 178—matching the numbered lock—poked it into the keyhole, turned it, and lifted the lid. Maureen had come to like the distinctive smell arising from the contents. *Old papers, like a closed-up library maybe,* she thought, *and something else—like fall leaves up in Massachusetts, and salt water.*

She'd already learned that the tightly packed contents had made paper items especially fragile. Very gently, she lifted a yellowed newspaper page, revealing beneath it a remarkably intact piece of sheet music. "The Dwarf's Marching Song," she read aloud. "Heigh-Ho." A Disney illustration in pastel tones showed Snow White and the Dwarfs. "This will look right at home on the old player piano in the bar," she told herself, picturing it opened up on the rail just above the keyboard. She couldn't wait to see it.

The instrument in question, a vintage Haines Brothers player piano with matching bench, gleamed from a recent polishing. It was pre-programmed to play piano roll versions of thirties and forties tunes while the keys moved up and down. "Ain't Misbehavin'" plinked in the background as though played by invisible fingers. Maureen had come to realize that from time to time, the ghostly fingers of Billy Bedoggoned Bailey, who'd long ago played piano in that very room, actually *did* tickle those well-preserved ivories with song choices of his own. His occasional impromptu performance of the 1980s hit song "Maureen" let her know when he was around.

She lifted the thing from the trunk; then, closing the lid, she carried the sheet music in front of her with thumb and forefingers of both hands. She left the office, feeling only the slightest pang of guilt for leaving the reception area unattended, considering the seasonal dearth of customers lately, and hurried through the dining room to the bar area.

"Got something for you, Billy Bedoggoned Bailey," she whispered to the long-dead musician. She debated whether to position the sheet open, the way it would look if Billy was reading the music, or closed so that the cute illustration showed. Deciding that Billy could probably play it by ear anyway, she opted for the Disney drawing, then stood back to admire the effect.

"So there you are, Ms. Doherty." That familiar voice again, but this time, Frank Hubbard's tone had an urgency that hadn't been present in their earlier encounter. "I presume you haven't heard the news."

"News?"

"There was a death in Haven this morning. A fellow named Terry Holiday turned up dead about half an hour ago. Aster Patterson found him in her petunia garden out behind the bookstore. We're looking now for next of kin. You know anything about that? Any feelings?"

"I'm sorry to hear it," she said, surprised that she *hadn't* already heard about it and somewhat annoyed that Hubbard was here, talking about her so-called feelings about death. "Is Aster all right?"

"Oh, come on, Doherty. You bought his book this morning. I saw it. You must have had feelings."

"Is Aster all right?" she repeated. "Finding a body is very upsetting." Maureen knew that to be true from unfortunate personal experience.

"She's not too shook up about it." He looked from side to side and dropped his voice to a near whisper. "Aster says that the ghost of her dead husband led her to it."

Chapter 4

It hadn't taken more than a few minutes after Hubbard's feeling-seeking visit that her housekeeping crew had burst through the front door to tell her about the sudden departure of the author. They had a few more details to share too, some circumstances that Haven's top cop hadn't mentioned. For instance, Gert said that she'd heard that the man had been strangled with a piece of heavy cord. Sam said that he'd bet it was the kind he'd helped Aster with when she'd tied up her Kentucky Wonder pole beans. George offered that over at the Quic Shop, the word was going around that some of the mystery writers had been at the bookstore and that the cops were questioning one of them. "Yeah," Molly agreed. "Someone had overheard the woman say that Holiday should be strangled."

"One of the writers did say that," Maureen acknowledged, remembering the slim dark-haired woman. "I heard her, but nobody took it seriously."

"You actually heard somebody say that about Holiday?" Sam wanted to know. "Weren't you shocked? Or at least surprised?"

"Not really. I don't know what surprises me the most about the whole thing. Is it the fact that Terry Holiday was found dead in Aster's petunia garden"—she looked around the lobby and, seeing that they were alone, whispered—"or that Aster told Frank Hubbard that Peter Patterson's ghost led her to the body?"

"Peter Patterson's ghost finally came home?" Gert forgot to keep her voice low, and clapped both hands over her mouth.

"Shhh!" Molly commanded. "You know the rules about that around here."

"Nobody heard me," Gert alibied. "But if Peter is home, does that mean we don't get free cookies anymore?"

"I'll bet it does," Sam grumbled. "Everybody is hooked on them by now, so she'll probably start selling a bunch of them."

"Maybe the new pastry lady can make shortbread cookies," George suggested.

"Shoot!" Molly interjected. "Anybody can make shortbread cookies. What was so special about Aster's was that she baked them for Peter. It's the sweet intention that makes them better than just plain old cookies you can probably get in a cellophane package at the Quic Shop."

"Molly's right," Gert agreed. "We should keep eating Aster's cookies even if we have to pay for them."

"Not to worry," Maureen assured them. "I'll make sure that Aster's cookies will be available at Haven House. I'll go out to the kitchen right now and ask Ted to put some on the lunch table every day. He can use one of Penelope Josephine's big glass cookie jars."

George halfway hid his mouth behind one hand and stage-whispered, "Maureen will use any excuse to go out to the kitchen to see her sweetie." Sam laughed aloud, and the two women didn't try to mask their giggles.

Maureen felt her cheeks coloring but didn't try to deny George's observation. She wondered why she and Ted tried so hard to keep the growing relationship under wraps—when clearly everybody on the staff knew the two were "an item," and undoubtedly wondered why they weren't sharing a bed as well as the morning runs on the beach. Ted was undoubtedly wondering the same thing. The urge was there, no doubt, for both of them. They'd shared some stolen moments, some much more than friendly kisses, but since Ted's room was on the same floor as the rest of the live-in staff, and since Maureen shared her suite with a ghost who might shimmer into view unannounced at any moment, opportunity for sleepovers had so far been non-existent.

Ignoring the knowing looks and more than one silly smirk from the rocking chair quartet, Maureen headed back into the lobby, through the dining room and on to the kitchen door. Looking through the glass panel to be sure no one was coming the other way, she pushed the door open and made her way past the refrigerator and freezer to the narrow space everyone called "Ted's office." Ted wasn't at his desk, but he spotted her entrance from his post at the salad counter. "Hi, Maureen," he called. "I'll be right with you. Have a seat."

She pulled the folding chair closer to the desk and acknowledged his invitation with a smile and a wave, appreciating once more the efficiency with which he managed the kitchen—including the staff, the preparations, and the consistently good quality of the food.

Not unexpectedly, several members of the kitchen crew paused in their work, eyes following Ted as he joined her at the makeshift office desk. They were clearly not being fooled about the boss/employee relationship any more than the porch gang was. They were undoubtedly encouraged in their suspicions when Ted grasped her hand in his as soon as he sat down, pulling his chair even closer to hers.

"What's up, sweetheart?" His voice was low, almost caressing. She hoped she wasn't blushing when she answered.

"Gert and Molly and the guys are concerned about what will become of Aster's cookies now that Peter has apparently come home," she explained. "They've become spoiled by the free cookies. I've promised them that Haven House will stock them every day. I wonder if you can dig up some of Penelope Josephine's big glass cookie jars to display them."

"My whole kitchen crew is gossiping nonstop about this Peter's ghost nonsense. No problem about the cookies though.

Everybody likes them. Did you know a lot of weddings these days are featuring cookie tables?"

"I've heard about that. Here's a thought. Maybe we should advertise that we can create cookie tables for weddings here in Haven. Joyce can make some of her own pastry specialties, and we'll include Aster's along with hers."

He reached with his free hand and touched her face gently. "Here's another idea. We could start with our wedding."

Had she heard him correctly? Was he joking? She stared into his eyes. "Is that a proposal?"

"It's not the official one I had in mind—like when I pick up your ring at Jimmy the Jeweler's and get down on one knee, but yeah, it's kind of a rehearsal for a proposal." It was his turn to redden a little. "Do you have an answer ready?"

"I do," she said. "I mean yes."

"Do I get to kiss you in front of everybody now?" He leaned forward. Eyes serious.

"I don't think it will shock anybody here." She leaned toward him. It was a long, sweet, memorable kiss. They shouldn't have been surprised by the burst of applause.

Chapter 5

"Gert and Molly were up here cleaning your place," Lorna announced from the couch where Finn leaned on—or more or less into—her knee. "I guess you and the cute cook were smooching it up down in the kitchen. They're both wondering if you two are sleeping together." She raised perfectly arched eyebrows. "Are you?"

Maureen hesitated for an instant. "No. It's complicated."

"Complicated? Why? He's a man. You're a woman. Pushing thirty-seven. You're not getting any younger, by the way."

"Thanks." Maureen sighed. "It's a matter of opportunity. He lives in a first-floor room between Sam's and George's. And I? I live with a ghost who's apt to pop in and out at any moment."

"Does he see us?"

"See who?"

"Us. Ghosts. Some do and some don't. You do. Gert does and Molly doesn't. Does Ted see us?"

"I don't know," Maureen said, wondering. "Now that you mention it, he told me once that he wished he could see the ghost that's supposed to haunt the bar. The woman they call Absinthe. I've even seen her once, myself, but I didn't tell him that. A lot of people claim to have seen her there at the end of the bar, and he's never seen her at all."

"I know her. The Goth chick. Dresses in all black and drinks that green stuff. He's never seen her?" Lorna shook her head. "She's there just about every night. Wicked show-off. Chances are he wouldn't be able to see me either." Lorna gave a shimmery wink of one long-lashed eye. "Want me to test him?"

"Yes. No. I don't know. How would you do it?"

"Easy," the ghost replied. "I'll just hang out with him until he's alone somewhere, then I'll materialize. I'll know by his reaction whether he sees me or not."

"See, that's just it," Maureen complained. "You can pop in and out at will. I mean you could be in my bedroom, and I wouldn't know you were there unless you decided to pop in."

"That's nuts. The only interest I have in your bedroom is your closet, and I only look in there when you're not around. Anyway, lately the shop is way more interesting, clothes-wise."

"I believe you," Maureen reluctantly admitted. "So okay, go ahead and 'ghost-test' him. Let me know what happens."

"Of course." Lorna stood, leaving Finn's surprised muzzle hovering above the edge of the couch. "I'll get started right away."

"Don't forget, Gert can see you," Maureen warned. "She works in the kitchen sometimes, and it won't do to have her notice you there."

"I'll wait 'til he's alone," Lorna repeated. "Don't worry. I know what I'm doing. I've been a ghost for a long time."

"I know. Since nineteen seventy-five. You were sixty-five years old doing Summer Stock at the Haven Playhouse. You tripped over an electrical cord and fell into the prompter's box."

Lorna took up the story. "Yep. Broke my darned neck and died on the spot. I was staying here at the Haven House, and all my clothes and stuff were here, so I decided to stay." Maureen knew that the reason Lorna looked much younger than sixty-five was because ghosts get to come back at their favorite age. In Lorna's case, that was twenty-eight. "I really like living here." Lorna pouted prettily. "Promise you won't evict me."

"Evict you? I didn't know I could. How does that work?"

"Forget I mentioned it," Lorna insisted. "It's complicated. Very complicated."

"Woof!" Finn agreed.

"I'm sure we can figure this out, without evicting anybody," Maureen said. "First, let's find out if my almost-fiancé sees ghosts."

"I'm on it!" Lorna popped out, then popped right back in. "What does 'almost fiancé' mean?"

"He sort of proposed today."

"Sort of? What does *that* mean?"

"It's complicated. Very complicated."

"Woof woof," Finn agreed.

"He's going to make it official. Ring, bended knee. All that."

"When?" Maureen shrugged. "I don't know. Soon, I think."

"Good. You're not getting any younger."

Maureen rolled her eyes. "Yeah. You already told me that."

"Okay then." Lorna began her shimmering exit routine. "I'll let you know what happens."

"Thanks, Lorna. Meanwhile, I've got an inn to run." As soon as Lorna had fully disappeared, Maureen filled Finn's special snack bowl with healthy treats, promising that she'd be back for his four o'clock walk.

"Woof," Finn objected. "Woof woof woof." He raced for the kitchen door and pulled his leash from its hook.

"You want to come and help me run my inn?" Maureen laughed. "Why not? We're pet friendly here." She attached the leash to his collar, paused to say hello to Bogie and Bacall, who watched from their individual perches on the cat tower, and left the suite.

Still smiling from the memory of Ted's "almost proposal," and the very satisfying kiss that had come with it, she took the elevator down, sniffing the air as usual for any traces of pipe tobacco. Finn raised his nose and sniffed too. Happily, she found none and passed the nearly empty dining room, admiring the new sheet of old music on the player piano, where the keys plinked out a lively version of "Tangerine." She greeted

Shelly, part-time waitress and all-around helpful employee, at the reception desk.

Once back inside her office, she removed Finn's leash and sat at her desk, making room for the golden to crawl under it, his head resting on her foot. She tapped the bright yellow cover of the book she'd so recently purchased from Aster, then pushed it toward the back of the desk. She hadn't looked inside the slim volume yet, even though Frank Hubbard seemed to think that just because she'd bought it, she had some kind of "feelings" about Terry Holiday's unfortunate death by strangulation.

All feelings aside, it was certainly possible—even probable—that the yellow book *did* have something to do with it. Once again, she reached for the book. This time, she opened it, flipped past the copyright notices and publisher's information, and concentrated on the page headed Chapter 1.

Who wouldn't want to live in a place—large or small—town or country—where others want to visit or stay, and most important, where others want to spend money—lots of it!

So the book, titled *How to Make Your City Famous and Attract Big Spenders*, began.

"I can relate to that," Maureen said aloud. "Haven could benefit from an influx of money. Anyway, the Haven House Inn sure could." Obviously, any small business just about anywhere would agree, she decided, and read further.

Every town or city is unique, and each and every one of them has something—some wonderful thing—that few other places have. Does your city have an excellent beach? Treasure Island in Florida hosts a sand sculpting competition every year that attracts visitors worldwide. Gloucester, Massachusetts dubs itself "the whale watching capital of the world" and a fleet of boats devoted to taking parties out into the Atlantic to see the magnificent creatures in their natural habitat has developed into a brand new industry for the old fishing city. Minot, North Dakota is known as "Magic City" commemorating its remarkable growth in a short time. The State Fair held in Minot, features big name country artists, spectacular auto events and NPRA bull riding and rodeo and draws upward of 300,000 people every year.

"Yes. I get it," Maureen thought. "Treasure Island has always had the sand, and Gloucester has always been visited by the great whales, and people in Minot have always loved all things country. They simply figured out new ways to use what's been there all along."

She closed the book. It had given her enough to ponder already, and she was just at the beginning of the text. It was certainly not badly written as she's been led to expect by the negative comments she'd heard about his previous books. She looked up at the old map of Haven over her desk. Haven had oceanfront, good beaches, a bird sanctuary, a lush forest, and even some historic Indian mounds.

"Florida is full of attractions," she said aloud. "They have a great State Fair over in Tampa every February, and Treasure Island owns the sandcastle gig. We already do an annual King Fishing tournament here in Haven. Sometimes it seems as if the thing people like best about us is that we're so laid back, so old-fashioned, that they can just relax here."

"WOOF," Finn proclaimed from under the desk.

She reached down and scratched behind his ear. "Haven is a dog-friendly place."

She sat bolt upright and said it again, louder. "Haven is a dog-friendly place!"

Chapter 6

"Brilliant!" She bent and kissed Finn on the nose. "You are totally brilliant!"

"Woof!" Finn agreed.

Shelly spoke from the reception desk in the lobby. "Are you talking to me?"

"Oops. Sorry. No. I'm talking to Finn. He just gave me a great idea."

"The dog?" Shelly laughed. "What did he say?"

"He reminded me that we're dog-friendly."

"I know," Shelly said, "and people really appreciate that. It's great that they can bring their dogs on vacation with them."

Maureen closed her office door, and she and Finn joined Shelly in the lobby as Maureen continued. "It seems to me that all of Haven is pretty much dog-friendly. We are, of course, and most of the restaurants have outdoor seating where they're welcome."

"You're right," Shelly agreed. "It's kind of a big deal around here, isn't it?"

"I'm thinking up a way to make it even a bigger deal." Maureen reached again for the yellow book. "I'm thinking of new ways to promote Dog-Friendly Haven that could 'make our city famous and attract big spenders.'"

"Wow," Shelly said. "Big spenders sounds good to me. Big spenders usually mean big tips. Especially at the bar. That reminds me. Are George and Sam still working on the Tiki bar for outdoors?"

"Yes. It's coming along. When they get the thatched roof done, we can start moving some of the wicker chairs and bamboo tables out there." Maureen smiled. "One of the previous owners or managers of the inn must have had a great fondness for them."

"Or a good friend in the wicker chair business," Shelly offered.

"Woof."

"Yes, Finn, the Tiki bar will be pet-friendly too," Maureen promised. "We'll have a special night for dogs so the guests' pups can get acquainted with each other." She laughed. "We can call it 'Yappy Hour.'"

"Brilliant." Shelly offered a high-five.

"I know." Maureen raised her hand to meet Shelly's. "And it was all Finn's idea."

"I'll go outside and see how the work on the Tiki bar is coming along," Shelly announced. "I can hardly wait to get Yappy Hour started."

Shelly headed for the side door exit just as Officer Hubbard pushed the green front door open and stalked, grim-faced, to the reception desk. He had a copy of the same yellow book Maureen had just read from in his hand. He placed it, with much more force than necessary, on top of the guest register. "I found the deceased's next of kin," he said. "A daughter. It wasn't easy. Terry Holiday wasn't even his real name. He used some kind of 'nomdy plomy.'"

"*Nom de plume,*" Maureen corrected. "A pen name. Lots of writers do."

"Apparently all of those Murderers Incorporated writers knew it wasn't his real name. His name was Trenton Hamburger. Same initials. Better-sounding name for a writer. Why didn't you tell me that?"

"Because I *didn't* know it."

"Oh." His expression softened. "Then you probably didn't know that for this book . . ." He poked a finger at his copy of *How to Make Your City Famous and Attract Big Spenders*. "For this book, he used a ghostwriter. He didn't even write the damned thing! His daughter told me so when she gave me the book."

"So who wrote it?" Maureen wondered aloud. "It's actually pretty good."

"Nobody seems to know—or nobody wants to tell me. The daughter doesn't know. Even Aster claims she doesn't know, and all of the creepy writers say the same thing." He dropped his voice and glanced around the lobby. "I guess you realize that Aster's entire backyard, including the potting shed, is a crime scene now. I've taped the whole area. I've already questioned Aster, even though she's probably too short and small to have killed a grown man like Holiday. Doherty, as soon as the medical examiner over in Clearwater releases the body, Trenton Hamburger's daughter Hannah will make funeral arrangements. When it's announced, will you do me a favor and go to the service? See if you get any feelings about it from anybody there?"

He was talking about those imaginary feelings again. Maureen decided that there was no point in denying for the umpteenth time that she didn't have "feelings" about murder and never had. Anyway, her curiosity was aroused. "If it's not a private service, I'll go," she promised. "It would help if I knew what I'm supposed to be looking for. The newspaper hasn't had much information. They say the murder weapon was a piece of 'strong cord.' Was it the cord Aster used to tie up her pole beans?"

"How do you know that?" he snapped. "There was a whole coil of it in Aster's potting shed."

"Sam told me," she said. "And the Quic Shop crew knew all about you questioning the Murder Inc. writers. Besides, I was one of the witnesses that heard a writer say he should be strangled."

"See what I mean? Sometimes those feelings of yours help you find answers before I get them. Help me out on this one, Doherty. First, I need to know who the ghostwriter is."

Exasperated, Maureen had no ready reply to the request. The conversation was interrupted when Gert burst through the front door into the lobby, with Molly close behind her. "You're not going to believe this!" she shouted. "Peter Patterson is back at the bookstore! I mean his ghost is there!"

"Yes, of course. We know. Don't worry about the cookies. We'll buy them from Aster." Maureen was puzzled. Everybody in Haven knew by now that Aster's bookstore was no longer without a ghost, and most people shared Aster's happiness about her beloved Peter's return.

"No. You don't get it. He's really there. I saw him myself. So did Molly." She pulled her friend by the hand. "Tell her, Mol. Tell her. You saw him too."

Molly's eyes were wide. "Oh, it's Peter all right," she gasped. "My first ghost! Right in the window of the bookshop. Big as life. He looks good, too. Younger. Thinner."

Lorna says ghosts get to come back at their best age.

Hubbard frowned. "You both saw him?"

"Everybody saw him. We came back to tell the boys," Gert said. "They're on the way down there now. You two go see for yourselves."

"We'll watch the desk," Molly said. "Go ahead. He's drawing quite a crowd."

"I'd better get down there and see what the hell is going on." Hubbard tucked the book under his arm. "Patterson's ghost. Sure! When will people figure out that there's no such thing! Damned foolishness." The front door slammed behind him.

Maureen didn't hesitate. She handed Finn's leash to Gert. "Will you watch Finn?"

"Sure. I'd better check with Ted too," she said. "I'll let him know what's going on."

I should have thought of that.

Maureen started for the front door. She heard the siren of Hubbard's cruiser. All of the rocking chairs were empty, including George's and Sam's. She hurried down the steps and onto the sidewalk and joined the parade of people heading toward the Haven Bookshop.

Chapter 7

There was quite a crowd assembled outside the Haven Bookshop. There were even a few people standing on top of the round table on the patio in front of the store—craning their necks to get a better look at the shop's large front window. Maureen finally wiggled her way through the excited throng close enough to get a glimpse of what was going on. She blinked a few times, shaded her eyes against the sun, closed them, then opened them wide.

Unbelievably, Peter Patterson sat there in a straight-backed kitchen chair, Erle Stanley curled up in a sleepy ball at his feet. He looked much the way Maureen remembered him, when he'd helped Aster around the store. She hadn't known him well. He was a quiet man and had kept to himself most of the time. Yet, there he was, on display before half the town, even though everybody knew he'd been dead for years.

"It's a trick," a man next to Maureen proclaimed loudly. "It's a hologram of some kind."

"Sure it is," said another. "Aster's playing a trick—and it's not a funny one. Disrespectful of a wife who's supposed to be grieving, I'd say."

The man in the window, who certainly appeared to be Peter Patterson, seemed to be making eye contact with some of the people in the growing audience. A brief smile flickered across the man's face, and he bent to stroke the snoozing cat.

"He looks like he's having a good time, doesn't he, Ms. Doherty?" Sam had reached her side.

"He does," she agreed. *Is it really Peter's ghost, or is it a trick?* Maureen felt conflicted. She'd read a lot lately about AI creations that look exactly like celebrities. They sometimes show the rich and famous doing things they'd never done—sometimes very naughty things. She believed wholeheartedly in ghosts, and she also understood the principles behind holograms. AI was fairly new, but celebrity holograms had been around for quite a while. Maureen remembered seeing Celine Dion perform a duet with an Elvis hologram on *American Idol* in 2008. But to be standing here in Haven, seeing a deceased neighbor petting his cat in the picture window of his house, was quite something else.

"It's a pretty good trick," Sam whispered. "How'd Aster do it?"

"Well, it *could* be some kind of AI manipulation, I suppose, but *if* it's a hologram, it would be pretty involved and quite expensive for Aster to do," Maureen explained. "Basically, you need angled glass and a pretty powerful color laser to project what looks like a 3D image."

"You don't think Aster is doing this?" Sam sounded doubtful.

"If that's not Peter's ghost"—she pointed to the window, where Peter was now eating a cookie—"somebody with a lot of technical know-how is trying to fool us."

The man who'd proclaimed it a hologram earlier spoke up again. "Ad agencies use it all the time. If you've got enough money, you can have Elvis playing a guitar on the beach to advertise your automobile dealership or have Michael Jackson moonwalk through your commercial for furniture."

By this time, Frank Hubbard had parked the cruiser, lights still flashing, and had pushed his way to the window, arms upraised. "Okay everybody, show's over," he shouted. "Move along. Go home now. You're all disturbing the peace. I'm going to start arresting people."

A ripple of laughter ran through the crowd while Peter's ghost—or Peter's hologram, whichever it was—stood up, saluted in Hubbard's direction, and slowly walked away from the chair and out of sight. Within seconds, Erle Stanley followed.

"Aster must be doing it for sure," Sam insisted. "She's right inside the store, listening to what the cop said. She doesn't want us to get arrested."

It made sense. Maureen knew Aster as a law-abiding person who wouldn't want any harm to come to her neighbors. But if it was Aster, where had she learned the necessary technology to pull this Peter-sighting off so perfectly? Was her desire to have Peter Patterson's ghost return great enough for her to have achieved what had just transpired on Haven's main street?

She moved away from the window, which now looked as it had earlier, with a display of recent mystery books and a sign advertising current movies and CDs.

Maureen joined the reluctant gathering of people leaving the area as Hubbard had firmly instructed under threat of imminent arrest.

Can he really do that?

Maybe more importantly, she thought, could Aster Patterson have somehow pulled off the quite spectacular impression of a ghostly visit that she, and much of Haven, had just personally witnessed? She needed to learn a lot more about holograms and artificial intelligence or whatever modern magic could produce such amazing things.

Gert was at the reception desk when Maureen returned, anxious to hear her reaction to what she'd seen. "Well, what do you think? Is that Peter Patterson's ghost, big as life, sitting in the window or what?"

"Maybe it's a case of 'or what'?" Maureen admitted. "Some of the people there think it's some kind of hologram." She knelt to accept Finn's happy doggy kisses.

"Like the ones where you can pay to go see a live concert from a band that doesn't exist anymore?" Gert asked. "They've got those things for bands that I really saw live when I was working in Las Vegas." She smiled broadly at the memory. "Those were the good old days. I think the Peter Patterson thing is some kind of fancy trick, though for Aster's sake, I wish he'd really come back to her."

"I feel kind of the same way," Maureen told her. "Thanks for watching over the inn. Any new business?"

"Just that one new check-in and a few early arrivals for dinner. They're in the bar talking about Peter's ghost. I told Ted what was going on down there, and now he's doing bartending duty, hearing all about it. I'm pretty sure he doesn't believe for a minute that it's really Peter."

"Thanks, Gert, for all you do."

"No big deal. I love living here. We all do. Molly took Finn for a walk while you were out, and the boys have gone to see a guy about carving some Tikis for the new bar."

"I'm working on some special plans for that bar," Maureen said.

"I know. Shelly told us about Yappy Hour. Everybody loves the idea."

News travels at warp speed in Haven.

Even with the rapid dissemination of information within the boundaries of the small city, Maureen wondered about the comparative lack of information about the recent murder of the author of the how-to book.

"A length of rope, a roomful of mystery writers—each with vocalized ideas on *how* to kill him, and the hoped-for return of a dead husband adds up to . . . what?" she wondered. "Even the police chief is casting around to a person like me for a 'feeling' about the sad situation. If there is a suspect, the name hasn't reached the Haven gossip grapevine yet."

When Ted appeared at the dining room entrance, Maureen's thoughts took an abrupt turn to happier ones—like shared kisses and talk of marriage. At the same time, she couldn't help wondering if he'd picked up anything new or interesting while doing bartending duty. People in bars often share information more freely than they might under more structured circumstances.

"Hi," she said.

"Hi, yourself." He moved toward her, his eyes focused on hers. "Got a minute?"

Maureen glanced at Gert. "Can you stay at the desk for a while?"

"Sure. No problem." Gert's grin was mischievous. "Finn and I can take care of things here."

"Woof." Finn waited for Ted's scratch behind the ears, then lay down behind the desk at Gert's feet. *On* one of her feet, actually.

"Want to go outside and see how the Tiki bar is coming along? The thatched roof looks good." He waved a hand in the direction of the side door. Maureen knew that George and Sam had gone in search of a Tiki carver. The bar-to-be would provide a reasonably private spot to spend "a minute." It would be for conversation only, of course. No shared kisses there. The place was in plain view to passersby along the boulevard.

She followed Ted around the brochure rack, past the laundry room, and out onto the new brick pathway leading to the thatched-roof area. He pushed two of the white wicker chairs together. "For a place that doesn't like to tell ghost stories, Haven is full of tales about Peter Patterson's amazing return from the dead," he said. "Everybody in the dining room was talking about it."

"The general consensus is that it's a trick. A hologram or something like that," Maureen said. "People are wondering how Aster could pull it off, though. From what I've learned, it's a pretty sophisticated thing to set up. What do you think?"

"Well, it obviously isn't old Peter come back for the cookies. Sure it's a trick. Somebody is pranking Aster, or possibly, Aster's found somebody to set it up for her." He frowned. "Why she'd do such a thing, I can't even imagine."

"I know Aster has been looking for ways to increase the book business." Maureen spoke hesitantly. "Maybe this is her attempt at doing it, though it involves everything all of Haven dreads about drawing 'ghost hunters' here."

"I should think it's a sure way to increase the book business," Ted said.

"Like, *How to Make Your City Famous and Attract Big Spenders*," Maureen said. "Letting the world know about Haven's ghost population would undoubtedly make our little city famous and attract big spenders."

"If Aster isn't responsible for it, somebody from out of town must be guilty," he said.

"I agree. I can't think of a single person in the whole city who'd try a stunt like this." Maureen shook her head. "The sooner it's revealed as a hoax, the better."

"Has Frank Hubbard talked to Aster about it?" Ted asked.

"Sure. She told him that Peter led her to Terry Holiday's body in the garden. I guess he's talked to all the mystery writers too."

"Is Aster a suspect?" Ted looked unhappy about that prospect.

Maureen didn't like the idea of her friend being suspected of murder, either. "At this point, I guess anybody who was in Haven and had access to Aster's garden during the time frame involved might be a suspect."

"I hope it was a stranger," Ted said. "I don't like to think there's a killer we might know—someone we might like and trust."

"In our business, we meet strangers all the time. A lot of the people who stay here at the inn with us *become* friends."

"True enough," Ted agreed. "I had a chance to talk with the new guest while I was working the bar. Carleton Fretham. He's an interesting guy. He looks a little bit like Clark Kent in all the Superman movies."

"You're exactly right," Maureen said. "Clark Kent for sure. Good looking in a nerd-type way, with brown hair and dark-rimmed glasses. I wonder if he looks like Superman when he takes the glasses off. I haven't talked to him except for my usual 'welcome to Haven House' speech. He seems to keep to himself. What did he think about Peter's ghost?"

"Like everybody else, he thinks it's a trick. A clever one. He's some kind of a researcher, so he's interested in just about everything."

"A researcher? What does that mean?"

"He studies a lot of things," Ted explained. "He claims he knows about thousands of topics. Mostly, he helps writers. They come to him with an idea, and he puts it into the correct words so that it's good enough so they can sell it."

Isn't that a pretty good definition of a ghostwriter?

Chapter 8

If she was going to promote Haven as a "dog-friendly" destination, Maureen would surely need the cooperation of the other businesses in the city. There wasn't an official chamber of commerce or visitor's bureau building in Haven, but any mail addressed to those entities went to a post office box belonging to the Haven Historical Society and were turned over to a committee of Haven merchants who met once a month at the inn. The Historical Society *did* have a building, and a very nice one at that. It was almost directly across the street from the inn, so Maureen tucked the sticky note on which she'd scribbled *Haven is a dog-friendly city* and *Yappy Hour in the Tiki bar* into her purse, asked Shelly to guard the reception area, and dashed onto the porch, down the steps, and across the boulevard.

Claire Davis, museum curator and expert on all aspects of Haven history, greeted her with a warm hug and undisguised curiosity. "What do you think? Is he real, or is he some kind of AI?"

"Peter Patterson?"

"Of course, Peter Patterson."

"He's an illusion of some kind," Maureen offered. "The real question is who's responsible for doing it, and why?"

"So you don't think it's possible that he's a ghost—come back because Aster has wanted him to for so long?"

Maureen sidestepped the question. "Aster has always claimed that Peter was a shy, retiring sort of man. He never wanted to draw attention to himself. I hardly think he'd be a show-off in the afterlife."

"I hope whoever is causing the apparition will shut it off soon. I've already had a call from one of those ghost hunter people. I just pooh-poohed the idea that it was really Peter." She glanced around the empty museum, then dropped her voice to a whisper. "But in Haven, you can't be sure."

"I know." Maureen sighed. "But I have an idea for attracting visitors to Haven that has nothing to do with—um—spirits."

"I'd love to hear about it. Come sit down in the art gallery." Claire led the way to a curtained alcove where softly upholstered benches faced a wall of Florida-themed paintings, ranging from George Inness Jr.'s sensitive renderings of Tarpon Springs; a small collection of Florida landscapes by some of the Highwaymen painters, including Al Black, Harold Newton, and Mary Ann Carroll; along with a pair of Laura Woodward's watercolor paintings of royal poinciana trees. "We're planning to have one of the St. Petersburg mural artists cover the blank wall behind us with a painting of Beach Boulevard. Your inn will be front and center."

"How exciting!" Maureen was delighted with that idea, and proceeded to tell Claire about her proposed "dog-friendly Haven" promotion.

"I think it's an idea worthy of a special meeting of the Merchants Association," Claire said. "Dog-Friendly Haven. Delightful! Most of the businesses and all of the restaurants already have special accommodations for them anyway."

"I guess we should specify exactly what kinds of dogs we mean." Maureen was thoughtful. "Should we be specific about how big they are, like some of the rental apartments do?"

"What about Great Danes and Irish wolfhounds?" Claire wondered. "Are they okay?"

"We accept them at the inn as long as they're well-behaved. This idea is obviously going to require a little more research, isn't it? I'll welcome whatever ideas the Merchant's Association comes up with, and maybe the muralist can paint in a few dogs along the boulevard," Maureen suggested.

"There are so many things we can do with this idea," Claire said. "I'll get going on planning the meeting. It'll be something that could keep their minds off the Peter Patterson matter for a while."

"And the Terry Holiday murder," Maureen finished the thought. "Did you read his newest book? Frank Hubbard says it was written by a ghostwriter."

Claire nodded. "I bought one when Aster got the first box of them. Written by a ghostwriter? An eerie coincidence?"

"Maybe. There's a new guest at the inn I've wondered about. Ted says he's a researcher."

"That can mean almost anything. He could be doing a demographic study for a chain store. Say, maybe we're going to get a real grocery store. He could be working for a politician, checking up on what Haven citizens think about government matters. Maybe he's even a lawyer representing Mr. Holiday's family."

"He told Ted that he helps writers."

Another knowing nod. "Newspapers. He might be scouting out sources for a feature about the death."

"You're probably right," Maureen agreed. "Researchers do a lot of things. Like us. We're about to research all the places where dogs are welcome in Haven."

"It will be interesting. For instance, some of the charter fishing boats allow dogs aboard."

"That's true," Maureen agreed. "Finn has enjoyed taking the half-day fishing trips on several of the charter boats. He always enjoys it and the passengers love him."

Maureen returned to the inn, pleased that Claire would be onboard with spreading the word about Dog-Friendly Haven, that she'd gained some insight into what Carleton Fretham might be doing in her small city, delighted with the proposal of a mural depicting Beach Boulevard. She found herself humming

"Heigh-ho, heigh-ho" as she approached the inn. She stopped, mid-"off to work," at the sight of Aster Patterson, wearing a flowered muumuu, black combat boots, and a Boston Bruins beanie, struggling up the front steps carrying a large tapestry carpet bag under one arm, and a well-worn cookie sheet under the other. Erle Stanley trotted along beside her.

Haven House was cat-friendly too, Maureen realized. Bogie and Bacall roamed the property at will and had been Penelope Josephine's pets before she'd inherited them along with the building and some of the staff, but so far, no visitors had brought cats along with them.

"Aster," she called. "Let me help you. What's going on?"

"We're checking in," the woman said. "The cop says I have to leave my place because of the dead guy in the garden. He says he has a warrant to search my house and the bookstore for some kind of newfangled movie machine or something of the sort. Total nonsense, but here I am." She lifted the cookie sheet. "I'll need a suite with a decent kitchen. And Peter will be along later."

Chapter 9

First things first. Maureen needed to find a place for Aster. "Follow me," she said. The two, with the cat following, climbed the stairs. Without being asked, Molly hurried to meet them, relieved Aster of the cookie sheet, and followed the other two women to the reservation desk. "Is the Dawn Wells Suite available?" Maureen asked Shelly. "Dawn was writing her cookbook when she was here doing a musical at the old Showboat Theater," she explained to Aster. "So her kitchen is still the best equipped in the inn, except for Ted's, of course."

"I can probably make do between the two," Aster conceded. "I expect everyone will want extra cookies now that Peter is back. I'll probably need help getting the cookie ingredients from my kitchen, though."

Sam and George returned in the pickup truck from their Tiki search just in time to help Aster check in. "Shall I take your bag up to your suite?" Sam asked.

Aster clutched the tapestry bag to her chest. "I'll handle it," she said. "You all could see if the cop will let you bring my flour and sugar and stuff over here, though. I'll give you a list."

The men looked to Maureen for approval. "That seems reasonable," she said. "I'll give Frank a call and tell him you'll be there with a list of cookie ingredients that Aster needs in order to make a living, since he's closed up her bookstore."

She reached for the house phone and hit Hubbard's number. He answered on the first ring. "Got anything for me, Doherty?"

She had to smile at his optimism. "Just a request this time, Frank," she said. "Aster needs to get some groceries from her house. You know, like flour and sugar and eggs and stuff for making cookies. Okay if I send Sam or George down there to get them?"

"Didn't you get anything else from her besides that? Does she know how to make hologram images or any of that technology they use to make fake ghosts?" He sounded genuinely perplexed. "We're not finding anything like that so far on the premises."

"I haven't asked her about it. She just got here. I just need to get her comfortably settled in. Can she have the ingredients?"

"Okay. Can you try to find out how she's making the ghost man appear?"

"I'll ask her about it," Maureen promised, knowing beforehand what Aster's answer would be. She'd declare that Peter's ghost was real, not manufactured. Maureen realized too that Aster's statement that "Peter would be along later" might be a cause for concern at Haven House Inn before long. The century-old inn already had more than enough spirits randomly drifting in and out of sight at any given moment—and the apparition that certainly appeared to be Peter Patterson was clearly wanting to be seen.

She thanked Hubbard, got Aster to write the list on Haven House stationery, and dispatched Sam to pick them up.

"I'd better go with him," Molly offered. "He wouldn't know baking powder from baking soda, sea salt from Epsom salts."

"You're right. You two get going so Aster can get comfortable here." She waved the two toward the door and watched as they stepped out onto the broad porch, where by now, several of the other guests were gathered—clearly curious about Aster's sudden appearance—including the reticent new man, Carleton Fretham.

George gestured toward the truck. "We picked up a couple of sample Tikis from a guy over in St. Petersburg. Want to take a look?"

"I sure do."

George dropped the tailgate and climbed into the truck bed, pulling a canvas cover away from two tall, carved Tikis. They were of a rich, brown hue, and the faces each wore a different expression. One looked happy, the other stoic.

"They look good to me," Maureen said. "What do you think?"

"There are several other carvers around," George said, "but we thought we might put these up now, just to get a Tiki vibe going, you know?"

"Yes. Let's do it. As soon as we get the bar set up, let's have a soft opening and see how it goes. We'll get Ted and Lennie to think up some exotic drinks, stock up on those little paper parasols, and start learning some Hawaiian words."

"Aloha," George offered.

"Good start. Aloha to you too."

"Excuse me?" Carleton Fretham, in an oil-spotted denim jumpsuit, had joined them beside the truck. "Excuse my appearance. I'm working on a biography for an auto mechanic. I couldn't help overhearing. I may be able to offer a few useful Hawaiian words. I take it this thatched roof structure and the carved heads are the beginnings of a Tiki bar?" His brown eyes behind thick glasses were warm and friendly.

"That's right," Maureen said. "Any help will be appreciated."

Sam and Molly rejoined them, each one carrying a bulging canvas bag. "Shall we take these up to Aster?" Molly asked. "The Dawn Wells Suite, right?" She nodded toward Fretham. "Hi, Carleton."

"Hi, Molly, Sam," he said. "I gather that Aster is joining us, and planning on doing some baking, while outside, the Tiki bar is gaining more character. Lots of things happening here."

"That's nothing new. That's why everybody likes Haven," Sam said. "Stick around. It's an interesting little city."

"I think I will. Mahalo." Carleton smiled.

"Mahalo?" Sam looked puzzled.

"It's the Hawaiian word for 'thank you,'" Carleton explained.

"You're Hawaiian?"

"I'm plain old New England," Carleton said. "New Bedford born. But I spent some time in Hawaii, and Maureen is looking for some authentic Hawaiian words to scatter around in the new bar. I've always been interested in foreign languages. I speak several with some fluency. So far we have aloha and mahalo. Aloha is usually a greeting, and mahalo is usually used to express gratitude, but they both have a few other meanings too. Hawaiian is a very versatile language."

"Cool," Sam said. "I'll stick with English, thanks."

"You mean mahalo." Molly giggled.

"I'm going to go talk to the Tiki heads," Sam declared. "They make more sense than you two do." He handed Molly his canvas bag and joined George beside the truck. "Here's the rest of the cooking stuff. I'll give George a hand out here."

The two went their separate ways, leaving Maureen and Fretham facing each other. "We'll put bowls of macadamia nuts around, and maybe we could offer pineapple pizza," she said. "Do you have recipes for any fancy Hawaiian drinks we might feature? I'm going to order some little parasols and swords and maybe some Tiki mugs."

"I sure do. I'll be happy to show your bartenders how to make them."

"You're very kind," she said. "I appreciate your interest."

"I have many interests," he said. "I think I'll do a little exploring around Haven. It's quite an old city, as Florida cities go. Founded in nineteen ten, I understand."

"Not old like St. Augustine." Maureen smiled. "The oldest continuously occupied city in America."

"Fifteen sixty-five."

Fretham's smile then was a bit on the smirky side, Maureen thought. *Smarty-pants.*

"That's right," she said, turning and heading back inside. Finn ran from under the reception desk to meet her, his leash trailing behind him. "Smarty-pants," she muttered.

"Woof," Finn agreed. "Woof woof."

"I'll take Finn for a short walk," she told Gert, "if you don't mind staying a little bit longer." She picked up the leash.

"I don't mind a bit. No more check-ins, though, except for Aster." Gert gave an eye-roll behind heavily mascaraed eyelashes. "She seems a bit miffed about Hubbard evicting her from her own house."

"I know. But she'll be fine once she gets to baking the cookies, I'm sure."

"Yeah, but cookies don't pay the rent. She needs to keep the bookstore running, doesn't she?"

"I'm sure once Frank gets through looking for whatever the apparatus is that he thinks might be there, he'll let her back in," Maureen said. "So far he hasn't found anything."

Gert snorted a laugh. "He won't find anything, either. Peter is back for sure, and he didn't need a fancy machine to do it."

Maureen had no ready answer.

Chapter 10

With Finn prancing ahead, Maureen deliberately took the long path around the inn so that she'd pass the kitchen entrance. She wanted to talk to Ted about appropriate bar snacks for the Tiki bar, and—perhaps more importantly—she felt that it was time to find out what he thought about ghosts. If the two had a future together, spirits would surely be a part of it. Had Lorna had a chance to pop in on him yet? What did he think about Peter Patterson's alleged return to Haven? It was surely a matter that had to be settled—one way or another—between them before the relationship moved further.

She pushed open the outer door, then tapped on the glass pane of the inner one. Finn's "woof" was loud enough to attract the new pastry chef's attention.

"Hello, Ms. Doherty," Joyce greeted her. "Hi, Finn. Come on in. We're serving my key lime pie tonight. Please try a slice. Ted's over there supervising the roux for chowder." She pointed.

"We'll wait outside," Maureen said. "Meanwhile, I'm thinking about food choices for the new Tiki bar. Any suggestions?"

"I do pineapple upside-down cake and coconut pie," she offered. "Not exactly pub grub, but I'm willing to learn."

"One of the guests has offered to share some drink recipes he learned about in Hawaii," Maureen said. "Hopefully he'll have some simple ones we can use."

"You mean Carleton? He knows a lot about food. We had a nice conversation about Caribbean cuisine. He seems very knowledgeable on so many things."

"Yes. He does," Maureen agreed. "Caribbean food, huh?"

"Yes. He speaks Spanish fluently, you know."

"Yes. He mentioned that he speaks several languages," Maureen told her.

"He's a bit full of himself though," Joyce said.

Smarty-pants. Maureen thought the words again, but didn't speak them.

"He even said that he knows how Aster made that ghost of her husband appear." Joyce gave an eye-roll. "He says it's an old parlor trick called 'Pepper's ghost'."

Maureen's immediate thought was of Hubbard's perceived "feelings." This time she had a "feeling" for sure—one that he needed to know about. She'd call him as soon as her visit with Ted was over. She gave a little fluttery wave of her fingers when Ted looked up from his roux-making project. He signaled that he'd join her near the back door.

Ted stepped outside with Maureen and Finn. Dog-friendly or not, the health department wouldn't approve of a dog in the restaurant's kitchen. After a quick peck on the cheek, his response to her questions about food for the Tiki bar was quick and decisive. "No worries at all," he said. "Everything we need is on line already. This type of bar is gaining in popularity everywhere. We'll even figure out special treats for our canine customers. Maybe some tiki-shaped dog biscuits. Any other worries?"

She looked around, as usual, before mentioning ghosts, making sure they were not being overheard. "Aster is settled in here at the inn, and she's told me that Peter will be along later. I've been wondering, Ted, what your feeling about ghosts might be. We've never actually discussed it, and—well—I want to admit to you that since coming to Haven, I've become a believer. I've seen some of them, and that's the truth."

He ran his fingers through his hair in a nervous gesture, and expelled a long "Whew! I'm so glad you brought the subject up. I've always said 'there's no such thing,' but actually—well—I've had a couple of what you might call 'encounters' in my lifetime. One of them fairly recently."

Her feeling of relief was palpable. The recent one was probably a pop-in from a cute blonde starlet. "I'm glad of that," she said.

"I'm not sure I am," he told her. "Life would be simpler if I didn't believe that what I've seen is real."

"If we could chalk it all up to holograms?"

"Holograms. Yeah. What do you think about the idea that Peter's ghost is a big fake?" he wondered aloud.

"I'm not sure about that one," she admitted. "I find it hard to believe that Aster has produced it somehow. Joyce says that Carleton told her it's an old parlor trick. Something they call 'Pepper's ghost'."

"Carleton? The research guy?"

"That's him. I'm thinking I should tell Frank Hubbard about it."

"Let's look it up and see what it means first."

The suggestion was logical. She pulled her phone from her pocket and asked the question. "What is Pepper's ghost?"

"A technique which uses angled glass to project a transparent, seemingly 3D reflection of an object hidden from the audience," came the quick reply.

"That doesn't *sound* awfully complicated," Maureen said. "Maybe Aster did do it."

Again, he spoke in a near whisper. "That thing in the bookshop window looked pretty damned real though, didn't it?"

She thought about the smiling, youngish Peter petting Erle Stanley. Was it the real Erle Stanley or a hologramlike representation of the familiar cat? A real ghost with a living cat? The whole puzzle approached silliness. "I don't even want to think about it anymore," she declared. "Let's change the subject to more pleasant topics."

"You and me, together forever," he said—no longer whispering, and loud enough so that anyone passing by could hear his words. "Isn't that a pleasant topic?"

"Absolutely," she agreed. "With or without Haven's ghosts."

"Want to go for an early morning run with me tomorrow morning? I may have a surprise for you."

"I'll be there bright and early."

"Woof," said Finn. "Woof?"

Ted laughed and ruffled the dog's shiny coat. "Yes, you can come too. You're part of the family."

Maureen was still smiling when she retraced her steps and entered the inn via the side door closest to the evolving Tiki area. The sound of the player piano tinkling out the notes of "Dangerous" made her pause, then frown. She was sure the Michael Jackson tune wasn't in the prerecorded rotation of old-time tunes. She moved closer, standing behind the piano bench, looking at the Snow White illustration on the fading sheet music she'd placed there.

"Okay, Billy Bedoggoned." She glanced around, making sure no one was within hearing distance. "Okay. What's dangerous? The old parlor trick or running on the beach? You're going to have to be more specific."

A plinkety-plink version of "Don't Stop Believin'" wasn't much help.

Chapter 11

"Officer Hubbard, I don't know if this is of any interest to you, but I've heard something—um—something new," she began.

"You got a feeling, Doherty? Spill it."

"Have you ever heard of a thing called 'Pepper's ghost'?" she asked.

"Ghosts again? No such thing," he scoffed. "But, let's have it. What have you got?"

She repeated what Joyce had told her that Fretham had shared about Peter's appearance. "I looked it up," she said, giving him the brief explanation she'd found. "It might explain the image in the shop window, I guess."

"Third-hand information," he mumbled. "I'll see what I can find out about it." Long pause. "And Doherty, thanks. Nobody around the department came up with that one. It's worth checking. It sounds like something that could have been set up, then taken down real fast. The moving parts have to be stashed around here somewhere. I'll find it, even if I have to dig up the whole damned garden. It's sure not in the house or the shop anywhere. I've taken the whole place apart—book by book."

Maureen thought about Aster's careful shelving system, hoped that the police had put things back where they belonged, wished Hubbard a good day, and put the phone back into her pocket.

With the bookshop closed, the Murder Incorporated bunch were without a meeting place. She checked her contact list. Three of the members had shared their phone numbers with her. The inn could provide a pleasant place to meet—she'd even provide coffee and cookies—Aster would enjoy seeing her authors, and Maureen might even pick up some information to share with Frank Hubbard. She dialed the first number. Elaine Cremonis, the woman who'd favored strangling as fitting punishment for Terry Holiday's terrible books.

Maureen introduced herself and reminded the writer that they'd met on the fateful Friday of Holiday's death. "Since the critique group has no meeting place at the moment, I'd be happy to welcome you all to meet here at Haven House. Aster is staying with us, along with Erle Stanley."

"Thank you so much." Elaine Cremonis sounded pleased. "What a great idea. We usually meet on Friday after lunch. Will that be okay?"

"Of course," Maureen agreed. "We can set you all up at one of the round dining room tables. Just let me know what time you'd like to meet, and we'll get things in motion. Aster will be so pleased."

"I hope you'll sit in with us again too," the woman said. "What did you think of us anyway?"

She'd thought their verbal attacks on Holiday had bordered on vicious, and that their individual preoccupations with various forms of murder were downright creepy. She paused before answering.

"It was quite unlike any other meeting I've ever attended," she said. It was true. "I'd never realized how much thought and research goes into planning a fictional murder."

Or probably planning a real one.

"Oh, it's even more complicated than that," was the blithe reply. "Some of us write in more than one genre. For instance, in addition to the murders, I write sci-fi for middle-grade kids along with YA dystopian stories. Judy Abbott writes erotic romance and horse stories for kids along with the murder books, and Lynn Ellen Crockett does true crime and medical romance—the kind with lots of naughty nurses." She ticked off the names on red-hued fingertips. "Paul Jenkins—he's the guy with all the tattoos—he writes a YA Navy Seal adventure series and some cowboy romances in addition to his murder mysteries. Wally—Walter Griffith—does ax murder, chainsaw bloody stuff, some early Florida cowboy books they call 'Cracker Westerns,' and some cute baby animal books for little kids. He also does ghostwriting for a few corporate types. I guess you might say we're quite versatile."

"Are any of you currently writing ghost stories?"

"Ghosts? Like woo-woo stories?" A laugh, then softly, "Are you kidding? In Haven?"

Maureen moved on to another question. "Do you all use pen names for the different categories?" Maureen asked.

"Sure. I'm myself and Tasha LaLonde and also Meri Payson. Paul is Lorraine London and Thatcher Winthrop. Judy and Lynn Ellen have a slew of names between them. Wally mostly uses his real name."

"Wow. I guess I'll have a lot of reading to catch up on." Maureen tried to keep the tone casual. "Was it Judy who wrote so convincingly about what strangling feels like?"

"Nope." Elaine chuckled. "That would be me. *The Corpse Cried Wolf*. One of my best."

Maureen knew that she'd be awake much of the night reading on her Kindle about the how-to of strangulation. Besides that, she needed to give some serious thought to exactly what dogs would be wholeheartedly welcomed in the newly conceived "dog-friendly Haven." She thanked the writer for her input, then made a mental note to learn more about Walter Griffith, Murder Incorporated's only known ghostwriter. Was he the author of Terry Holiday's final book? And what about Carleton Fretham? What was his position in all this? Was he capable of writing a successful book, or did he stick to doing research for others?

Once alone in her office, Maureen tried to cast aside her varied errant thoughts and googled "Pepper's ghost." Perhaps she could find a more detailed explanation for how it worked. There was no shortage of information. Briefly stated, the trick uses an angled reflective surface to project a transparent, ghost-like, seemingly 3D reflection of a person or object offstage so that it seems to be in front of the audience. The reflective surface could be a plain sheet of window glass, or a mirror, a section of Plexiglas or even a piece of aluminum foil. The ghostly effect could be enhanced with gauze or scrim.

Maureen glanced around the office. "If that's all it takes, practically anybody could do it. We all have window glass and mirrors. Ted has Plexiglas cutting boards in the kitchen, and everybody uses aluminum foil."

She returned to her online study, learning that there was a history of the trick dating back to mid-nineteenth century London. It was named for a John Henry Pepper, who popularized the effect back in 1862 for a stage show. This launched a vogue for ghost-themed plays. Even in today's Florida, Maureen learned, the old technique is still used at Walt Disney World's *Haunted Mansion* attraction. With a smile, she remembered her twelve-year-old self, riding beside a ghost as she and her parents traveled through that darkened waterway maze.

There were a few YouTube examples of do-it-yourself experiments, along with comments about failed attempts at duplicating the illusions. Could Aster actually have done this by herself to produce Peter's image? Hubbard seemed to be convinced that she had, and that he'd find the working parts of the illusion buried somewhere on the property. "Even if he had to dig up the whole damned garden."

If her research on Pepper's ghost had been correct, he didn't need to dig up anything. He could walk into any house in Haven and find all of the components it took to produce the illusion. Even so, the idea saddened her, as she thought of Aster's orderly, color-coordinated rows of seasonal and annual blooms. If he chose to dig anyway, she was comforted by the thought that gardens can be replanted and beautified, just as century-old inns can be updated and improved.

She tried to shake away Aster's remark that "Peter would be along later," almost hoping that Hubbard was right. That the Peter she'd seen in the bookshop window was a trick—an illusion Aster had done with smoke and mirrors—not the realistic 3D healthy-looking husband the woman had been wooing with cookies for years—tempting him with the very cookies she was undoubtedly baking right now upstairs in the Dawn Wells Suite of the Haven House Inn.

But wouldn't it be kind of fun if the real ghost of Peter Patterson showed up at one of the round table meetings of the Murder Incorporated writers? She folded her hands together, relishing the thought. Then, noticing a couple of chipped fingernails, she reached for the phone and made an appointment for a quick manicure at the Heavenly Haven Nail Salon, then buzzed Gert and asked her to man the front desk. If Ted's surprise in the morning was going to be a ring, her hands had better look pretty.

Chapter 12

Hands soft and lotioned, nails short and pearly pink, Maureen returned to the reservation desk, where Gert and George were involved in an animated conversation about Peter's ghost. "It's some kind of a trick," George insisted. "No way that old man looks that good. He's been dead damn near ten years."

"Could be, I guess," Gert agreed somewhat half-heartedly. "They say it's some kind of thing Aster could have rigged up with a pane of glass and lights. Do you remember that little tiny mermaid that was in a fishbowl over at Webb's City in St. Petersburg years ago?"

"Webb's City!" George's smile was bright with remembrance. "The world's biggest drugstore. Long gone now, along with the little mermaid and the dancing chicken! I'll bet you're right. That was a good trick though. You think Aster's that smart? That she could have fooled everybody?"

Gert shrugged. "Why not? She's read a thousand books or more." She faced Maureen. "Hi, Ms. Doherty. Do you think the cop is going to find the pieces of the whatchamacallit that makes things look real when they aren't?"

"Maybe not. I read that you could do it with aluminum foil instead of a mirror. That wouldn't be hard to get rid of," Maureen offered.

"Maybe," Gert allowed. "Your nails look nice. I like that color on you." She inspected her own long red nails. "I like bright red or black myself."

"Thanks, and thanks for running the desk. Anything new?"

"No new guests, if that's what you mean." She lifted a sheaf of papers from the counter. "Claire from the museum dropped this off. It's the Florida State Parks dog policy. Claire thought you might find it useful. You thinking of getting another pet besides Finn and the cats?"

"Not me. We're working on an idea about calling Haven a 'dog-friendly city,' and we need some guidelines about what that means."

"We're already pretty dog-friendly here at the inn. Dogs on leashes inside the building. Clean up after your dog and keep it quiet in the room at night."

Maureen accepted the papers. "I'll read this in my office with the door open so I can watch the lobby." Claire had been right. The park rules were useful. Maureen typed out a few of them.

"Dogs that are noisy, vicious, dangerous, disturbing, or intimidating to other persons or pets, or which damage premises, are considered to be nuisances and will not be permitted to remain in the facility."

That's a good one.

"Some animals may be prohibited on city property."

I hadn't thought of that.

"Dogs must be vaccinated. Florida Law."

Yep.

"Individual parks, buildings, or facilities may have specific areas prohibiting dogs."

Some beaches don't allow them.

She was off to a good start.

"Hello? Ms. Doherty?" She looked up at the sound of Carleton Fretham's voice. She stood and approached the reception area.

"Yes, sir. How can I help you?"

"I have those Tiki bar drink recipes for you." With both elbows on the counter and a big smile on his face, he handed her a colorful brochure. Having studied much of the paper memorabilia that Penelope Josephine had stashed in an old steamer trunk, Maureen immediately recognized the midcentury modern artwork on the cover. "It's a real 1950s drink booklet from the original Mai Kai restaurant over in Fort Lauderdale," he told her. "A treasure."

"It certainly is," Maureen agreed. "Are you sure you want to part with it?"

"No problem." He waved away her concern. "As a researcher, I've managed to collect a wide variety of miscellany. I have to weed it all out occasionally. Enjoy!"

Maureen glanced through the bright pages, noting names like Fog Cutter, Blue Hawaii, Zombie, and Trader Vic's original Mai Tai. "I'll share it with Ted and Lennie," she promised. "I'm sure some of these will be new to them. Thank you so much."

"No problem," he said again. "My pleasure. I'm really enjoying my stay here in Haven. It's an intriguing little place."

"I hope you'll stay with us for a while," she said.

"I'm planning to," he said. "The entire area is interesting. Yesterday I took a trolley ride along some of the Gulf beaches." He ticked them off on his fingers. "St. Pete Beach. Madeira Beach. Treasure Island. Redington Beach. I hopped on and off. Came home with a pocketful of seashells—coquina, auger, a tiny wentletrap—a few picture postcards—mostly aerial views. I drank a craft beer on Blind Pass Road and even got my fortune told by a Zoltar machine in an ice cream parlor on Treasure Island. Quite a busy day!"

A Zoltar machine?

She said it aloud. "A Zoltar machine?"

"Yes. It's one of those arcade machines with a life-sized man with a turban in it. It dispenses cards with wise sayings." He reached into an inner jacket pocket and displayed a blue card. "See?"

"Uh-huh. I saw one of them when I was on my way here. It was at South of the Border in South Carolina." Even as she spoke, she felt her heart rate speed up at the memory.

"South of the Border. One of the country's great roadside attractions," he said. "It's been there for over seventy years. Did you get a fortune card?"

"Yes."

She had kept that card with its prophetic message. From time to time, she still read it over to herself—although she knew it from memory.

With a message from the dead
On a journey you've been led.
Another message from a stranger
Holds an answer, comes with danger.
A riddle, a puzzle in plain sight.
An answer, a vision in black and white.
You'll know the where but not the why.
Beware the place one comes to die.
ZOLTAR KNOWS ALL.

That cryptic message was printed on a pale blue oblong card in dark red ink. It had been dispensed by a turbaned mannequin from an electronic machine in a popular amusement arcade where she'd stood in line with several other fortune-seekers, waiting her turn to put a couple of dollars into a slot. Had all of those people received cards with an amazingly accurate, personal, frightening rhymed warning like hers? She thought not. There was a second Zoltar card she'd found among Penelope Josephine's old Christmas cards. It too had carried a cryptic message.

If she dared to visit the Treasure Island ice cream shop Zoltar, would she get an ordinary "You will take a journey and meet an attractive stranger" message? Or would another pale blue card change her life?

Chapter 13

After Finn's four o'clock walk, Maureen and the golden climbed the stairs to her suite. Abba's "Dancing Queen," one of Lorna's favorites, issued from inside. Finn gave a soft, happy "Woof."

A shimmering, almost transparent Lorna, wearing a floral tiered sundress that Maureen recognized as an Erdem original from the downstairs shop's show window, danced gracefully to the music. Maureen had selected the pricey Hawaiian print dress in keeping with the inn's growing Tiki identity. She'd also stocked a line of men's Hawaiian-print shirts along with some Panama hats. Both had begun to sell nicely. Lorna took on a slightly more solid shape when the two entered. "Hi, Maureen. I love this dress. Your taste keeps getting better all the time." The ghost paused her dance to pat Finn, then sat on the nearby couch.

"Thanks." The dress was actually blue and white, but on Lorna, it appeared to be black and white, as usual.

"I heard that old Peter Patterson is back in Haven," the ghost said. "Have you seen him yet?"

"I've seen something that looks a lot like him," Maureen admitted. "I guess you'd know whether it's really him or not. Is it?"

"I haven't had a chance to check him out yet. I went to see the red carpet at the Metropolitan Museum of Art Gala; then there was the annual country and western blast at Nashville. Then Reggie and I popped over to London to see what's going on with the Royals." Reggie is one of Lorna's gentleman friends who's become more or less a regular visitor at the inn. She pretended not to notice when Bogie walked through her and sat on the arm of the couch. "Do you think the Peter thing might be a trick?"

"Apparently it could be. Maybe a hologram or maybe something they call Pepper's ghost."

"Oh yeah. When I was at the Actor's Studio, they did a production of Dickens's *The Haunted Man*," she recalled. "They used that Pepper's ghost trick." Bogie strolled through her once again, in the opposite direction. "Cats are weird," she observed. "I heard over at the Quic Shop something about Haven being dog-friendly."

Maureen offered a brief explanation of the proposed promotion. "I'm hoping it would draw some tourist interest."

"Sure. Everybody likes dogs." She gave Finn a little scratch under his chin and stuck out her tongue at Bogie. "A cat-friendly promotion wouldn't work at all."

"I don't think cats would enjoy a waterfront vacation anyway," Maureen said. "I guess cats don't like water much."

"Some do," Lorna corrected. "There's quite a history of seagoing cats. Sailors like to have them onboard because they can control rats. Cats seem to like it too, because there are so many places to climb. I'll bet Aster has books about them. Maybe someday I'll read to Bogie and Bacall about cats on ships."

Bogie seemed to like the idea. He walked carefully around her, hopped down from the couch onto the floor, purred loudly, and performed a definitely friendly figure eight around her ankles.

"Weird, but in a good way," Lorna observed, bending to give Bogie a tentative, shimmery pat on the head. The cat returned to the cat tower, resumed his usual spot, while Bacall, unruffled and always gorgeous, licked one dainty paw, smoothed long whiskers, and looked on without any apparent emotion.

Maureen hung Finn's leash behind the kitchen door and filled his bowl with his favorite refrigerated food. He made short work of the dinner; then, giving a wide, pink-mouthed yawn, he headed for the bedroom. "I guess you've had a busy day. Nighty-night. I'll join you after dinner. Now I'm going down to the shop and pick out something new to wear—maybe something pink to match the new nails."

Finn gave an approving "Woof."

The gift shop, occupying most of the right-hand side of the porch, was a fairly new addition to the century-old structure. The wraparound porch with its protective roof was similar to those on many of Florida's older homes and hotels—providing both shade from the sun and access to cooling breezes, and a perfect spot for comfortable rocking chairs. However, a most unfortunate incident had occurred on this part of the porch when Maureen had first arrived in Haven. A man had been found dead, murdered in his rocker there, and after that it seemed that no one wanted to sit on the right side of the porch anymore. Building something attractive and useful to cover up the bad memory seemed like a logical and productive way to go. Using new construction techniques and incorporating decorative aspects from Penelope Josephine's amazing hoard of items stored in a gigantic storage locker, the gift shop had evolved successfully and quite beautifully.

When Maureen arrived, there was already a good-sized before-dinner group occupying the front porch rockers, and several customers were already inside the well-stocked shop. One of the young women Maureen had hired from the St. Petersburg College distributive education course was behind the counter, ringing up a sale of several T-shirts, while Shelly, still putting all the hours in that she possibly could, stood ready to bag the merchandise and at the same time, make sure that the sales procedure went properly.

Pausing briefly to welcome her customers, Maureen headed for the stockroom. This was the plainest part of the structure—strictly utilitarian with every inch of space used as efficiently as possible. George had installed a secondhand ironing board so that it folded up against the wall like a Murphy bed, easily put into use when an item arrived wrinkled. A narrow pink enamel-topped table that had once graced somebody's nineteen-fifties kitchen now served as a marking table where price tags and special hangtags were attached to garments, and stickers were applied to decorative articles and jewelry boxes. One of the ubiquitous white wicker chairs provided seating at one side of the table. On the opposite side, a sturdy wooden shipping crate, open on one end, served as storage for cleaning products. Topped with a quilted cushion, it made an adequate, if unlovely, bench.

From a plain pipe rack, Maureen selected a rose-colored strapless sheath, removed the clear plastic garment bag, and tucked the tags inside the back zippered closure of the dress. She slipped on a pair of her own high-heeled white sandals, checked hair and makeup in the secondhand full-length mirror she'd bought at the Second Glance Thrift Store. She liked buying things there. All of the proceeds went to a women's shelter in St. Petersburg.

She returned to the lobby. From inside the dining room, the familiar sounds of subdued chatter, the clink-clink of china and glassware, along with the tinkling of the piano, plinking out the familiar melody of the old Peggy Lee hit, "Mañana." Was that one part of the regular rotation? She thought it was.

"*Mañana* means 'tomorrow'," she reminded herself. "Is that a message or a coincidence?"

She walked into the room toward the piano and stood behind the empty piano bench, facing smiling Snow White depicted on the sheet music. *Lucky girl. She had seven cute little guys to help her out.* With her lips barely moving, she whispered. "Okay, Billy Bedoggoned, is it a message? What about tomorrow?"

Without missing a beat, the piano keys merrily moving up and down in their usual rhythm, "Mañana" eased into "Tea for Two." That one was definitely in the pre-programmed rotation. It often played several times a night. But what the heck did it mean to her right now?

She had no time to reflect on it at that moment. She returned to the doorway. It was time to seat her guests, be the hostess, say all the right things, try hard to remember everybody's name, make suggestions and recommendations about the evening's menu. That was easy. Everything coming from Ted's kitchen was good, and she proudly told them so.

Many of the incoming people were staying at the inn. Carleton Fretham was there in blue scrubs, indicating that he was working on a medical story. The McKennas were present. A few were regulars from the neighborhood like Dick and Ethel Flannagan. A surprise was Walter Griffith from the Murder Incorporated writers' group. His companion was Elaine Cremonis in slinky black spandex.

The phrase *dressed to kill* crossed Maureen's mind.

Chapter 14

Not unexpectedly, dinner went smoothly. Assorted appetizers, soups, and salads began the meal. A huge prime rib was the star of the main course, perfectly cooked, pink in the middle, yet nicely browned on the outside. Baked potatoes with a choice of toppings were offered, and roasted asparagus spears were buttery and flavorful. As promised, Joyce's key lime pie with whipped cream was the dessert.

Maureen made more than one stroll around the dining room, moving from table to table ostensibly to inquire if everything was satisfactory—actually to catch whatever snatches of conversation might be relevant to the various things going on in Haven—from Peter Patterson to John Henry Pepper, from Tiki huts to friendly mutts, and—overriding everything else—the brutal strangulation murder of Terry Holiday.

Once dinner service had begun, the player piano was stilled, replaced with the less-intrusive canned instrumental contemporary classics, allowing for easier conversation among tablemates. *It allows for easier eavesdropping for nosy inn proprietors too*, was Maureen's guilty thought as she hovered behind Walter Griffith's chair, offering unnecessary extra linen napkins to the varied group assembled at the round table. Elaine Cremonis was seated on the writer's left with Carleton Fretham at his right. Beside Elaine was the St. Petersburg carver of the much-admired Tikis, who didn't try to disguise his admiration of Elaine's quite provocative black spandex, very short dress, while Mrs. McKenna involved the entire group in a lively discussion of the possibility that the Yankees might dominate the coming baseball season.

Nothing. She moved on to the next table. The more information she could gather to share with Hubbard, the faster the killer would be caught. At least that's what she *hoped* would happen. Having a potential killer in Haven was surely a deterrent to anyone thinking about taking a Gulf Beach vacation and quite likely was one major reason for too many vacant suites at the Haven House Inn.

Longtime Haven residents and frequent diners Dick and Ethel Flannagan greeted her warmly and introduced *their* visiting guests from Massachusetts, Dick's sister Janie and her husband Robert Taylor. She quickly learned that brother-in-law Robert was a police detective in his home state, and had a great interest in Haven's current murder mystery. She recognized two more of the Murder Incorporated critique group—Paul Jenkins and Lynn Ellen Crockett. Maureen recalled that Lynn Ellen was a true crime writer. Perfect. The conversation here would undoubtedly be all about murder. The table was one of the larger ones that seated eight. There were two empty chairs. Did she dare to take one? Could she?

Shelly appeared with the cold shrimp appetizer course.

"My goodness, doesn't that look good? I'd forgotten how hungry I am. These are locally caught Gulf shrimp," Maureen enthused. "None fresher or more delicious anywhere. I'm tempted to join you."

"Please do!" Always a gentleman, Dick Flannagan stood and pulled one of the vacant chairs away from the table, and at the same time, signaled to Shelly to bring another appetizer. Ethel echoed her husband's invitation and added, "That's a lovely dress, Maureen. I'll bet it came from your shop." She turned to her sister-in-law. "Maureen has the dearest little shop out on the porch. You'll love it."

It would be hard to walk away from such an opportunity. Murder talk and more sales for the shop. A win-win.

She accepted the proffered seat.

Dick's brother-in-law began the conversation immediately.

"Do you have any particular feelings about the murder, Ms. Doherty?" he asked.

"Feelings?" He sounded just like Frank Hubbard. *Do all police detectives think that way?* "At this point," she explained, "I'm still mostly concerned about Aster Patterson, the bookstore owner who discovered Holiday's body in her garden."

"Do you think she might be guilty?" he prodded. "I understand that she knew the man. A nonfiction writer of some kind."

Paul Jenkins laughed out loud. "A writer of the worst kind. His books are notoriously awful."

"I believe in Aster's innocence," Maureen answered the officer's question. "But it seems that anybody who was in Haven and had access to her garden at the time could be a suspect." She turned toward Paul. "Some say the newest book, the one about attracting big spenders, was created by a ghostwriter."

"I've heard that," he agreed. "I bought the book, but I admit I haven't read it yet."

"I've read it," Maureen said, "and it gave me what I think might be a good idea to attract those big spenders to Haven."

At the urging of her tablemates, Maureen offered a brief explanation of "dog-friendly Haven," including the concept of Yappy Hour in the Tiki bar. The reception of the plan was enthusiastic. It seemed that all concerned were dog lovers. She tried to think of a way to turn the conversation back to Holiday's murder. "Of course," she said, "having an unidentified killer roaming around town doesn't encourage tourism."

That worked. Dick's detective brother-in-law picked up the topic immediately. "I presume that local law enforcement is well into the investigation." He aimed a questioning look in Maureen's direction.

"Officer Frank Hubbard," she stated. "Yes. He's quite focused on it." Although she knew that Hubbard was also focused on the Peter Patterson ghost quandary, she was positive that none of the other three Haven residents at the table—Dick, Ethel, or Paul—would touch *that* topic with the proverbial ten-foot pole.

"As a murder mystery writer, I'm paying particular attention to the details of the crime," Paul said. "Why was the body in a garden? Why was he strangled with a piece of cord that may have come from Aster's potting shed? Was it a crime of convenience or had it been planned to throw suspicion on Aster? Did she do it?" He gave a smiling, nonchalant shrug of broad shoulders. "It doesn't matter to me. It's all just book material."

Maureen thought about the other members of Murder Incorporated in the room. Were Elaine and Walter simply gaining material too? Was Walter the ghostwriter who'd turned Terry Holiday's idea into a readable how-to book? And how about Elaine's newest novel? Was *The Corpse Cried Wolf* actually a how-to manual on how to strangle somebody?

Paul's mention of his books prompted a round of questions from the others about the titles of his books, his various pen names, and about writing in general. Maureen found the courage to ask about the possibility of putting together a book from Penelope Josephine's trunk full of Haven memorabilia. She was surprised by the positive reaction she received. Paul offered to help her organize it, and Janie suggested that such a book would be a wonderful souvenir for her to sell in the shop.

She felt a momentary pang of guilt. She'd been neglecting the contents of Penelope Josephine's trunk lately. Yet, whenever she'd taken the time to lift the curved top, to investigate just a bit of the tightly packed contents, she'd found something useful—something surprisingly timely. She made a silent vow to take time—no, to *make* time—to see what the trunk had to offer—and to do it soon.

Shelly had begun to serve the main course when Aster entered the dining room from the lobby. She was, for her, quite conservatively dressed in navy blue overalls and a white button-down shirt. She hesitated in the doorway, looking around the room.

She looks hesitant, Maureen thought, and stood. "Shelly," she said, "could you fix up another place setting? I'm going to invite Aster to join us."

The Flannagans, Paul Jenkins, and Lynn Ellen Crockett were well acquainted with Aster, and all four welcomed her warmly. Maureen, confident that Aster would remain true to Haven's unwritten rule about never mentioning ghosts aloud among outsiders, introduced the bookshop owner to the Taylors.

After some brief how-do-you-dos and pleased-to-meet-yous, Police Detective Taylor lost no time in pursuing details of the death of the departed how-to writer.

"I'm sure this is a difficult time for you, Ms. Patterson," he said. "Finding a body in your own backyard is a shock, a truly traumatic experience. I'm sure as time has passed, you've gained some clarity of the details surrounding that moment."

A flicker of sadness crossed Aster's face. Maureen hurried to change the subject. "You look very nice, Aster. That shade of blue is becoming."

"Thank you." She smiled. "The overalls were Peter's, and so was the shirt. I like wearing his clothes. They still smell like him."

Taylor didn't give up. "Memories are important." He leaned closer to Aster. "You must be remembering details of finding Holiday as time passes."

Aster favored him with a smile. "Oh, yes indeed. Officer Hubbard said almost the same thing. I talk with him every single day as bits and pieces occur to me." She made a *tsk-tsk* sound. "Though he keeps insisting that I'm familiar with lighting and cameras and such that I know nothing about. I know about books and baking, baking and books. That's me." Another sweet smile, followed by another flicker of sadness.

"That's interesting, about the details," Lynn Ellen put in.

Aster nodded. "I guess so. That piece of cord on the poor fellow's neck came from my potting shed. I was sure of it. So tight it made his tongue stick out. I told Frank Hubbard where to find it. And just yesterday I remembered that Terry Holiday had told me the first time I talked to him on the phone that since the new book had come out, 'certain people were gunning for him.'" Another vigorous nod of bouncing gray curls. "That's what he said. 'Certain people are going to be gunning for me.' Does that mean people with real guns? Or did he just mean that the usual reviewers were likely to give him one-star reviews again? I guess we'll never know."

Aster's dinner had arrived. "This is delicious, Maureen. You and your staff have been so kind. Did you people know that Maureen's housekeepers Gert and Molly got Frank Hubbard to let them into my place to bring me everything I needed to make my cookies? I don't know what I would have done without them. I have my flour and sugar and eggs and my favorite egg beater and my aluminum foil and my . . ."

"Aluminum foil?" Maureen interrupted. The words had just slipped out.

"Sure. To line my old cookie sheet. I need it to make the bottoms of the shortbread cookies brown nicely."

"Is foil important?" Taylor asked.

"No," Maureen said. "I just wondered what it had to do with cookies. I'm not much of a cook."

"Me either," Lynn Ellen, who'd undoubtedly been one of the one-star reviewers of Holiday's books, said with an undisguised glare in Taylor's direction. "Can we change the subject? Dinner and dead bodies don't go well together. Let's stay with books and baking."

"Speaking of books," Maureen said, thankful for a change of subject, "a friend of mine is looking for books about seagoing cats. Do any titles come to mind, Aster?"

Robert Taylor frowned and concentrated on his dinner. Aster put down her fork and leaned forward. "Oh, yes. I've read some of them to Erle Stanley. There's a lovely true one called *Cats in the Navy* with lots of pictures of real navy cats. Did you know that some cats have even been awarded medals for bravery? Another one Erle Stanley likes is *Seafurrers*. It's about cats who traveled the world with mapmakers. Then, there's the story of *Unsinkable Sam*, a cat who survived three World War II shipwrecks."

There was a fast round of cat stories from the tablemates about smart cats they'd each known and loved. Maureen told about how she'd inherited Bogie and Bacall along with the inn. The topic had been successfully steered away from the as-yet unsolved murder. So Aster had aluminum foil. So did everybody else in Haven. But *was* Aster planning to make her dead husband appear at the Haven House Inn via Pepper's ghost? Or had Peter finally learned to materialize on his own? Maureen wholeheartedly hoped neither one would happen—at least not right now, when she had so many irons in the fire. She had an inn to run, a Tiki bar to complete, a gift shop to stock, and a dog-friendly promotion to sell to the city. She needed to take a quick peek into Penelope Josephine's trunk, too. She still hadn't decided whether or not to visit the ice cream shop Zoltar, and most importantly, she was looking forward to the happy possibility that she might soon be an engaged woman.

Oh yeah. And help Frank Hubbard figure out who killed Terry Holiday.

Chapter 15

"Another cancellation phoned in, Maureen." Night manager Hilda sounded apologetic. "Sorry."

Dinner guests had adjourned to the front porch or the cocktail lounge, and the lobby was empty except for Molly, tidying up the vacant white wicker chair-and-table seating arrangement across from the reservation desk.

"It's not your fault," Maureen said. "It's nobody's fault. The weather is perfect. The inn looks fine. We had a couple of early checkouts this afternoon before you came. There were even empty seats in the dining room tonight. People just aren't comfortable in Haven since—since—you know. The murder."

"A headline like this one doesn't help." Molly lifted a discarded newspaper from under a chair. "No Progress in Flower Garden Murder," she read aloud. "People are afraid. Heck. *I'm* afraid. But the paper is wrong. There's been plenty of progress, no doubt about it."

"There has? Progress? What do you mean?" Maureen asked.

"I heard about it over at the Quic Shop." Molly squirted some spray cleaner onto the table top. "Everybody's talking about it."

Quic Shop. Of course.

"About what?" Maureen prodded. "What kind of progress?"

"The ghostwriter. The one who really wrote Holiday's new book," Molly reported, "has been talking to the daughter.

Hannah Hamburger. Somebody heard them arguing on the phone when the writer was in there buying chocolate-covered pretzels. I thought you knew all about it, what with the ghostwriter staying here at the inn. That dress is fabulous on you, by the way. Got a late date?"

"Thank you." She didn't answer the part about the late date. Meeting Ted after the kitchen and the lounge were closed for the night had become a regular thing. Maureen knew without asking that Molly was talking about Carleton Fretham. "Carleton," she said.

"Right."

"What about him?"

Molly moved across the lobby to the reservation desk and lowered her voice. "Money. The squabble was all about the money."

"What squabble? Who's arguing with who about what money?" The answers were becoming more confusing than the questions.

"Why, the daughter and the writer," Molly said. "Haven't you been paying attention?"

I've been thinking about little else!

"I thought I was, but I sure missed this part. Go on," Maureen encouraged.

"When Holiday died, everything he had automatically went to his daughter." Molly's tone was conspiratorial. "It seems that his agreement with the ghostwriter was for fifty thousand dollars in cash. Half up front and the rest when the book was published. Plus Holiday agreed to split the profits from sales of the book."

"It sounds as if ghostwriting is nice work if you can get it."

"It sounds good to me too," Molly agreed. "Terry Holiday—I mean Trenton Hamburger—gave Fretham an IOU for the second twenty-five thousand payment. The daughter doesn't want to honor it."

"Oh-oh."

"Yeah. She said he had no business paying the first twenty-five, since his books never sell," Molly explained. "She said writing books was just her father's hobby. Paying Carleton now would just be throwing good money after bad."

"I can't blame her for thinking that way," Maureen said. "Even though the new book is actually pretty good."

"You read it?"

"I did. It might actually sell enough copies around the country to show a nice profit."

"Wow. I'll bet the daughter doesn't know that." Molly raised an eyebrow.

And I'll bet Frank Hubbard doesn't know about the money squabble. Maureen stepped into her office and called Hubbard.

"I was just about to call you," he said. "The medical examiner has released Holiday's body. His daughter says the funeral will be next Wednesday. Two o'clock in the afternoon at the Community Church. She says it won't be much of an affair, since his books never amounted to much. He's only famous for getting himself murdered. You promised you'd go and see if you can pick up anything interesting."

"I remember. I'll go," she agreed. "Listen, Frank, maybe you already know about the money squabble that's going on between Hannah Hamburger and the ghostwriter who wrote her father's last book."

"How do you come up with this stuff, Doherty?" Exasperation sounded in his voice. "What's going on about money that nobody's told me about?"

"It may just be Quic Shop gossip," she apologized, "but there may be some truth to it." She related the conversation she'd had with Molly.

"Quic Shop, you say? I never shop there."

"Neither do I," she agreed. "It's too expensive, but it's apparently where people go to swap stories."

"So have you got any feelings about all this?" he asked.

"Feelings." She smothered a laugh. "Detective Taylor asked me the very same thing at dinner tonight."

"Taylor? There's no detective on my staff by that name. Who in blazes is Detective Taylor?"

"Oh, he's Dick Flannagan's sister's husband. He's from Massachusetts," she explained.

"And this Yankee cop is working *my* case and nobody told me?" Hubbard sputtered. "Why is he questioning you?"

"He wasn't questioning me." She tried to explain. "He was mostly talking to Aster. He's not working the case. It was just part of the general conversation. I mean, everybody's talking about the murder."

"Not a good subject for a dinner conversation. I never talk business over food. What did he ask Aster about?"

Maureen paused, thinking back to the conversation. "Details. The importance of details. Some of it *was* kind of gruesome. She talked about the cord on Holiday's neck and that his tongue was kind of sticking out. Some of the Murder Incorporated writers were there, so they got involved in the conversation. Paul Jenkins said something gross about a Mexican restaurant he goes to that serves cow tongue tacos. Then Aster said that Holiday thought somebody was gunning for him. Everybody looked relieved when Lynn Ellen changed the subject, and we started talking about cats."

"Lynn Ellen from the Murders Incorporated gang?" he asked. "The one who writes about real crimes? And she didn't want to talk about the one that happened right here in Haven?"

"We all felt sorry for Aster, being quizzed like that, and besides, Dick's sister Janie was looking kind of pale," Maureen recalled. "She'd ordered the taco salad."

Hubbard brought about a fast ending to the call. In the ensuing silence, from across the lobby, Maureen heard the plinkity-plink of the piano playing the 1940s hit, "It's Been a Long, Long Time." She glanced in the direction of the neglected steamer trunk. "Thanks, Billy Bedoggoned," she murmured. "You're right. Let's see if there's anything interesting on top of the pile tonight." Pulling a jangling ring of keys from a desk drawer, she selected the key marked with the number 178 and opened the curved cover.

Maureen took a deep breath, wondering briefly why she liked the smell of what certainly must be decaying paper so much, and leaned forward in her chair, peering closely at the interior. Some yellowed newspaper, a torn magazine cover, a brown envelope, a slim red booklet marked ASTROLOGY. *Discover what the stars have in store for your love life.* The booklet was dated thirty-seven years earlier—the year she was born.

She touched it, not picking it up. It felt warm.

Chapter 16

Several minutes had passed before Maureen felt comfortable picking up the red booklet. She lifted the edge of the cover carefully. Would the pages be stuck together? Would the whole thing fall apart in her hands? She'd experienced both things happening before with items from the trunk. *Maybe*, she thought, *just maybe I'd rather it* did *disintegrate somehow, so I wouldn't have to read it.*

The player piano had switched tunes again—back to "Don't Stop Believin'." "Believing *what*?" she asked aloud. Ever since she'd moved from Boston to Haven, from her solid, dependable New England background, to the topsy-turvy, ghost-filled existence that marked her new home, she'd experienced myriad ups and downs. Yet, she had to admit, much of it was pleasurable, fun and, in its own way, quite exciting.

So am I supposed to believe whatever this little book is about to tell me? She lifted the cover all the way. The first page was headed LOVE LIFE. She took another deep breath.

"A beautiful love story has begun," she read. "Make sure your relationship is full of affection, great conversation, emotional connection, and shared dreams and projects. Trust and sensitivity are the foundations of love, so don't overcomplicate things. Let your intuition guide you." *Okay. So far, so good.* Ever so carefully, gently, she turned the page. "Your feelings for each other will be intensified during a romantic trip." *Wow! I like that idea!*

"Ms. Doherty? Are you busy?" Sam's voice startled her. She closed the booklet quickly, hoping even as she did it that she hadn't handled the aged paper too roughly. Carefully, very carefully, she returned it to the spot where she'd found it, and gently, very gently, she lowered the lid.

"No, Sam. What's up?"

"The Tiki carving guy brought over another really good looking Tiki. This one is carrying a camera. It's kind of funny, and it's the same price as the other ones. Can we get it?"

"Business is kind of slow, you know," she said. "Tell him I'll take a look at it and let him know."

If the next page in the red booklet is about money, maybe I'll figure out exactly what to do. She'd deal with astrology and a Tiki with a Kodak later.

As usual, after the kitchen had closed, Maureen and Ted met in the lounge for what Gert liked to call her "late date." She sat beside him at the bar. He had a light beer. She sipped on a wine cooler. The admiration in his eyes made her glad she'd chosen the rose strapless number for the evening—and halfway convinced her to buy it.

"You look so beautiful," he told her. "I sneaked a peek into the dining room tonight, just to look at you. It seemed like there was a lively conversation going on at your table. I'm glad you invited Aster to join you. Is she okay?"

"She seems quite convinced that Peter's ghost has finally shown up, and that makes her happy. She's baking the cookies in her suite, so I'm sure you won't run out of them in your kitchen."

"Everyone likes them." He took her hand. "I'm not forgetting about that cookie table for our wedding."

She repeated the words softly, almost to herself. "Our wedding."

He smiled, and said the words again. "I know. I keep repeating it to myself. It'll be official soon. It just has to happen in the right place at the right time. Soon. Really soon."

She was positive that tomorrow morning's run would take them to the right place at the right time and that when they returned to the inn, she'd be an engaged woman. She could hardly wait for him to surprise her with a ring.

They chatted briefly about business—or rather, the lack of it. She told him about the cancelled reservations and the early checkouts. "As soon as the police arrest Holiday's killer, everything will be back to normal, I'm sure." Her tone was hopeful.

"Do you think it's somebody we know?" he asked.

"I hope it isn't."

"Does Hubbard think it is?"

"I don't know. If he does, he hasn't shared it with me."

"It's tough," Ted said. "No fingerprints, no witnesses, not even any video. That's strange. It seems as if these days, there's *always* a camera watching you, no matter where you are."

"If there was one, no one has come up with it so far. Aster has one in the front of the store and a couple of them inside, but there wasn't one in the back. After all, there's nothing out there except the flowers and a few vegetables. Aster always said she never minded if anyone wanted to swipe either one. Her property extends back another two or three acres, but that's all hills and trees and a lot of squirrels and birds. Beyond that, there's an old nineteen-fifties style neighborhood of around a dozen tract houses. A few of them have cameras, but nothing interesting has shown up there."

"She still insists that it was Peter who led her to the body?"

"She seems quite positive about it," Maureen agreed.

"So no one knows if she imagined it, or if it was a person in disguise, or a hologram, or a mirror image of some kind, or a . . ."—he glanced around in true Haven fashion to be sure no one was listening and whispered the last words—"a ghost."

"No one knows that," she agreed, "but I'll bet someone knows who Holiday's killer is, and someone is protecting him—or her."

"What makes you think so?"

"Too many people disliked him, or at least disrespected him," she explained.

"Like his fellow writers, who said they thought he should be shot or hanged or poisoned or strangled."

"Exactly. And even his own daughter says he was a terrible writer and that he's only famous for getting himself killed. I have to go to his funeral on Wednesday, because I promised Hubbard that I would." Maureen focused her attention on the lazily swimming angelfish over the bar. "I'm not looking forward to meeting a daughter who seems not only disrespectful, but mean. Now she's refusing to pay the ghostwriter her father owed money to."

"No kidding? Where'd you hear that?"

"From Molly—via the Quic Shop," Maureen reported. "She says Carleton charged him fifty thousand dollars to write *How to Make Your City Famous and Attract Big Spenders*—half to start and half the balance when it was published, and half of the royalties. Hannah Hamburger says writing was just her father's hobby and that paying Fretham is like throwing good money after bad. I'm quite sure she isn't expecting any royalties."

"What does Fretham say about it?"

"I don't know. I haven't mentioned it to him," she said. "It's none of my business."

"But you like the book?"

"I do. That book, along with Finn, gave me the idea for the 'Pet-Friendly Haven' promotion."

"How's that coming along?"

"I'm encouraged by the response so far," she said. "But famous or not, until the killer is caught, I don't think *any* promotion is going to attract big spenders to Haven."

"We're feeling the effects of it in the kitchen now," he said. "I may have to let some of my part-time high school kitchen helpers go if the dining room gets much emptier."

Maureen knew that Ted wouldn't want to do that. Haven, like the rest of Florida, was growing fast. A brand-new high school was being built to accommodate the larger classes, and meanwhile, the old high school was on double sessions. Ted had two shifts of willing teenaged workers—a morning crew to help with breakfast and an afternoon group for dinner prep.

"I hope it doesn't come to that," she told him. "Honestly, if it wasn't for you and Sam and George and Gert and Molly, I might not be able to stay afloat at all." It was true. She was grateful to all of them. "Wouldn't it be awful if after a century in business, Haven House Inn had to close?"

"We won't ever let that happen," he promised. "Can we do anything to help Hubbard, besides keep our eyes and ears open?"

"I'm doing my best at that." She told him about the evening's interaction with Detective Taylor, and that she'd shared what she'd learned with Hubbard. "I think he feels that Taylor is working *his* case."

"It seems to me it would be helpful if they could work together instead of competing with each other," he suggested.

"You're right," she said. "That might be really helpful. I'll try to get them into the same room together somehow and see if they can cooperate. Maybe they'll mesh perfectly."

"Maybe they'll explode." He smiled. "But it's worth a try."

"I'm going to do it," she said. "I have a feeling it will work."

Wow! Finally. A feeling. After all this time!

Tomorrow she'd tell Frank Hubbard about the feeling.

She could hardly wait for the Tuesday morning run and Ted's special surprise. "A beautiful love story has begun," the astrology book had said. "Let your intuition guide you," it had advised.

Tomorrow was absolutely going to be a wonderful day.

Wasn't it?

Chapter 17

Finn woke up before Maureen did, and insistently tugged at her bedcovers. "Woof!" he insisted.

"Oh sure. That's easy for you to say." She sat up and yawned. "You were sound asleep before dinner. I was up until almost midnight. Okay. I'll take a shower, and we'll go to the beach."

She was as anxious as he was to get this day underway, and she hummed happily as she ran the warm shower. She'd decided to wear a pink shorts-and-shirt combination again, partly to complement her fingernails, and partly because she'd had so many compliments on the previous night's pinky-rose outfit—which still hung in her closet. She thought again about buying it. Maybe.

Finn fetched his own leash from the kitchen, and carried it in his mouth to the front door, where he deposited it gently on the floor. "Woof?" he pleaded.

The clock showed nearly six. It wasn't too early to head downstairs, where she'd arranged to meet Ted at the side door. She leashed Finn, and the two went down the stairs. She wished Hilda a good morning and promised to be back to relieve her soon. "Any phone action?" she asked.

"One call for you. Elaine wanted to know if the Friday writer's meeting is still on. I checked your calendar and told her it's on the schedule."

"I hope they're not going to cancel. It's a freebie, but at least it'll be an almost full table." Maureen was justifiably proud of the way the aged round tables looked in the recently redecorated dining room. Each of the tables was topped with a vintage snowy white, real linen, round tablecloth. Penelope Josephine had never skimped on quality, and even though some of the tablecloths had been carefully mended, Maureen had no intention of ever replacing them with plastic cloths or paper placemats as so many other eating establishments had done to save money. Gert and Molly and some of the neighborhood women laundered and ironed the tablecloths after every use. Even if the writers weren't paying, it would look good to have one of the largest tables in use.

Hilda looked appropriately sympathetic. "If you need me to help out with anything at all, day or night, just call me. Have a nice run," she said.

Having a nice run today was one thing Maureen was quite sure about. "We will," she said. Finn gave a positive "woof," and tugged her toward the side door.

Ted waited on the path between the inn and the evolving Tiki bar, and Maureen ran to where he stood, his arms spread wide to embrace her. He held her close for a long moment, whispered "I love you" into her hair, then stood back, his hands on her shoulders. "This is such a special day for me. I want to remember every single minute of it. I want to remember how you look and what you're wearing and how good you smell."

"I love all the memories we're making together," she told him.

"Woof woof woof," Finn announced.

"Yes, you're a big part of our memories too." Ted laughed, bending to pat the golden. "Let's run and make some more."

With Finn in the lead, they jogged down to the hard-packed sand along the shoreline, then began the familiar run toward the long pier in the distance. The early morning sunrise had painted the sky with pink and orange streaks, and a fading half-moon was still visible in the western sky. It was a perfect day for running—cool, with just a hint of a breeze and barely any humidity. Maureen gave herself up to the pure exhilaration of it all. Thoughts about business worries or even about the expected surprise at the end of the run were momentarily banished.

Before long, she spotted the familiar weather-beaten sign in the distance. They were still too far away for the words on it to be legible, but they both knew them from memory: LONG PIER FISHING CHARTERS.

The memories of the old sign came flooding back. The fish she'd caught, the picture in Penelope Josephine's office, the place where the fish had been cooked all those years ago. So many questions. It was in front of this sign that she and Ted had shared their very first kiss. There was no question about that! It made sense to Maureen that they would officially become engaged at that spot. In fact, she was positive of it.

Of course she was right. Finn reached the sign first and sat in an expectant position, just as if he knew something special was coming. As Ted dropped to one knee, in the traditional posture, she felt her back pocket to be sure her phone was there. Would there be someone around to snap the picture?

Ted presented the open blue velvet ring box. Finn gave a soft "woof," at the sound of running feet coming from the opposite direction.

"Will you marry me?" Ted said.

"Oh, yes." Her eyes were misty, her voice strong.

"Ooops," came a woman's voice. "Am I interrupting an intimate moment?"

"Not at all." Maureen beamed and handed the woman her phone. "You're just in time to capture it for us." A couple of seconds later, the phone was back in her hand. Ted stood once again, kissed her soundly, and the woman was gone.

"Thank you," Maureen called.

"You're welcome." The voice drifted back, but the woman's form was lost in the early morning mist.

Chapter 18

The run back to Beach Boulevard was somewhat slower than the earlier run had been. Maureen kept looking away from the sandy shoreline and the distant Casino building to admire the glitter of the diamond ring on her rosy-nailed left hand.

The modest-sized emerald-cut diamond, set horizontally on a simple gold band, was a perfect combination of the traditional solitaire with a contemporary twist. She loved everything about it—and told Ted so —many times during the run back to home. He grasped her right hand tightly in his, holding Finn's leash in the other, and beamed broadly at her words of loving praise. "I've been saving up all of my tips for quite a while," he admitted.

That made her love the ring—and the man—even more.

Once back on the boulevard, the two slowed to a walk. "Now that we're officially engaged, we can walk down the street holding hands and stop trying to pretend we're just friends," he said.

"I don't think we've fooled anybody." She suppressed a giggle. "Not for a long time."

"Have you ever been to Key West?" he asked.

The question surprised her. *What does Key West have to do with anything?*

"No. I've always meant to. Why?"

"Do you think we could both take a couple of days off and check it out? We could leave on Friday afternoon and be back on Sunday morning."

She squeezed his hand. "I think it's an excellent idea. Business is slow anyway," she alibied. *And this avoids pop-in ghost visits in my room and thin walls and next door co-workers in his.*

"There was enough tip money left for a motel, but if we're going to fly, you'll have to pitch in. We could drive, and save some money," he added, "but it's at least seven hours on the road each way."

"We'll fly."

"I can prepare menus ahead for a weekend, and Joyce is capable of directing everything," he said. "No problem."

"Hilda has offered to work the desk some days, and Shelly is always looking for extra hours," she pointed out.

Not unexpectedly, the first people to see the new ring were the four early risers in the rocking chairs at the head of the inn's front stairs. The women *ooh*ed and *aah*ed over the style of the setting and the brilliance of the stone. The men pumped Ted's hand and pounded his back, and all four voiced sincere congratulations and no one claimed to be one bit surprised.

The announcement of the engagement, the calls to Maureen's and Ted's parents, the showing off of the ring in person and on social media, arrangements for staff to cover both jobs and to care for Finn during the planned vacation, and with Friday only two days away, even the plans for the Key West weekend including flight plans and the motel reservation, all happened within an hour after their return to the inn. They'd leave Friday afternoon, flying from Clearwater airport, arriving in Key West in less than two hours.

"We'll be there in time to see the sunset ceremony at Mallory Square," Ted said. "You'll love it. Everybody does."

"I've read about it," she said. "This is going to be so much fun! I can hardly wait."

He pulled her close. "I can hardly wait either."

She understood exactly what he meant. "Me too," she whispered. "Me too."

Maureen called Shelly to watch the front desk while she took an afternoon break to begin the process of packing for the proposed trip to Key West. She'd put the open suitcase on her bed, and selected a sundress from her closet, when Lorna shimmered into view. Finn voiced a happy woof of welcome.

"So you're engaged, and you're going on a honeymoon to the Keys, huh?" the spirit asked, attempting a spectral pat on the head for Finn. "Can I see the ring?"

Maureen extended her left hand proudly.

"Cute." Lorna's comment was dismissive. "*All* of my diamond rings were much more—um—significant. But, a diamond is a diamond, I guess. Things are moving pretty fast. You're taking that?" She pointed a shimmery finger toward the spaghetti-strapped sundress with a nautical blue-and-white print.

"How did you find out about the engagement? It just happened." Maureen held the dress at arm's length. "Yes. I like it. What's wrong with it?"

"I heard Gert and Molly talking about it. Nothing's wrong with the dress, but you have some much cuter ones in the shop."

Wow! The news didn't even have to filter through Quic Shop. "I'm not going to spend my vacation tucking in price tags and being careful not to spill anything," Maureen pointed out. "Anyway, I need all the sales I can get from the shop while I'm away." She took a simple black crepe dress from the closet and put it on the bed.

"You're not planning on taking that old rag, are you?" Lorna looked aghast at the prospect.

"Of course not. I have to go to a funeral tomorrow."

"Oh, that. The dead writer. Listen. At least take one of the cute sun hats you have in the shop window with you on your trip. I wore one of them to Beach Week in Panama City and everyone raved about it," Lorna insisted.

"Okay. I can do that." Maureen folded a lacy blue nightie and added it to the suitcase, then held up a one-piece black halter top swimsuit for the spirit's inspection. "How about this?"

Lorna made a face. "No. Take the red bikini. Trust me."

She packed the bikini, putting the one-piece aside. The back-and-forth conversation and the folding and unfolding of garments went on for longer than it should have, but finally, the suitcase was filled to the satisfaction of both women. "I wish you'd packed some of that high-priced lingerie from the shop though." Lorna pouted.

"It'd be pretty hard to hide the price tags on those. They're practically transparent," Maureen pointed out.

"True," Lorna agreed. "Anyway, I don't think you'll need to try very hard to entice the man after all this time."

"True," Maureen echoed, quickly steering the conversation away from enticing lingerie. "While I'm gone, you'll keep an eye on Finn, won't you? And maybe you could read some nice dog stories to him at bedtime. He loves that."

"I'm way ahead of you. We're rereading *The Incredible Journey*. He never gets tired of hearing that one. The cats like it too."

"Thanks, Lorna. I appreciate you." Even as she spoke, Maureen realized how strange it was to have such sincere feelings about a ghost. The inheritance of Haven House Inn from Penelope Josephine Gray had changed her life in so many unforeseeable ways.

She looked once again at the ring. *Thank you, Penelope Josephine.*

"So you've invited the murder mystery writers to have their meetings here." It was Lorna's turn for subject-changing.

"I have. Do you still think it's bad karma?"

A shimmery shrug. "It doesn't have to be. Maybe going to the dead writer's funeral will help, and having the meetings here is a good omen."

"How so?"

"That bunch knows more about murder than both of those stuck-up cops put together do. I think you should throw the whole gang of them around the table and see if they can figure out who offed the dead writer."

"Ted told me once that he thinks the detectives should try to work together."

"Ted is right."

"And you're right." Maureen closed the suitcase firmly. "I'll call Hubbard and tell him I have a feeling. The writers meet on Friday right after lunch. I'll invite Hubbard and Taylor to meet with us."

"You're going to sit in with them?"

"I wouldn't miss it for the world," Maureen declared. "We'll use one of the biggest tables. There's plenty of room for all of us."

"In that case," Lorna suggested, "you might as well invite the uppity ghostwriter. Carleton. He thinks he's smarter than anybody else, anyway."

Chapter 19

Packing finished and ready to go, Maureen relieved Shelly at the reservation desk, pulled up her list of phone numbers, and began calling, starting with Elaine. All of the Murder Incorporated writers were delighted by the idea that they'd get to share murder plot points with a couple of professional detectives, and at the same time have a chance to quiz the men about details of police work. Frank Hubbard was not exactly delighted, but agreed that he valued having an opportunity to quiz the writers—who were, after all, along with much of the population of Haven, among the possible suspects. He seemed okay with the idea of a possible face-to-face meeting with his out-of-state counterpart, Robert Taylor.

Maureen called Dick Flannagan to find out if the Taylors would still be in Haven on Friday. They would be. She asked for the detective's telephone number and was pleased when he readily agreed to join the proposed meeting.

"It'll be an interesting break from laying around on the beach and eating great seafood, and fishing from my brother-in-law's motor boat," Taylor told her. "It's a fascinating case. The idea of involving people who study and write about murder is—well—brilliant."

I'll be sure to share that with Lorna, Maureen thought.

With the meeting time and place established, and with participation by all of the participants, including Carleton Fretham, confirmed, Maureen tried hard to refocus her attention on the pressing need to fill up the suites and rooms of Haven House Inn. The Dog-Friendly Haven idea was a good one, she was sure, but it would take a while to gain enough momentum to show up in the bank account. Meanwhile, she needed a quick promotion to stimulate business right away.

She thought back to her department store days. What had they done to move people through the doors of that grand old store? There'd been special sales, of course, usually with the cooperation of manufacturers. They'd arrange a price break with a TV manufacturer, or a maker of brand-name cosmetics, or a fashion line, and pass on the savings to the customers. But with the hotel business, there were no helpful vendors to share expenses with. Sometimes there was a general price break—like a twenty percent day, when everything in the store was twenty percent off. That wouldn't work either. She'd be losing money at that rate.

What did other businesses or organizations do? They offered amusements. She remembered bingo night at a local church back in Massachusetts. People had paid to get into the hall. They paid for the bingo cards. They'd paid for soda and chips. Prizes were cash—or sometimes they might be other things of value—like a weekend stay at a beautiful inn. Or a week of free breakfasts.

She could do it with signs and paper flyers. The minute she and Ted got back from the Keys, she'd set it in motion. They could use the Tiki bar! She could see the signs in her mind.

WEDNESDAY NIGHT BINGO AT HAVEN HOUSE INN.

She could hardly wait to tell Ted about it. The opportunity to do so came when he appeared at her office door just as the early-bird dinner folks began to trickle in. It was a pretty slow trickle, she noted. If business didn't pick up soon, she'd be in financial trouble. She shook away the bad thought and greeted Ted with a smile. "Hi," she said. "I was just thinking about you."

"I think about you nonstop. Day and night," he responded.

"Aw, thank you," she said. "But, seriously, we need to think about business if we plan to keep this particular roof over our heads much longer." She pointed upward. "We can't live on love."

"Oh yeah. Business. Actually that's what brings me out of the kitchen right now. A guy who was here for the breakfast buffet this morning wants to know if we can cater a small beach wedding. About fifty people. It'll be in a couple of weeks, and he wants to see a sample menu of the food we can provide." He held out a stapled stack of paper. "Here're a few menus and cost estimates for each of them. Shall I tell him it's okay?" He sat in the chair facing her desk.

She studied the pages. *A relationship is made of shared dreams and projects,* the astrology book had advised. "It's a really good idea if you and the staff can do it without stretching yourselves too thin," she told him. "The cost estimates seem reasonable and the profit sounds really good."

"We can do it. I already checked with everybody," he assured her. "A beach wedding sounds like fun, doesn't it? Let's look into that idea for us when we get back from our trip."

"I love the idea. When do you think it should be?" Maureen wondered. "My parents will be coming all the way from California, so they'll need time to plan."

"When our parents meet each other, wouldn't it be amazing if somebody remembered that day when you were twelve and caught a fish and had it cooked at a restaurant?" he asked.

"That would be just too hard to believe, even in Haven," she told him. "Meanwhile, here's an idea we can put into motion soon." She told him about the bingo game. "Maybe we can use the Tiki hut for it."

"I like it," he said. "But I think the dining room will be the place to hold it. It's the biggest space we have, and all the tables are in place. How about this? On bingo night, while we're setting up for bingo inside, we'll serve a Hawaiian buffet in the Tiki Hut. It'll give me a chance to try out the new gas grill."

"And we'll be able to sell them dinner in the Tiki and then sell them on bingo in the dining room. Win-win." She smiled. "I like it too."

"I think we've managed to find answers to all of our pressing questions," he said. "We've done everything we can to keep Haven House afloat."

"You're right," she agreed. "We can relax knowing that we've done the best we could with what we have to work with. We can go on our much-deserved vacation with pure hearts and clear consciences." There was a hesitant tap on the partly open office door. "Come in, Aster," Maureen called. "Is everything okay?"

Aster attempted a tentative smile. She carried a tray bearing two flower-sprigged teacups, matching sugar bowl, cream pitcher, and a plate of cookies. "I thought you might enjoy a nice tea break." She placed the tray on Maureen's desk. "It's that good English tea that you like. I have something to tell you."

Ted moved a white wicker chair closer to the desk. "Here. Sit down. What's going on?"

"It's Peter," Aster said. "He wants me to follow him into the woods behind my garden. You know he wanted to save that poor Mr. Holiday. He saw the length of cord all laid out like a noose, and he tried to get Mr. Holiday's attention, but the poor soul was one of those people who can't see ghosts, so Peter came running to get me so I could warn him, but I was too late. What if there's another dead person out there? That's something I don't ever want to see again." She put both of her hands around her own throat in a choking motion, rolled her eyes back, and stuck out her tongue. "It's not a pretty sight."

Maureen had a feeling that she'd better call Frank Hubbard.

"I'll call the police, Aster. Don't worry. They'll take care of it."

"Oh, I almost forgot. Peter said he's sorry he caused such a stir when he sat in the store window and Officer Hubbard had to come and break up the crowd. He promises he won't do anything like that again."

"Officer Hubbard will be pleased to hear that." Maureen picked up one of the cups, added two lumps of sugar, and sipped the steaming brew.

Tea for two?

Chapter 20

"So are you going to tell me that you saw the old man's ghost again?" Hubbard demanded.

"Nope. Not me. I'm just telling you what Aster said. I'm sure not going into the woods to check it out." She spoke with conviction. "She also said that Peter won't be showing up around town again. He's sorry he caused you trouble last time."

"The ghost was a trick. Aster is messing with us somehow." Long pause. "But I'll send someone out there. It's in the woods behind the garden, you say?"

"She didn't actually say there was anything there. Just that he wants her to follow him." Maureen was beginning to feel sorry that she'd called Frank. Although she'd promised Aster that she'd tell the police about Peter's invitation to take a walk in the woods, Maureen had hesitated to make the call. After all, Peter hadn't actually *said* there was somebody being threatened or maybe even dead among the trees. Why should she bother a busy police officer who doesn't believe in ghosts, with such an unlikely tale? But when once again the player piano had—unbidden—plinked out a honky-tonk version of "Don't Stop Believin'," she'd reached for her phone. "I appreciate your looking into it, Frank," she said, "even though I guess it's possible that Aster is imagining these things. It's been stressful for her. For all of us. The whole town is on edge."

"Don't rub it in, Doherty," he growled. "We're doing the best we can. There just isn't much to go on when all you've got is ghost stories and a real unpopular dead man. Even his own daughter doesn't seem to have much respect for him. You probably won't get much information by going to that funeral. I guess he didn't have a lot of friends. I'm hoping the get-together you've planned for Friday will help me narrow down the field of suspects, though." Another pause. "You haven't told Taylor about this, have you?"

"Are you kidding? Would I talk to an outsider about a ghost in Haven? Not me. Not anybody."

"Okay, then. I'll send a uniform over to look around. If anyone asks, I'll blame it on reports about somebody shooting squirrels in there," he said.

"Is that true?" she asked. "Somebody's been shooting squirrels?"

"I'm afraid so. You know how college kids have always sneaked into the woods to drink beer and leave their beer cans around. Somebody got the bright idea of using the cans for target practice. You know, setting up beer cans against a hill and plinking away at them. Aster never objected to it. But killing squirrels is something else. Not that squirrels aren't pests sometimes, but there are humane ways to get rid of them. Anyway, it's private property. We'll check it out."

It was with a sense of relief that Maureen sent Molly to the Dawn Wells Suite to return Aster's clean tray, cups, and plates. The message, ostensibly from Peter, had been delivered to the proper authority. Had the "Tea for Two" tune been a message from Billy Bedoggoned, or just a random selection from the pre-programmed recordings? If it was a message, and it was linked to Aster's tea and Peter's most recent pronouncement, she'd handled it properly by calling Hubbard. She dusted her hands together in a motion of "that's that," and focused her attention on the upcoming writer's meeting—to be followed by what she was beginning to think about as a much-anticipated early honeymoon.

Since the writer's meeting was a freebie, she'd planned only coffee and Aster's shortbread cookies for the requisite snacks—and even those small items cost money. The sooner Frank Hubbard could bring the killer of Terry Holiday to justice, the sooner business in Haven would return to its healthy, bustling, normal touristy self. Maybe the meeting, involving all of the writers along with the presumed ghostwriter and two detectives, would shed some overdue light on the subject and get the proverbial ball rolling in the right direction.

Vacation wardrobe selected, and suitcase packed with Lorna's approval, Haven House Inn business attended to as well as possible under the trying circumstances, Maureen decided to take Finn for an extra walk, and maybe stop at a few of the other businesses along the boulevard to see how they were coping with the visitor slowdown. Molly cheerfully volunteered for desk duty. "It's not as if I'll have to do anything. There's no business anyway," was her good-humored reasoning.

Maureen took the elevator up to the third floor, listening for Finn's welcoming "woof" as she hurried down the hall to her suite. The woofing was happy, and there was prancing and kissing and no visiting ghosts when she opened the door. She grabbed the leash from behind the kitchen door, and they were off.

Maureen and Finn had just stepped onto the sidewalk in front of the inn, when the familiar Ford Victoria pulled up beside her. Hubbard leaned out the window.

"What are you trying to pull, Doherty? And don't give me that ghost crap either." He didn't ever try to lower his voice when he uttered the Haven-forbidden g-word. She took a fast glance up at the porch, where—fortunately—no one except Gert, Sam, and George were present.

She put a finger to her lips, warning him against repeating such an indiscretion, and approached the police car. "What is it, Frank?"

"Just stop wasting my valuable time with stupid stories Aster is feeding you. I feel like I have to follow up, because

Aster and my mother are best friends. I sent a perfectly good cop tramping through those woods, halfway expecting to find another victim, and all he came up with after wasting an hour was a couple of target shooters with twenty-twos, and a case of poison oak that'll put him out of commission for a week." Hubbard glared.

"I never said there was a victim in the woods. Neither did Aster." Maureen kept her voice low. "I just told you what Peter said."

"Well, stop it. Don't bother me with this nonsense again. Got it?"

"Got it," she said, "and tell him to try calamine lotion for the poison oak."

Hubbard didn't answer, just raced the engine a couple of times, then drove away.

Gert called down from her regular spot at the head of the stairs. "Old Frankie's got his panties in a wad over something. What's he so mad about?"

"No big deal. I gave him a tip that didn't work out," Maureen said. "He'll get over it." Finn tugged at the leash, and the two hurried away from the inn, avoiding more questions. If Hubbard didn't want any more information from her, there wouldn't be any, she vowed. "I was just trying to help," she told the dog.

"Woof," he agreed. "Woof woof."

Maureen's first stop was at a place she rarely visited—the Quic Shop. If there was a lot of talk around Haven about the slowdown of business, that would be the place to hear about it. She tied Finn's leash to the railing on the narrow porch in front of the store and went inside. She'd tucked a few dollars into the pocket of her shirt. After all, the least she could do was buy something while she snooped for information.

She didn't have to do much snooping. The topic of conversation the second she stepped inside was the recent dearth of customers. "Hey there, Ms. Doherty, how's business at the inn? It's slower than marked-down molasses in here." She was greeted by the store's proprietor from behind the counter. That, in itself, was unusual. Mr. O'Leary usually watched over his domain from inside his glass-windowed office. Perhaps some of the part-time employees had had their hours shortened. Maureen felt blessed that she had such loyal live-in help. *Thank you again, Penelope Josephine.*

"Not so good," she told him honestly. "Cancelled reservations and even a few early checkouts."

"We're feeling the same thing. So's everybody else in town. The word is that it's because of all the publicity about the murder of that writer." He frowned. "There were a few curiosity seekers right after it happened, but then the cops closed up the bookstore and made the garden a crime scene, so there was nothing for the lookie-loos to see. People are afraid to come to Haven until the Flower Garden Killer is caught, and that's the truth of it. It's still in the headlines." He pointed to a newspaper rack, where the *Tampa Bay Times* headline proclaimed, "No Progress in Garden Murder." The *Haven Beach Beacon* had similar news. "Locals Questioned About Killing."

Maureen picked up a copy of the *Beacon*, wondering if it gave the names of the people being questioned, then added a too-expensive package of refrigerated dog food. Mr. O'Leary nodded his approval of the dog food purchase. "Glad to see you're not cutting back on Fido. A lot of people have switched to the cheap canned stuff." He gave a disapproving sniff.

"It's for Finn," she said. "He's worth it." She walked around in the store, where she recognized most of the few customers there. She spoke to each one, with a noncommittal greeting like "How's everything going?" or "How are things with you?" All of the answers were negative, some more downbeat than others. One woman had lost her job, and several admitted to cutting back on movies and eating out. She paid for her purchases, wished Mr. O'Leary a nice day, and left the store.

Maureen and Finn's next stop was the Second Glance Thrift Store. Surely the low prices and the fact that all the proceeds went to a women's shelter would assure that at least their business would hold steady. Finn was always welcomed inside the thrift store, and he was greeted with the usual enthusiasm by Mr. Crenshaw, the manager. "Good to see you, Maureen, and I'm always glad to see this big fella, too," he said. "How're things?" He asked the question before she'd had a chance to voice it.

"Slow," she said. "How about you?"

"Could be better. Could be a lot better," he admitted. "Worse than that, the donations have slowed down too. It seems like people are holding onto their old stuff. Do you think it's because of the killing over at the bookstore?"

"I do," Maureen said. "I can't think of any other reason. Things seem to be normal for this time of year in Tampa and Orlando. I'm trying to think up promotions to perk things up."

"I've heard about the Dog-Friendly Haven idea." He smiled and gave Finn an extra chuck under the chin. "We're sure friendly to dogs here." She told him about the proposed Yappy Hour and her idea for bingo nights at the inn. "I've got quite a few boxes of bingo cards for sale here," he offered, "and some of the daubers to mark the cards too." He quoted a reasonable price.

"Mark 'em sold," she said. "I'll bring you a check later today. I need to get home and put Finn's food in the refrigerator."

"Maybe things are looking up," she told Finn as they crossed the boulevard and walked toward the inn. "It looks like bingo night is good to go."

Finn's "Woof" was doubtful.

Chapter 21

When Maureen and Finn climbed the stairs to the front porch, Gert, George, and Sam were in their usual spots, all three leaning forward in their rockers, obviously anxious to speak.

"What's going on?" she asked.

"We don't know," Sam said. "Something's up with Aster. She's been sitting at the table in the lobby waiting for you ever since you left. She won't talk to us about whatever's bugging her."

"Oh dear. I hope she's okay." Maureen moved quickly toward the green door.

"Let us know what's going on," Gert said. "We all worry about her ever since—you know."

"I know." She handed Gert the Quic Shop bag. "Would you put this in my refrigerator, please? I'll see if Aster will talk to me." She pushed the door open. As Sam had described, Aster sat in one of the wicker chairs, eyes closed, hands folded in her lap. Molly, from behind the reception desk, lifted her hands in an *I don't know what's going on* gesture. Maureen took the seat across the bamboo table from the silent woman. "Aster? Are you okay?"

Aster opened her eyes. "Oh, Maureen, I'm glad you're back. I'm sure it's all my fault that Officer Hubbard scolded you the way he did. Right in front of everybody too." She made a disapproving "tsk-tsk" sound, then whispered. "Actually it was Peter's fault. Naturally he apologized, but you'd already left."

Maureen looked around, hoping no one else was listening. *Oops*. The McKennas, along with Snicker, had just entered the lobby. Had they overheard? If so, maybe the name "Peter" didn't mean anything to them. She stood, greeted the couple, and patted the labradoodle. "Are you folks enjoying your stay?" she asked, hoping for a positive response.

"Loving it," Mrs. McKenna responded with a wide grin. "We had our pictures taken in front of Babe Ruth's house today and went over to the ball park to buy some Tampa Bay Rays gear for the grandkids."

"Delighted to hear it," she said, relieved, thinking, *maybe things really* are *looking up—or else the McKennas don't read the local papers*. Either way, it was good news. She reached for Aster's hand and spoke softly, gently. "Let's discuss this in my office, shall we?" The woman followed obediently, without comment. With only a sidelong glance at the closed steamer trunk, Maureen closed the office door and directed Aster to the chair closest to her own. "Now tell me all about Peter, won't you?"

Aster leaned forward. "It wasn't totally his fault, you know. He *still* wants me to follow him into the woods, but not until he tells me to. He's worried that something bad is going to happen there. Don't you worry about anybody else seeing him. He'll make sure they don't this time. But something is going to happen in there, Maureen. And it won't be something good. He wants me to be ready when he says it's time. I'm not going to do it. It was too awful before. I thought he meant I should go right then, as soon as he told me. I misunderstood, but when he tells me he'll lead me there—whenever that is—I'll have to tell him no. I'll tell you about it, though, and you can tell Officer Hubbard."

No, I can't, Maureen thought. *Hubbard told me explicitly not to bother him with this stuff again. If Aster is right, and there's going to be another victim in the woods, somebody will find him—or her—sooner or later.* It was a cold reality. She faced Aster. "I think you need to tell Peter that you can't do it," she said. "Do you think he knows who the victim will be? Maybe we can figure out how to warn him—or her—somehow."

"That's a very good idea, Maureen." Aster's eyes brightened. "I'll tell him I'm not going to do it, and I'll ask him about the victim when I see him later today. He likes to watch me when I make the cookies." She stood, smiling. "I feel better already. By the way, I'm a little short of butter. Do you think Ted could lend me a quarter of a pound?"

"I'm sure he could." The two women crossed the lobby and made their way to the kitchen entrance.

The requested stick of butter was foil-wrapped, brown-bagged, handed to Aster, and she'd taken the elevator back up to the Dawn Wells Suite to do her daily baking and to confront Peter. Molly had returned to her regular duties, and Maureen was once again at the reception desk when George burst into the lobby from the front porch to deliver the latest news from the Haven grapevine at the very same moment that an out-of-breath Aster dashed from the indoor staircase with almost the same news from Peter.

A target-shooting teen had called 911, an officer had been dispatched to the woods behind the garden crime scene, and the still-warm body of Walter Griffith had been identified, the apparent victim of a bullet wound.

Now Haven had two unsolved deaths to deal with, and both of the victims were writers—one of them whose funeral she expected to attend the following day and the other whom Maureen had expected to see in her dining room on Friday afternoon. She wasn't surprised when Frank Hubbard called to see what she knew about the departed ghostwriter.

Yes, she'd met him. She'd heard that he wrote thriller mysteries of the bloody variety along with some others about animals. No, she hadn't read any of them. Yes, he'd been at dinner in her restaurant on Monday night. No, she hadn't noticed whom he left with. She thought about that. Had Elaine

Cremonis been his date? It had looked that way. He hadn't tried to hide his interest in her. But had they left together? She honestly didn't know. Was it important enough to mention to Hubbard?

"He could have left with Elaine Cremonis," she said. "I think they arrived together."

"You *think* they arrived together? He *could have* left with Elaine? Can't you do better than that, Doherty?" There was exasperation in his tone, and she couldn't blame him for that.

"I'm sorry, Frank. It didn't seem important at the time. I understand that Walter was shot."

"Where did you hear that?" he rasped. "I haven't released that information."

She hesitated. He wasn't going to like her answer. "Aster says that Peter told her about it, and besides that, George knew about it too—from the Quic Shop, I suppose."

Hubbard didn't bother to say "goodbye" when he hung up. Aster would surely have uttered a stern "tsk-tsk" over such a lapse of manners.

Chapter 22

Maureen's Wednesday morning run on the beach had to be cut short so that she'd have time to take care of morning business and then get into the black dress for Trenton Hamburger's ten a.m. funeral. She ran only halfway to the fishing sign, told Ted she'd see him later at the inn, and returned with Finn to the lobby.

Hilda held up an early-edition newspaper. "Another one, huh? It says here that writer everyone's talking about died of a gunshot wound. Wasn't he one of the ones you invited for Friday afternoon?"

So Hubbard had released the news. "Right. Walter Griffith. Does the paper give any details about what happened? Any witnesses? Videos? Anything?"

Hilda studied the front page. "Nothing much here. The police are asking anybody who was in the vicinity of those woods yesterday morning and heard or saw anything unusual to call a special number. They're asking neighbors with outdoor video cameras to check their footage to see who might show up on it."

"What kind of bullet? Does it say?"

"A twenty-two caliber."

"No kidding. Did they get the names of the people who were shooting in the woods yesterday? I heard that they were using twenty-twos."

"No names. It says here they've interviewed several people who've been known to fire weapons in the woods. Here's a sad note about that poor man who got shot. It seems that he wrote books about small animals and really cared about them." She made a "tsk-tsk" sound worthy of Aster Patterson. "He was worried about the squirrels. He used to go in there and talk to the young people about protecting them. He posted signs in there about how important the small animals like squirrels and possums are to the environment. He even gave away some of his books."

"Poor Walter. I didn't know him well, but I liked him. And now Haven has not one, but two unexplained deaths keeping people away, and I'll be going to another funeral. Say, can you stay here until Shelly arrives?"

"Of course. Your plate is awfully full right now, isn't it?" Hilda folded the newspaper. "You've barely had time to enjoy getting engaged, and you're working extra hard thinking up ways to keep Haven House afloat. I heard about the bingo parties. Everyone is excited about that idea. I'll be a customer for sure."

I haven't even made the flyers yet. News travels fast in Haven. "I hope it will help. Right now I need to be sure the dining room is set up for breakfast and that today's menus are in all the guests' mailboxes." She slipped a menu into each of the nine unblocked slots and put one into her own pocket. "We going to need more than nine suites filled, though."

"We'll be fine." Hilda's words were encouraging, even though her eyes seemed sad.

Finn's "woof" was definitely positive. "Woof woof," he insisted.

Maybe, Maureen thought, *if the service for Terry Holiday isn't too long, I'll have time to zip over to Treasure Island and see what Zoltar has to say about all this.* After checking the dining room and greeting Ted with a kiss when he returned from the beach, she and Finn climbed the stairs to her suite. She opened the new dog food and fed Finn, then checked the menu to see what her own choices for breakfast were. One of Ted's giant blueberry muffins and plenty of coffee would make a good start to this busy day.

By nine thirty, she'd made the promised return visit to the thrift store, paid for and picked up the bingo cards and daubers, donned the black dress, gassed up the green Subaru and run it through the nearby Mister Carwash, and headed for the funeral for the man she'd never met but that she'd promised Hubbard she'd attend. She hoped the effort would yield information to help her adopted city get back to its normal, if haunted, self.

There were few cars in the parking lot at the small community church. The foyer was cool and dimly lighted, and slow, measured strains of organ music issued from inside. The aisle leading through the nearly empty sanctuary to the altar looked very long indeed from where Maureen stood in the doorway.

There was a coffin at the front of the church, and two women sat together in the first pew. As she drew closer, Maureen remembered Aster's graphic description of how the man's face had been distorted in death and was glad that the coffin was closed. She tiptoed down the aisle, grateful for thick carpeting muffling her footsteps, and sat directly behind the women. She assumed a prayerful posture and leaned as far forward as she could.

Since both women sat with heads bowed, backs to her, she couldn't distinguish their features. Maureen assumed that one of them had to be Hamburger's daughter, she who, according to Quic Shop reports, had said that her father was a terrible writer who was only famous for getting himself killed.

The organ music halted when a man wearing a black academic robe with a blue stole across his shoulders entered the room from a side door and approached the coffin. He looked quite young to be a pastor, and appeared nervous as he began to read from a black-covered book."We are gathered here to pay our respects and to celebrate the life of . . ." He paused, consulting a white index card. "Trenton Hamburger." He looked up and nodded in the direction of the women. "He leaves behind . . ." Again he consulted the card. "A loving daughter, Hannah. This is a most difficult day for her." He placed one hand on the coffin. "Trenton, thank you for all that you were and all that you gave and may you now rest in peace. Amen."

He moved toward the first pew, extending his right hand toward the woman closer to the aisle. Both women stood, and he gave each one a solemn handshake, murmuring low-toned condolences. Maureen leaned closer. "So sorry. Praying for you." He exited by the same door he'd entered from.

That may have been his first funeral, Maureen thought, *and I'm sure he's glad it's over.* It was obvious from his hesitant words that the youthful pastor hadn't known the deceased or anything about him. If she was going to learn anything new, she may as well approach the daughter—whichever woman that might be. She made the first bold step, moved to the front of the pew, and stuck out her hand toward the woman the pastor had shaken hands with first. "Hello. I'm Maureen Doherty from Haven, and I'm so sorry for your loss." She knew she'd chosen correctly even before she'd finished the words. The woman standing beside Hannah Hamburger was Judy Abbott, the erotic romance and murder mystery writer.

"Hello, Maureen," Judy Abbott greeted her. "I'm looking forward to our meeting on Friday. It was nice of you to come to say goodbye to Trenton."

"Thank you for coming," Hannah Hamburger said, and put out her hand. "My father didn't have many friends. Did you know him well?"

"I didn't know him," Maureen spoke hesitantly. "But I liked his most recent book, and I wanted to meet you and perhaps learn a little about him." *I'm also here to snoop and pry and pick up any little thing that might point to his killer.* "It's nice to see you, Judy," she added, wondering why a representative of the group who'd suggested numerous ways Terry Holiday should be murdered was here acting like family.

The organ had begun playing what sounded like a recessional hymn, and Hannah Hamburger moved into the aisle, followed by the writer, and motioned for Maureen to follow.

"The church ladies have set up a little coffee and cake reception for us, although the Lord only knows why. My father surely wasn't a churchgoer, and I don't know any of them. I guess it's just something they do for funerals."

"Yes," Maureen said. "People are kind."

Hannah looked surprised. "They are?"

Chapter 23

It was an awkward celebration of Trenton Hamburger's life. There were more church ladies present in the room adjoining the sanctuary than mourners, and much more cake than necessary. Maureen hoped that the church would find a worthy place to donate it while it was still fresh. She accepted a dainty teacup full of coffee and a good-sized piece of cake. Vanilla with excellent vanilla cream frosting. She made sure to stay close to Hannah Hamburger. Judy Abbott did the same. When the pair chose seats at a long table covered with a white linen tablecloth, she followed and took a seat directly across the table from Hannah, all the while searching for the right words to get the conversation headed in the direction she wanted it to go.

Hannah was the first to speak. "Thank you for coming—both of you. I had no idea what to expect. If my father hadn't pre-paid for his funeral a long time ago, I probably would have just had him cremated and put the ashes out in the Gulf. He and my mother were divorced years ago, so she has no interest in having them." She helped herself to another slice of cake. "I know that Judy here was one of Dad's writer friends. Do you write too, Maureen?"

Calling Judy a "writer friend" was quite a stretch, Maureen thought, but didn't comment on that. "No, I'm just a fan of his most recent book. I own an inn in Haven, and I found the promotional suggestions in *How to Make Your City Famous and Attract Big Spenders* quite useful."

"No kidding?" Judy asked. "You liked it?"

"Oh, yes," Maureen agreed. "I've already put one of his ideas into motion, and the next one won't be far behind."

"That's nice," Hannah said.

"He used a ghost," Judy mumbled.

"Is your inn that nice old one that Penelope Gray used to run?" Hannah asked.

"That's it. We've made a lot of improvements since she left it to me."

"She left it to you? I didn't know Penelope had children." Hannah put both elbows on the table and leaned toward Maureen, clearly interested in the topic.

"I wasn't a relative," Maureen explained, offering a brief rundown of the circumstances of the unexpected inheritance. "I'm still working on figuring out exactly how it all happened, but yes, it's mine now."

"Lucky you," Judy said. The comment had a sarcastic edge.

"Lucky is right." Hannah frowned. "Maureen gets a hotel from a stranger, and I get a stack of unpaid bills from my own father."

The conversation wasn't going in a helpful direction. Maureen gave it a push. "Tell me about him, please, Hannah. You must have some happy memories of him."

The woman's eyes took on a distant look. "He always wanted to be a writer," she said, "even when I was a little girl. He had other jobs, of course, real jobs—enough to keep a roof over our heads—just barely. My mother got tired of it and left him, and I shuffled between the two for years. She remarried and moved out of state. I was grown up by then and liked Florida, so I stayed. He kept writing. Some of the bills are from a stack of unsold books he had in a storage locker."

"Maybe you can sell them," Judy suggested. "A lot of writers get more famous after they're dead."

Maureen had no response to such an insensitive remark.

Hannah replied with a hesitant "Maybe."

"Especially since he was murdered," Judy went on. "There was a lot of publicity. You told me yourself that he was only famous for getting himself killed."

"That's true. I said it because I was angry." Her eyes were moist. "After all, he was my father."

"Hold onto the happy memories," Maureen suggested, hoping against hope that "friend" Judy would just shut up.

Fortuitously, one of the church ladies intervened at that moment, with a small square box tied with a white ribbon. She handed it to Hannah, who by then had real tears on her cheeks. "This is for you, Ms. Hamburger," she said. "We always make a CD of pastor's remarks as a memorial of the departed dear one."

Hannah grasped the package eagerly. "Thank you so very much," she said. "And thank you, Maureen and Judy, for well—for just being here—and of course there were happy memories with Daddy."

It was the first time Maureen had heard Hannah use the affectionate term *Daddy*. Maybe she was getting close to learning more about the man—and maybe more about why he had died in such a terrible way. "Tell us about him," she suggested.

"Let him rest in peace, like the man said." Judy's voice had an impatient edge.

"I don't mind talking about him," Hannah said, "if you don't mind listening."

Judy looked at her watch. Maureen poured another cup of coffee. Hannah helped herself to another slice of cake. "Writing those books made him happy," she began. "He really believed the subjects he chose were things that would make people's lives better. Even that last one—the one he paid somebody else to write—was his idea."

"Paying somebody else to write it was the best idea he ever had." Judy smirked. "You actually read it, didn't you, Maureen?"

"I did. You bought one too," Maureen reminded her.

"Sure. It has to be a verified purchase to get a review up on any of the worthwhile sites. Everybody in the Murderers Incorporated group bought one. We bought all his books so that we could . . ."

"So you all could post those one-star reviews," Hannah interrupted. "I understand. But not *everybody* hated his work. He had a few fans, and he relished those two- and even three-star comments. Heck, he didn't even mind the mean reviews. He said that just mentioning the name Terry Holiday in a review was a good thing. Daddy was an eternal optimist, no doubt. He trusted everybody. I never heard him say a bad word about anybody. That's why he's dead, I suppose. He must have trusted his killer."

Yes. He must have trusted someone enough to turn his back on whoever it was—at least long enough for that someone to slip a strong cord around his throat.

Maureen had a quick mental picture of how that would have looked. "Hannah," she said. "How tall was your dad?"

"Oh, he was average height. Slim but wiry. He was in good physical shape. He worked out often—at a gym when he could afford it, and in the house or out in the yard when he couldn't." She smiled at what must have been one of those happy memories. "I guess you never met him in person, Maureen."

"No, I never had that pleasure." She looked at Judy. "You knew him, Judy?"

"Sure. He used to hang around the bookstore when we had our meetings there. We all knew him." Her eyes narrowed. "What about it?"

"I'm glad you came to represent the group, Judy," Hannah said. "He'd be so proud."

The church ladies had begun to clear away the cups and saucers, and to sweep up cake crumbs from the tablecloth. "I don't mean to rush you ladies," was the soft-spoken comment, "but we have another funeral today at noon, and we need to prepare for that."

All three women stood. Hannah held the square package high. “Thank you all so much for this, and for making us welcome.” Maureen and Judy murmured thanks too. The three left the church and parted company with brief goodbyes in the parking lot.

Chapter 24

The clock on the Subaru's dash said 11:15. A scoop of ice cream would top off the vanilla cake nicely, and she'd save time by skipping lunch. At least that was the excuse she made to herself for heading the Subaru toward Treasure Island, the ice cream shop, and Zoltar.

There was plenty of room in the small parking lot for the aging green Subaru. She took that as a good omen. Snatching a few extra minutes out of this jam-packed day couldn't do any harm. She'd already checked to be sure there were enough singles and a credit card in her wallet—not sure what manner of payment this Zoltar might require. She recalled that she'd paid in quarters for the Zoltar fortune she'd bought from the amusement arcade at South of the Border a year ago.

This lone machine was not part of an arcade. In fact, it stood all by itself outside the little ice cream shop. Maureen noticed that it was on wheels, so it must get pushed inside the building at night or when it rained. This one accepted dollar bills. She deposited the required amount and watched as the bearded, turbaned figure locked inside his glass booth passed his pale hands over a glowing crystal ball as music played and Zoltar's mouth began moving. The kindly voice promised that Zoltar is wise and powerful and sees the future. The expected clicking and whirring took place, and an oblong blue card spilled into the tray in the front of the machine. She hesitated for only a second or two before snatching the thing up. Should she read it right here in front of the store?

She supposed it would only be courteous to go inside and buy something. She tucked the card into her pocket, noting only the zodiac design, not looking at the words at all. She bought a cup of soft-serve chocolate with hot fudge sauce, whipped cream and a cherry, then climbed back into her car.

She lay the card, face down, on the seat beside her while she savored the ice cream treat. The cake and ice cream lunch was a far cry from the healthful and delicious meals she'd become accustomed to from her own dining room, but was somehow quite satisfying.

She got out of the car again to deposit the paper and plastic wrappings into a nearby trash barrel. She stood there for a long moment. Maybe she should throw the blue card in too—unread.

But she knew she wouldn't.

She drove a short distance down Gulf Boulevard to the public parking lot overlooking the beach. It offered a pleasant view of white sand, calm azure water, colorful umbrellas, frolicking kids, tanned people relaxing on towels or beach chairs. She read the card.

You've traveled far to reach this place
With new decisions yet to face.
Watch for a gift-horse bearing news
Of two possibilities—which to choose?
Help a friend. Do what you can
To find the truth; to save a man.
There's safety in numbers so they say.
Read the words to find your way.
ZOLTAR KNOWS ALL.

Great. This card didn't make any more sense than the first one had. Ditto for the one she'd found among Penelope Josephine's Christmas cards. "But the words on that first card eventually all came true," she reminded herself, and so had the second. It had just taken time and circumstances to sort it out. "Maybe Zoltar *does* know all. Are these the words I'm supposed to read to find my way?"

She looked at the clock on the dash. "I'd better find my way home right now. It's nearly noon," she said aloud, tossing the card into her handbag. "I'll deal with you later. I already have plenty to do and a short time to do it."

On the drive back to Haven, Maureen tried to figure out whether or not she'd actually learned anything of value to Hubbard while attending Terry Holiday's funeral. She ran over the details of that sad occasion in her mind, trying to put into words her impressions of that morning. "That's about all it was. Impressions," she realized. "There was nothing concrete—nothing I could put a finger on and say 'here's a clue,' or 'Hannah told me this' or 'Judy said that.'"

Had she wasted her time? Had Hubbard's confidence in her been misplaced? "Read the words to find your way," Zoltar had commanded. "What words? What way?" she asked herself. "I have to come up with something to tell him. Now he's got the death of another writer to deal with. The two are obviously connected somehow."

She turned onto Beach Boulevard, where everything looked so normal, so pleasant, she thought about the proposed mural for the wall at the Historical Society. This was what it would look like— the beach, the pastel buildings, the people, the dogs, the inn, the grocery store, the bookshop. The bookshop. On a sudden whim, she turned onto the narrow street beside the shop, the street that passed Aster's house, her garden, the tree-filled acreage where Walter had been found. The yellow tape that had once encircled the flower beds now extended along the entire edge of the acres-long property—from the back of the house to as far as she could see down the street, where there appeared to be a small gathering of people.

Lookie-loos already gathering at the scene of the crime?

She moved as far as she could to the right, avoiding an oncoming yellow school bus—realizing in an instant that the people ahead were the morning double-session students returning home and the afternoon crowd heading for their classes. Maureen hoped once again that Ted would be able to keep his high-school crew employed. Some of them had already shown a real aptitude for working with food, and the experience they gained at the inn might lead to satisfying careers in the future. Mindful then of the current precarious positions of everyone at the inn, and of much of Haven itself, she made a tight U-turn and headed to work.

Shelly greeted her with unwelcome news. "No new check-ins, and the McKennas say they have to leave tomorrow but that they had a great time and will be back again as soon as they can." She gave Maureen a studied up-and-down look. "You look good in black. Hilda said you went to the funeral for that dead writer. The first one, I mean. How was it?"

"Sad," Maureen said. "I didn't know the man, but I felt bad for him. There was hardly anybody there. Just his daughter, a writer from the critique group that's going to meet here on Friday, and me."

"I guess you'll be wearing that dress again soon," Shelly commented, "for the other writer's funeral. Maybe he'll have better attendance."

"He probably will. He was a much more successful writer than Terry Holiday was," Maureen said. "Walter Griffith was a member of that same Friday critique group."

"I haven't heard anything new about him. Just that he was shot." Shelly held up the same paper Hilda had referred to earlier. "I wonder if anybody has come up with any home videos yet that will be helpful to the police."

Read the words to find your way.

That's what Zoltar had advised. Maureen didn't need to read the words in Hilda's newspaper. She remembered what the woman had told her earlier. "They're asking neighbors with outdoor video cameras to check their footage to see who might show up on it."

"It's not the neighbors!" Maureen exclaimed. "It's the kids!"

"What?" Hilda asked, puzzled. "What kids?"

"The school bus. I need to tell Frank." She reached for her phone.

Chapter 25

"Frank? I know where you might find videos of whatever went on around the woods when Walter was killed. Maybe when Terry Holiday died too."

"Slow down, Doherty. What videos? We haven't found a single one that's of any use."

Maureen tried to tone down the excitement of what she'd just discovered. "This morning, I took a little side trip down the street beside the bookshop—where the wood lot where the bodies were found is."

"Yes. We've already gone over the whole area with a fine-toothed comb. What's your point?"

"Did you know there's a school bus stop at the end of that road?"

"No. But what does that have to do with anything?" He was beginning to sound impatient.

"Cell phones. High school kids have cell phones. They sit on the curb waiting for the bus, and every one of them is on a cell phone. They take pictures of everything. All the time."

He got it.

"Thanks, Doherty. You're right. I'm on it. 'Bye."

It was with a great sense of relief that she put the phone down. She'd done what she could to help solve Haven's most pressing problem. Now on to the next item on her very full plate.

First of all, she put the new Zoltar blue card into her top bureau drawer next to the two old ones. Since Ted had the Key West plans well in hand, and her bag was already packed, the Friday critique group meeting was next on her mental to-do list. Did the other members of the group know that Judy had attended Terry Holiday's funeral? Maureen had every intention of calling it to their attention. Was Judy there to represent them? Was she the token apologist for all the terrible things they'd said about Trenton Hamburger and his books? Also, she needed to check with Ted about the availability of fresh shortbread cookies for the meeting. If Aster wasn't up to providing them, Joyce would have to be ready for backup. Were there enough bingo cards on hand? She'd already found a source in Tampa in case she needed more. Her previous department store career had proven good experience in finding providers of merchandise—wholesale and retail. She'd already had lunch, such as it was. She'd neglected Penelope's trunk, and she was anxious to get back to her recent finds, but it could wait. That old trunk wasn't going anywhere, that was for sure. She'd speak to Ted about the cookies, and after that, it looked as if she could afford to take a bit of time off. Nor nearly enough time for trunk-digging, but maybe she'd sit on her balcony and work on getting a little tan. She'd been indoors too much lately.

Sitting on the narrow balcony just outside the living room window for Maureen was easier said than done. First, she'd have to make sure that Bogie and Bacall weren't already spread out on the wood-paneled surface of the structure. She'd get the folding sand chair from her closet, hang the black dress carefully in the closet, don the previously discarded halter-topped one-piece suit, move the cat aside, and slide the chair into place, taking advantage of the early afternoon sun overhead.

That accomplished, with the cats watching from the branch of the nearby oak tree, and with a satisfied sigh, she closed her eyes, feeling completely relaxed for the first time in days. The luxury was short-lived. From inside the suite, she heard the insistent buzzing of the phone she'd left on the coffee table.

"If it's important, they'll call back," she told herself. The buzzing continued. "They'll leave a message," she murmured aloud. The sound by then had alerted Finn, who added an urgent "Woof woof woof." "It's just a nuisance call. Someone selling something," she insisted, addressing Bogie, who'd reached across from the branch to tap her shoulder.

"Okay. Okay. I give up." She began the process of reversing her oh-so-recent preparations, climbing inside, pulling the sand chair in behind her. She snatched up the phone. Her "Hello" was less than courteous. "Who is it, please?"

"Sweetheart?" Ted's voice was concerned. "Is everything okay? I've been trying to call you. I got worried when you didn't answer."

"I'm fine," she said, softening her tone. "Finn and I and the cats are all snug and safe right here in my lovely penthouse. There's nothing at all to worry about. My phone was just out of reach for a little while." She knew as she spoke the words that there was plenty to worry about in Haven, but it hadn't occurred to her that Ted might be worried about her personal safety. She explained about her attempt to get a little pre-Key West tan.

"I feel as though I should be with you all the time." His voice was warm. Comforting. "All this involvement with the police, going to the funeral of a stranger, hanging around with the creepy murder mystery writers—and keeping the inn business afloat at the same time. I'll feel better when we're married."

"So will I, about everything," she agreed. "Meanwhile, we'll be together this weekend. I'm all packed and ready."

"Are you coming downstairs for lunch?"

"I already had a . . . um . . . a light lunch on the way home from the funeral," she said, sort of truthfully. She glanced at the lunch menu she'd left on the coffee table earlier. She'd missed a hot Cuban sandwich, sweet potato fries, and a house salad. "Maybe I'll come down and have a salad. It's a good excuse to see you."

"You don't need an excuse anymore. Everybody knows we're engaged. Come on down."

She changed into shorts and T-shirt, gave Finn one of his tooth-cleaning green doggie treats, and hurried down the corridor toward the elevator.

Still in deep thought about Haven's current slowed-down economy, she felt the elevator bump to a stop too soon. Had there been a power outage? No. The lights were still on. The door slid open, admitting Carleton Fretham from the second floor. He wore faded jeans and a T-shirt bearing the name of a well-known Clearwater sport fishing fleet, the words FIRST MATE embroidered on the breast pocket.

"Oh, hi, Ms. Doherty." Big smile. "I hope I don't smell like fish. I'm working on a 'careers on the ocean' series. I don't have time to change. By the way, have you noticed this elevator smells like tobacco? I know you have a no-smoking rule. When I first got in, it was so strong it made my eyes water." He pushed his glasses up onto his forehead and dug at his eyes with a fist. "I'm on my way to see a lawyer about collecting my money from Terry Holiday's daughter. Jackson, Nathan and Peters. Do you know anything about them?"

"Yes. They're my attorneys. Good people."

"I'll mention your name. I don't like going the legal route after someone who just lost her father, but a contract is a contract." He shrugged. "I'm enjoying my suite. I've been researching the namesake. Arthur Godfrey. I remember my grandmother talking about him."

"I gather that you truly enjoy your work," she told him. The elevator came to a halt, and the brass door slid open.

"I can't help myself. I have to know the answers to everything. See you later." He offered a brisk wave in her direction. "After I meet the lawyers, I'm going over to the Historical Society to see what I can find out about the Native American tribes who lived here. Then I'll need to arrange for a trip up to Maryland. The university up there has more than four thousand of Arthur Godfrey's audio tapes, covering his fifty years in broadcasting. What a treasure!"

"Have a nice day." Shelly waved toward Carleton's retreating back as the green door closed behind him. "I swear," she said. "That man is a walking AI. There's probably not a subject in the world you could mention that he wouldn't know a lot about."

"You're right," Maureen whispered. "AI with a little OCD thrown in." The two shared a quiet giggle, and managed straight faces when George pushed the green door open.

"Ms. Doherty, maybe you'd better get over to the kitchen." He pointed toward the side of the building. "There's a cop down there questioning the part-time high school kids. About their cell phones."

Before she could respond, the door swung open again, and Carleton reappeared. "What's going on? Are the kids in trouble?"

"No, not at all," Maureen said. "I'd better get over there and straighten it out."

"Can they do that? Can they question minors without their parents present?" George was indignant.

"They sure can," Carleton said, "but the kids can refuse to answer. They can ask for a lawyer—and I'm going to see that they get one. In 2014, the Supreme Court ruled that unjust search and seizure of your phone is a civil rights violation. How many high school children work here anyway?" He led the way to the kitchen entrance. "Come on, Ms. Doherty. Fair is fair. I was on my way to the lawyer's office anyway."

"That's not really necessary," Maureen protested. "It's a simple matter that has to do with their cell phones. There are only three of the kids who work here altogether, two in the morning and one in the afternoon." But Carleton had already opened the kitchen door. *There was no need for Frank to be heavy-handed about this*, she thought. *Those kids are probably scared to death*. She hit Hubbard's number. He answered immediately.

"I told you, Doherty. I'm on it. We found the bus driver. It's a short stop—only half a dozen kids altogether. We'll have those pictures in no time. Hopefully there'll be something we can use in one or more of the cameras. That was a good idea you had."

"It just got a little more complicated," she said. "One of my tenants has offered to get the ones who work here lawyers. You might not be seeing those pictures for a while."

Long, exaggerated sigh. "How did you let that happen, Doherty? Lawyers? Why? It's not as if they're under arrest. I don't have warrants. It's just a simple request to let us see their recent pictures taken near the woods—to see if there's anybody of interest there in the background. It's for the good of the community—for Haven—for Pete's sake!"

"I know that. You know that. I'm sure Mr. Fretham means well."

"Fretham? So the do-gooder is one of your writer friends, right?"

"That's right," she mumbled.

"Will this 'concerned citizen' be part of the get-together you roped me in on this coming Friday?"

"Yes."

"Get ready for some fireworks." His "goodbye" was abrupt.

Chapter 26

Maureen was pleased to see Larry Jackson approaching the front steps of the inn. Larry, who always reminded her of a young Jamie Foxx, had been the lawyer who'd kindly, gently, and carefully led her through the various legal complexities of inheriting Haven House from a person she'd never met and had been her personal and business attorney ever since. A smiling Carleton Fretham was just a few steps behind him. Surely Larry could make some sense out of the increasingly complicated questions about photos and videos taken in the vicinity of the bookshop crime scene by some high school students—photos and videos which might—or might not—have some bearing on Haven's most recent crimes.

Maureen met the two men at the head of the stairs. Four interested pairs of eyes watched the process. Gert, Molly, George, and Sam occupied their usual rockers, each leaning forward so as not to miss a word of conversation. She greeted Larry cordially.

"Did the officers stop the questioning?" Carleton wanted to know. "I told the kids not to answer until their lawyer got here."

"I don't know," Maureen said. "I've learned not to interfere with police business. I'm afraid it might have interfered with kitchen business, though. Our high school staff is really helpful with prep work."

"We'll handle this as quickly as possible, Maureen," Larry said. "It's good to see you. I understand that congratulations are in order for you and Ted."

"Thank you."

"Let's get this show on the road, shall we?" Carleton urged. "The kitchen door is over this way, Larry."

Larry knows where it is. He probably knows more about the building than I do.

The lawyer, smiling, said hello to the four rocking chair occupants and followed Carleton through the lobby and into the dining area. With a nod to Shelly at the reception desk, Maureen followed the men.

Other than the presence of the uniformed police officer, who was seated by himself in a white wicker chair at the far edge of the room, the situation there seemed to be normal. Ted, moving easily between the various work stations, pausing occasionally to speak to one of the white-uniformed workers, looked up as the kitchen door swung open, admitting the visitors.

Carleton approached the officer. "The children you're questioning have legal counsel." He pointed his finger at the man. "You'll need a warrant to look at their phones."

The officer stood, towering over Fretham. "Who are you?"

Carleton produced his wallet, displaying a driver's license. "My attorney is here with me."

"I know." The officer handed the wallet back. "Hi, Larry."

"You need a warrant," Carleton repeated.

"I haven't asked to see their phones, Larry." He addressed the attorney. "We're just asking them to look through the photos they've taken anywhere behind the bookshop and to show us pictures where anyone, probably an adult, shows up who they haven't seen there before. A stranger."

"There's no problem with that," Larry stated. "Any results so far?"

"Two so far. Nothing yet from the kids here. Pictures of two different men. We've ID'd one of them as a man who collects the shot-up beer cans in the woods for scrap metal. No ID yet on the other one, but it looks like he's wearing a face mask. Some people still do, you know. Jeans, cotton shirt, bucket hat, and he has a backpack. Neatly dressed. Might be a teacher."

"So the youngsters are being cooperative?"

"Absolutely. They all want to help if they can. I've suggested that they tell their parents about what's going on. I'm just waiting around now for the next kid to show up for work here. It was a good idea to ask them all to help," he added. "So far we've been up against a stone wall—or maybe a forest. We've come to depend on videos for so long, we forget sometimes that there are still spots where there simply are no cameras."

"I'm sure all of Haven appreciates what the police department is doing," Maureen said. "We're all anxious for the killer to be found and for Haven to get back to normal."

"Thanks, Ms. Doherty. We're doing our best."

Carleton, with an eye-roll but without further comment, turned and pushed open the door leading back to the dining room. Maureen, relieved that any aspects of confrontation seemed to have been resolved amicably, made her way quietly to the elevator and pushed the button for the third floor. The odor of tobacco in the glass and brass confines of the elevator was unmistakable.

"Reggie?" she asked aloud. "You know this is a no smoking hotel. I had a customer complaint." The gentleman ghost with a clipped British accent and a bad pipe-smoking habit shimmered into sight as they passed the second-floor landing.

"So sorry, luv," he said, covering the bowl of the pipe with one hand, "but something's come to my attention you may need to know about."

"If you'll go and put the pipe back to wherever you keep it, we can talk in my suite."

"I'll be back straight away." He disappeared just as the door whirred open on the top floor. Maureen heard Finn's welcoming "Woof" when she reached her front door and turned the key. Reggie, without pipe and smelling like Aramis, was already inside, seated on the long blue couch. "That better, luv? I stashed the pipe at my digs in Brighton and dabbed on a bit of cologne."

Finn gave an approving "Woof."

Reggie patted the cushion beside him. "Now sit down and let me tell you what I overheard Aster Patterson telling her husband."

"You've heard her talking with Peter?" Maureen asked, still marveling at Reggie's speedy travel mode.

"Yes. They're in that suite where she bakes biscuits every day. Some sort of American shortbread things." He gave a dismissive sniff.

"Cookies," Maureen suggested.

"Exactly. I was interested in the baking process, but I couldn't help listening to the conversation. You know I'm a bit of a busybody. Anyway, Aster was chattering away about somebody named Walter that she knew who'd died recently. She said he'd been murdered and that she thought she knew who might have done the deed but that she was afraid to tell anybody, because the killer might come after her next. It seems that the dead fellow was a writer of some kind, and she said he was Haven's second dead writer in a week. She says Peter led her to the first one in her own flower garden, hoping she'd be able to warn the victim, but she'd been too late. Is that true?"

"She found the body in her garden, yes."

"She scolded Peter, because he'd wanted to lead her to the second one, to warn him, but the killer had had a change of mind about who was going to die next, and this Walter died—shot dead—with no warning at all from anybody."

"Next?" Maureen was startled by the word. "You mean the killer isn't through yet?"

"That's what Aster thinks, and she's afraid to tell anybody."

"So you're handing it over to me," Maureen said. "Thanks a lot."

Reggie gave a shimmering shrug. "Kind of a grim gift, isn't it?"

Watch for a gift horse bearing news.

Chapter 27

Maureen could picture herself trying to explain to Frank Hubbard that her live-in ghost roommate's ghost boyfriend had overheard a conversation with Hubbard's chief suspect chatting with *her* ghost husband about the recent murders. She wanted very much to tell Reggie to keep the grim news to himself and to shimmer himself the heck back to Brighton.

"So Aster thinks she knows who the killer is?"

"It seems that way. She said that she doesn't know *why* Terry Holiday was killed, even though he was apparently disliked by many. I gather that he was the first victim?"

"Yes. He was a writer. I went to his funeral."

"Oh, I say, so sorry. I didn't know he was a friend of yours," Reggie apologized.

"He wasn't. I never met the man. Go on," she said.

"You Americans have strange customs," he mused, but continued. "Aster believes that Walter, the most current victim, had figured out who'd killed the first man, so *he* had to be eliminated."

A gift horse bearing news of TWO possibilities?

"Definitely a possibility," she agreed. "I expect that the police have thought of that. Did Aster happen to tell Peter who she thought the killer might be?" Maureen's curiosity overcame her initial reluctance.

"She did," Reggie said. "Do you know a writer named Elaine?"

"Elaine?" She gasped the name at first, questioning, then spoke it more firmly. "Elaine Cremonis? Not a bad guess. She was one of Terry Holiday's louder critics, and she actually 'wrote the book' on how to strangle someone."

"So you agree with Aster?"

"I didn't say that. But Elaine and Walter have been pretty chummy lately."

"How so?"

"Like maybe dating. They were both here for dinner a couple of days ago, and I think they might have left together."

He frowned. "That's quite a bit of *maybe, they might have,* and *I think*."

"I know," Maureen agreed. "There's certainly nowhere near enough of anything there to accuse somebody of murder."

"Unless Aster knows something we don't."

She smiled at the *we*.

"That's also a possibility," she said. "Aster has the advantage of having Peter on her team. A ghost can do things the police can't do."

Reggie drew himself up to his full height and gave a brisk salute. "At your service, Ma'am. First Class Detective Sergeant Reginald Yardley. Scotland Yard."

Maureen began to extend her right hand, but remembering how unsatisfactory shaking hands with a ghost is, returned the salute. "Welcome to the team," she said. "Scotland Yard? No kidding?"

"One doesn't joke about such things. Now tell me about this Elaine person."

"I don't know a lot about her," she admitted. "She writes murder mysteries as well as some other books. One of her books is what some have called 'a textbook on how to strangle someone.' *The Corpse Cried Wolf*. I haven't read it. She's quite attractive looking. Tall, dark hair, model's figure."

"If I'm understanding this situation correctly, the deceased—this Terry Holiday—was associated with writers, but was not popular among them?"

"That's right. There's a local group of half a dozen or so murder mystery writers who call themselves 'Murder Incorporated.' Terry Holiday was the author of a number of how-to books which were, for some reason, the constant butt of jokes and bad reviews by the mystery writers," Maureen explained. "I happened to be present at a meeting where every one of them suggested that Holiday should be killed—and each one suggested a means of doing it."

"They couldn't have been serious!"

"I didn't think so. But, what if one of them was?"

Reggie looked up at the ceiling, appearing deep in thought. Maureen remained silent. Finn looked back and forth between the two, and after a moment gave a soft "woof."

"You're right, Finn," Maureen told the dog. "We just need to figure out which one of them is the likely killer—and why."

"We'll go about it in an orderly way," Reggie declared. "We'll prepare a thorough dossier on each one, just as we did at the yard."

Maureen nodded agreement. "Since Aster thinks it's Elaine, we may as well start with her."

"Agreed," Reggie said. "Since she's a published writer, I assume that her publisher has released a biography on her. It will be a puff piece, of course, but there should be some basic facts there."

"She writes under several names," Maureen recalled. "And in several different fields."

"All the more for us to learn about her then. To the computer?" He stood and started across the room to where Maureen's computer stood on a sleek, mid-century modern desk. "You run your business from here?"

"No. I have an actual office downstairs. Room twenty-seven." She watched to see if he had any reaction to the room number.

"Ah-ha! Lorna has told me about that room. It was once quite haunted, I understand."

"It's fine now. John Smith has 'gone to the light,' as they say. But this computer will serve the purpose. Pull up a chair, and let's get started."

"Move a chair? Do you think I'm some kind of blasted poltergeist?" Reggie grumbled and produced a portable seat that folded into a walking stick. "I'll bring my own. Haven't used it since last rugby season at Twickenham."

Maureen sat in her swivel desk chair, and Reggie appeared to be comfortable on his seat-on-a-stick. She typed *Elaine Cremonis books in order* into the search bar. "Wow," she murmured when the requested list appeared. "This may take a long time."

Reggie leaned closer, the cologne not quite masking the pipe tobacco, but all in all, she decided, not an unpleasant combination. "It appears that she used different names for the different series. Shall we start with the ones she wrote under her own name?"

"The murder mysteries. Yes," Maureen agreed. "See? There's the one I told you about. *The Corpse Cried Wolf.* I downloaded that one to my Kindle. I haven't read any of it."

"The one that describes how to strangle somebody."

"Right."

"The bio says she was born in Tarpon Springs, Florida. Went to local schools," Reggie read aloud. "She graduated from Florida Southern College in Lakeland with a bachelor's degree in communication and media studies. Look at this. She minored in criminology. An interesting combination, eh?"

"It says here that she hosted a radio show in Clearwater for a while in 2020. Maybe we can get transcripts," Maureen said. "This is going to be fun."

"Investigating a murder isn't supposed to be fun," he deadpanned, then winked. "But sometimes it is."

"There are five more books in that series, beside the crying corpse one," Maureen pointed out. "Do we have to read all of them?"

"I don't think so. Let's just read some reviews and then read something from one of the other series," he suggested. "I used to love sci-fi books when I was in middle school. Let's try those next."

"Are you volunteering?"

"Will you order one for me? I don't have a credit card." He made a sad face. "I'd love to read *A Pup in Time*. It's about a cocker spaniel puppy who can time travel. She wrote that one as Tasha LaLonde."

"Time travel would be a handy gift to have just about now," Maureen said, and ordered the book about the sci-fi pup. "We could travel back to Aster's flower garden and see who strangled poor Terry."

"Next comes the YA series. They look like girlie books. Twin girl sleuths who play soccer. Maybe Lorna can read those," he suggested.

"And you can read the puppy book to Finn."

"Fair enough. Now back to business. Let's see what else we can learn about Elaine. Aster must have some good reason to believe she could kill a man."

"Here's a bio from the YA publisher." Maureen focused on the screen. "It says here that Elaine was quite an athlete in high school."

"Soccer? Like the crime-solving twins?"

"Exactly. As Paul Jenkins says, 'For a writer, everything is material.'"

"Who is Paul Jenkins?" Reggie wanted to know.

"Oh, he's another one of the Murder Incorporated writers. Besides the murder books, he writes romances about cowboys and some other things," she said. "Nice guy. Everybody likes him."

"In the mystery books I've read, nice guys often turn out to be killers." Reggie gave a shimmery wink. "We should take a really close look at him. We have a lot of work ahead of us. Maybe we're getting a bit ahead of our skis. Back to Elaine. One suspect at a time."

"Right. Back to the bios." Maureen pointed to the screen again. "Here's something interesting. Elaine designs and makes her own clothes. When she was in college, she made costumes for the drama department."

"A multi-talented woman, for sure," Reggie observed.

Maureen recalled the black spandex number Elaine had worn to dinner when she may or may not have been Walter's date. "Maybe we should look into the costume-making thing a bit more. Can she make disguises?"

"I think you've got the hang of good investigating methods," Reggie said. "You can continue on your own. Tie up any loose ends on what we know about Elaine, then move on to the others—one at a time. Think about who's next on your list. The process of elimination is a tried-and-true way to find the answer. I'll check in on you once in a while. Ta- ta for now."

Chapter 28

After Reggie had left, Maureen tried to put murder-solving out of her mind so that she could attend to more current problems. Had Carleton Fretham's interference in the cell phone search messed up the project entirely? She hardly dared to call Hubbard about it and really hoped Fretham wouldn't mention the subject at dinner. She needed to check on the inventory in the gift shop, almost hoping that she'd need to order more merchandise, because that would mean business was picking up. She wasn't surprised when Shelly reported that Aster had called to request that dinner be delivered to her suite. The woman was genuinely frightened for her life.

By four thirty, the early dinner arrivals had begun to trickle in. Maureen returned to the third floor to change her clothes for dinner. She took special pains with her outfit, hair, and makeup, anticipating another "late date" with Ted. It wasn't time for Hilda to arrive yet, though, and Shelly was needed in the dining room, so Maureen once again took her place at the reservation desk. She found herself staring at the telephone, willing it to ring, hoping for a new reservation and at the same time, fearing another cancellation.

She was pleased to see Dick and Ethel Flannagan arrive, along with the Taylors, and greeted them with smiling appreciation. "I'm so happy to see you all," she told them.

"You know Ethel and I love dining here, and Rob and Janie are hooked on Ted's dinners as well," Dick said. "Besides that, Rob wants to get a little more information about the Friday meeting, right, Rob?"

The detective gave a positive nod. "I can see that you're busy, Ms. Doherty," he said, "but perhaps you can stop by our table during dinner for a minute or two. I have an idea I'd like to run by you."

"An idea?"

"Yes. About the recent deaths."

So is this Yankee cop working Hubbard's case?

"I'll be happy to do that," she fibbed. She was not happy about it at all, but what if Taylor was on to something helpful? Maybe his idea was about one or more of the suspects she and Reggie had focused on. She could be sure of one thing. Robert Taylor's idea couldn't possibly have anything to do with ghosts, and that in itself simplified things. The group moved toward the dining room just as the player piano began to plink out a familiar tune. "Thank You for Being a Friend." The familiar theme song from *The Golden Girls* long-running TV show almost asked for a sing-along, and Maureen hummed the melody to herself. She was sure the song wasn't part of the old instrument's pre-programmed repertoire. Billy Bedoggoned Bailey had picked it out just for her ears.

Why?

She thought of Zoltar's most recent pronouncements.

Help a friend.

The ringing of the phone on the desk drove thoughts of the mechanical mystic away. Maybe, just maybe, it meant new business. She smiled and picked up the receiver, hoping the smile would show in her voice. "Haven House Inn. Good evening. This is Maureen. How may I direct your call?"

"Maureen? It's Claire, from the Historical Society. I need to ask a favor, and I hope you can help. I just had a call from a relative who missed his flight and needs a place to stay until tomorrow. I know it's short notice, but do you possibly have a room for tonight? For a friend's uncle?"

The smile stayed in place. A room? She had three-quarters of a hotel. "Of course, Claire. That's not a problem at all. Send him over."

Billy Bedoggoned's song was still playing while Maureen thanked Claire and assured her that a suite would be ready when her relative arrived. "Help a friend," Zoltar had instructed. "Do what you can to find the truth; to save a man."

She was absolutely focused on finding the truth, and at the same time, on filling those empty suites. The smile was still in place when Hilda arrived to take over. Maureen relayed the information about Claire's uncle's imminent arrival.

"It's nice to have somebody checking in." Hilda was enthusiastic. "Things are getting better."

Maureen hoped Hilda was right, and that Billy's song about friendship was about Claire's uncle. If it was, was he the man they were supposed to save? *The more information I get, the more confused I am*, she thought. *And now I have to go into the dining room and see what the Yankee detective's idea is all about.*

She stood, smoothed the skirt of her blue silk shirtdress, and did a slow walk across the lobby to the dining room. The player piano had stopped, and the piped-in dinner music had begun. She searched the room for the table where the Flannagan party was seated. Ethel raised her hand and motioned for Maureen to join them at one of the smaller tables at the far edge of the room, which seated six.

Maureen rejected the offer of dinner, but accepted a glass of Chablis. They'd saved a seat for her between Robert Taylor and Dick Flannagan. She'd greeted them all at the desk when they'd entered, but welcomed them again. They all smiled and acknowledged her words, but then grew silent. Robert cleared his throat. "I have an idea," he began, "that applies to the recent killings here in Haven."

All heads turned toward Maureen. "Go on," she encouraged.

"I've been studying one of the murder mystery writers in particular," he said. "I've begun gathering facts about one of the women."

A dossier?

So far, all three of the Murder Incorporated women were alive and well, while Paul was the only man left standing. Was Detective Taylor gathering facts about Elaine, Judy, or Lynn Ellen? Maureen sipped her wine and waited for the answer.

She wasn't too surprised when he said "Judy Abbott interests me."

Judy Abbott had interested Maureen too, especially because of her attendance at Terry Holiday's strange funeral. She assumed that the Yankee cop already had that bit of information. She waited. Since it was, after all, dinnertime, and the two couples were there to enjoy their meals, any conversation about murder was necessarily interrupted by comments about the tenderness of the filets and the excellent seasoning of the green beans almondine. Maureen was, however, able to garner a couple of snippets of what Taylor had learned about the writer of mysteries and romance and animals before the dessert, a simple yet elegant vanilla flan with fresh raspberries, was served.

"Ms. Abbott, in addition to her prowess as a writer of both murder mysteries and erotic romance, holds a degree in forensic toxicology from the University of Florida and works part-time for a veterinarian in Tampa," Taylor said, then turned toward Maureen. "I haven't read any of her books yet. I assume she writes quite capably about both poisons and animals?" He phrased it as a question.

Maureen answered that she hadn't read Judy's books either.

The detective's raised eyebrows indicated surprise, but he said, "It was an assumption. I thought perhaps you were friends, since your names were the only ones in the Hamburger funeral guest book."

"Just an acquaintance," Maureen told him, not about to confide to the Yankee detective that she'd gone to the funeral simply because Frank Hubbard had asked her to.

"I see," he said. "I did take time to browse through one of Walter Griffin's cowboy books. He is—was—quite knowledgeable about horses. It occurred to me that Ms. Abbott, with her veterinarian skills, might have collaborated with him."

"I'm sorry," she said, absolutely meaning it. "I wish I could be more helpful."

"No matter," he said. He turned to face Janie. "This is a lovely dessert, isn't it? Simple and healthful and beautiful to look at."

The idea that Judy Abbott and Walter could have been collaborators would never have occurred to her. She had a lot to learn about building dossiers. Her phone vibrated. She glanced at a new text, passed on the offered after-dinner cocktail. "I need to greet a new guest," she said. "A friend of a friend is just checking in."

She met Claire's uncle, a pleasant gray-haired gentleman who seemed delighted to find attractive lodging so close to his niece's home. Maureen was more than delighted to see him, and her "Welcome to Haven House" speech was even warmer than usual.

There now. She'd helped a friend, as Zoltar had instructed. She asked Hilda to assign him to one of the best-coveted ocean view suites and assumed that he hadn't heard about the recent murders, or perhaps wasn't bothered by them.

Help a friend. Do what you can
To find the truth; to save a man.

Was Claire the friend Zoltar meant for her to help? Would she find the truth, and more importantly, could she save a man? She watched as George escorted Claire's Uncle Everett Davis into the elevator. George had reached for the man's lightweight carry-on bag, but Mr. Davis had shaken his head in a scowling "no," and clutched the bag to his chest. Maureen smiled as the small tableau played out. Some travelers, especially the elderly ones, guarded their possessions carefully, while the young ones sometimes seemed almost careless about theirs. *Perhaps things were harder to come by in earlier times*, she thought.

Chapter 29

Maureen was first to take her usual seat at the bar for her late date with Ted. She had so many things to talk to him about, and there hadn't been time or opportunity during the brief moments they'd had together during the day. The player piano tinkled out a ragtime version of "Ain't Misbehavin'" when Ted strode across the lobby to the lounge area, took the seat beside her, and greeted her with a kiss. He'd changed from his chef wear to jeans and a bright Tommy Bahama shirt.

"You've been shopping in the gift shop," she said. "It looks great on you."

"I used my employee's discount," he said. "I bought a couple of these for our vacation, and they'll be good for when the Tiki hut gets operational too."

"I bought a sarong," she admitted, "for exactly the same reasons."

"Great minds," he said.

"Mine's not so great." She fake-pouted.

"What's wrong?"

"I've been trying to help Frank Hubbard by gathering up as much information as I can about the mystery writers, and I missed something I should have caught." She wasn't going to mention Reggie's involvement. It would just complicate things. "I have plenty about Elaine Cremonis, but I missed something big about Judy Abbott that Dick Flannagan's brother-in-law found right away."

"So at least now you have it. Does it matter where it came from?"

"No. It doesn't. You're right. Thank you."

"You're welcome. One of my high school helpers came up with an interesting new snippet of video today."

"Tell me about it."

"It's interesting, but kind of sad. It was Walter. He even waved at the camera. The photo was date and time-stamped. So we know what time he entered the woods on the day he died."

"Has Frank Hubbard seen it yet?" she asked.

"I'm not sure. Sad, isn't it?"

"It's more than that. Frank will want to see every picture taken during that time frame. Who else went into the woods—or came out? I'll text him about it." She reached for her phone, tapped in a few sentences, and returned the phone to her handbag. "Has the officer sitting in the kitchen questioning the part-time kids been disruptive?"

"Not really. The ghostwriter who hired the lawyers is kind of a pain in the butt, though."

"Yeah. I can believe that," she agreed.

"I met our new guest this evening," Ted offered a welcome change of subject. "Maybe people are starting to come back to Haven."

"He's Claire Davis's uncle," she said. "He says he might stay for a few days, instead of just overnight. I hope it's the beginning of a trend."

"I hope so. You've been working so hard on ideas to bring people here."

"I'm trying," she said. "Bingo games, 'Dog-Friendly Haven.' I'm going by Terry Holiday's book . . . *How to Make Your City Famous and Attract Big Spenders.*"

"You haven't said much about his funeral."

"There isn't much to tell," she said. "I met his daughter, Hannah. The man apparently had few friends. The only ones there were Judy Abbott and me."

"Judy is one of the writers you met at the bookstore."

"Yes. And Judy is the person Dick Flannagan's detective brother-in-law is gathering information about. He knew I'd been at the funeral with her, and he shared that she has a degree in chemistry and that she works with animals."

"She hadn't told you that?"

"She barely spoke to me at all, and I hadn't had a chance yet to read her bio."

"It's going to be so wonderful to spend hours together this weekend," he said. "This snatching moments here and there with bits and pieces of conversation is not enough. I'd hoped to see you at lunch today."

"I know. I'm ashamed to admit to you what I actually ate." She described the cake and coffee repast the church ladies had provided. Ted pretended to be horrified, making a cross with his fingers as though warding off a vampire.

"It gets worse," she promised, and told him about having ice cream at the Treasure Island shop. "They have a Zoltar machine out front, just like the one from the movie *Big*. I've always been fascinated by them. There was one at South of the Border where I stopped on the way to Florida. I couldn't very well just get my fortune told and not buy anything, now could I?" She didn't mention the blue cards hidden in her bureau.

Someday I'll have to tell him all my secrets, but not yet. Not yet.

"It's okay," he said. "There are times when ice cream and cake for lunch are just what we need. And if there's a Zoltar machine somewhere in Key West, we'll get our fortunes told together."

Maureen barely sipped from her wine glass and Ted ignored his beer entirely. They talked of the beach wedding they planned to cater, and about their own future beach wedding. Maybe they'd figure out how to have it near the sign that meant so much to both of them.

"Finn will have to be the ring bearer," Ted joked.

"I found out that Elaine Cremonis is a costume designer," Maureen said. "I'll bet she can make him a doggie tuxedo." They laughed together at the mental picture that created.

"We could have our reception at the Tiki hut," Ted suggested. "And we could wear Hawaiian wedding clothes."

Maureen's department store ready-to-wear buyer expertise kicked in. "I know exactly where to order them," she said. "The bridal gowns are amazing, and the groom wears a beautiful embroidered white shirt." She giggled softly. "Here we are planning what to wear at our wedding, and the only time we've ever even been alone together is on a public beach and here in a cocktail lounge with a bartender, some angelfish, and an occasional Goth ghost looking on."

"We'll correct that this weekend," he whispered.

"I know," she whispered back. The two leaned toward each other. The kiss exchanged held promise of fireworks, shooting stars, a total eclipse of the sun.

"Excuse me. Ms. Doherty?" Hilda interrupted. "The new guest, Mr. Davis, wants to know if we can change his suite. He's in the Joe DiMaggio. He says the smell of perfume in the bedroom is so strong it's making him sneeze."

Chapter 30

Maureen sat up straight, trying to focus her thoughts. "Pick a nice suite for Mr. Davis, will you, Hilda? Maybe the Burt Reynolds?"

Ted frowned, reaching awkwardly for his beer glass. "Perfume?" he asked. "Perfume in the bedroom?"

Of course, Hilda and Maureen both knew about—and accepted—a long-dead movie star's occasional visits to Joltin' Joe's suite, but that information had never been shared with Ted—and this was surely not the moment to do so. "Who knows?" Maureen pretended ignorance. "It's an old building. Night-blooming jasmine outside of a leaky window? I'll have the boys air it out properly in the morning. No big deal. Now, where were we?"

"We were planning our wedding," he said. "Hawaiian wedding outfits and Finn for ring bearer."

"And ice cream and cake," she added. "Or was that another story?"

"Another story," he recalled. "The one about a funeral and Judy Abbott and pictures of people in the woods and the fortune-telling machine."

"Everything is much too complicated around here," she said. "We need a vacation."

"Let's leave right now." He grasped her shoulders, his eyes sparkling. "We can do it. Joyce can take care of the kitchen.

Your crew can handle things here. Grab your suitcase and we'll drive down tonight."

If only I could be that spontaneous.

"Oh, Ted, I wish I could. I truly do. But there is so much to do here. I'm worried about Aster. She's terrified and she won't leave her suite. I may have to go to another funeral, and I've set up that meeting with the writers and the detectives and the ghostwriter for Friday afternoon." She didn't add that she needed to do everything possible to help Frank Hubbard with his investigation—to find a killer and to get Haven back to its cute, touristy, profitable self—and while she was at it, to prepare a Reggie-type dossier on Judy Abbott starting tomorrow morning.

She ended with a weak, "I'm sorry, but right now, I need to get to bed so I can get up bright and early for a nice run on the beach with my man."

"It's a date," he promised. "Come on, I'll walk you to the elevator."

Maureen stepped out of the elevator onto the soft carpet in the hallway and heard Finn's welcoming "woof" after she'd taken just a few steps toward her suite.

"Hello there. I was just leaving." She heard Reggie's voice before he shimmered into view, materializing just outside her door. "I just dropped your roommate off. We were polka dancing tonight in Texas." He tipped a large Stetson hat and gave a quick two-step in tooled boots. Tight jeans, embroidered shirt, leather vest, and red neckerchief gave off true cowboy vibes. "Sengelmann Hall in Schulenburg, just outside of Houston, has a ghost polka band that plays there every night. See you later. I'm going to ride down in your beautiful lift."

Maureen heard the elevator whirr as she turned the key to her suite, where Lorna, in a cute short-skirted cowgirl outfit that matched Reggie's, held Finn upright by his front paws in an apparent attempt to teach him to boot-scoot. "Hi, Maureen. Can you buy Finn a western collar? Maybe something leather with silver conchos?"

"I guess the budget can stretch for that," she promised. "But no more dancing tonight. We have a busy day planned, and I'm going away for the weekend, so maybe you'll get to doggy-sit him."

"So the romantic weekend is finally going to happen for you two, huh?" She gave a long-lashed wink that looked even naughtier because of the shimmering effect.

"I'm just hoping the place he picked for us to stay isn't haunted," Maureen spoke fervently.

"Key West? I know of at least six of them that are definitely haunted." Lorna was matter-of-fact about it, and began to tick off names on her fingers. "The Artist House, Marrero's Guest Mansion, the Curry Mansion, the Ridley House, Old Town Mansion, and La Concha Hotel. Are you staying in any of those?"

"I don't know. It's going to be a surprise."

Lorna giggled. "If it's one of those, it sure will be!"

"Come on, cowdog Finn," Maureen said, and headed for the bedroom. "We'll worry about all that later. We have a date for an early beach run in the morning. Goodnight, Lorna."

Finn was already sound asleep beside Maureen's bed when, showered, cold-creamed, pajamaed, and yawning, she stepped over him and snuggled under the covers. But sleep did not come quickly. A kaleidoscope of thought buzzed around in her head—Judy Abbott and Elaine Cremonis—were they the "two possibilities" Zoltar had warned about? Cell phone pictures from high school kids—were they important? Bingo games and friendly dogs—helpful for Haven? Aster Patterson hiding in her room—is her fear justified? Peter Patterson's ghost—smoke and mirrors, or the real deal? Mystery writers and detectives meeting together—helpful or dangerous? Walter's funeral—would she miss it by going to the Keys? A red-covered astrology book in Penelope Josephine's old steamer trunk? Overriding it all—the calm, mechanical voice of Zoltar and the words on blue cards. ZOLTAR KNOWS ALL.

Chapter 31

A red sun streaked the Florida morning sky with vivid color. Maureen and Finn waited for Ted at the inn's side door. "Red sky in the morning, sailor take warning," Maureen recited the old rhyme to the dog.

"Woof?" he queried.

"Never mind," she said. "It doesn't apply to us anyway. We're runners, not sailors."

"What about sailors?" Ted pushed the door open and joined them.

She repeated the rhyme. "I told Finn not to worry about it. We're not going for a boat ride today. Anyway, it's just a myth."

"Generally, it simply means it's going to rain. Red sky at night, sailor's delight," he countered. "When we get a red sunset, we usually get a nice day."

They did their warm-up exercises, establishing a comfortable rhythm between them. "If it's going to rain, we'd better get going then," she suggested. "Race you!" She handed him the leash.

"You're on. Come on, Finn." The man and dog quickly took the lead. Maureen moved to the water's edge, where the sand was hard-packed, and soon caught up with them. Ted slowed his pace, and they ran together toward the distant sign. "Finn wins," he announced, dropping the leash and letting the dog run free as they approached the goal.

"I think when we have our beach wedding," she said, "we should take our vows right here under the sign, even if it makes for some odd-looking wedding photos."

He laughed. "I know. How will we explain to our kids about the ratty old sign instead of a beautiful altar full of flowers?"

"We can have flowers too," she said.

"Under the sign."

"And over the sign and all around the sign. Why not?"

"Woof woof." Finn agreed.

"Our kids," she repeated the words. "I hadn't thought about them."

"I had," he said. "Almost from the minute I first saw you." They shared a long kiss, and hardly noticed the beginning sprinkles of rain.

Returning from their run, the two were quite soaked when they reached the inn. The four porch-sitters had backed their rocking chairs away from the usual stair-top positions, staying beneath the sheltering overhang. "Hey look, two drowned rats," George called, as Maureen and Ted jogged around the corner toward the side entrance.

Once inside, another kiss reminded Maureen that Ted's corridor-mates were both safely seated in their chairs on the porch. The two could be alone in his room. She was positive that he was thinking about the same thing. She shook the tempting thought away, and whispered "soon." Ted headed for his downstairs room, while Maureen and Finn passed the guest laundry on the way to the lobby.

"I'll be back to relieve you as soon as I change and dry my hair," she told Hilda. "This rain isn't going to help business."

"Take your time," Hilda advised. "I'd rather be here than home. You've made this place so attractive, I'm going to stick around and dawdle over coffee and breakfast anyway. Maybe I'll even stay and have lunch too. And a Bloody Mary. Why not? It's that kind of day—and it isn't hurting business. A friend of Mr. Davis's has reserved a room for the weekend. He says he's a shoe salesman, and he'd like to talk to you about some sandals for the gift shop. He'll be here later this morning."

"Good news! That makes two new guests, and we can always use cute sandals." As soon as she spoke the words, Zoltar's cryptic message about "two possibilities" once again came to mind. She climbed the stairs to the third floor, the air-conditioning making the damp clothing feel even more uncomfortable. She noticed that Finn was shivering too. "I'll give you a good rubdown with a warm towel as soon as we get home," she promised.

There were two grumpy cats indoors on their tower and no ghosts in sight. Maureen kept her promise. Wrapping Finn in a fluffy beach towel, she gave him a brisk rub, then swaddled him in a blanket she'd usually reserved for winter-cool Florida days. She took a hotter-than-usual shower, then dried her hair, enjoying the warmth of the hair dryer. She pulled on black-and-white-striped tights and a lightweight French terry white sweater. "Sometimes a rainy day is a good thing," she told the dog. "You stay indoors and attend to things you might have put aside for 'someday,' because there were more interesting—or more important things—clamoring for your attention."

"Woof?" Finn asked.

"I mean like vacuuming the rug or ironing that darned ruffled blouse or washing the cat-nose prints off the window or starting a dossier on Judy Abbott." She knew which one she'd choose. It took only seconds to pull up and print the publisher's biography on Judy Abbott's author page. She read the back-cover copy on three of Abbott's books and ordered them for both Kindle and audio. She could read or listen whenever she had a spare minute.

"Spare minutes—that's a laugh," she told herself, but remembering Hilda's offer to stick around for a while, she started reading the first page of the Kindle of *Sipping Death*, because the back cover promised "a glimpse into the dark side of big city nightlife when poison invades the wine cellars of the rich and famous." She was sure Judy had been the writer who'd shouted that Terry Holiday should be poisoned, and it appeared after only an hour of reading that Judy's mystery novel could be as much an instruction manual on how to poison someone as Elaine's had been on strangling.

Maureen had read enough Agatha Christie mysteries to recognize that an accurate and detailed knowledge of poisons was critical to the believability of the tale being told, but Christie's careful detailing never distracted the reader from the plot. Abbott's vivid descriptions of the throes of agony endured by the victims displayed her medical knowledge of human biology and, at the same time, bordered on what amounted to a weird form of eroticism. The means of administering the poisons themselves was so specifically spelled out, so precisely measured, that Maureen wondered if Abbott's methods of murder had ever inspired the real thing.

"Not my cup of tea for sure," she said aloud, not caring to finish the book. "And I wonder how many readers gave up drinking wine entirely after reading this. I think I'd rather iron ruffles than read another Abbott murder mystery. I hope the romances and cozies aren't as graphic as *Sipping Death*, but I have a feeling they might be."

Finn gave a sleepy "woof" of agreement.

"We're better off reading about time-traveling puppies or seagoing cats," Maureen declared. Finn snored softly, and Bogie gave Bacall a gentle lick behind her right ear. "You guys might as well have the rest of the day off. I think I'll go downstairs and think up some more ways to bring Haven back to life." Closing the door softly behind her, she took her time walking along the corridor, appreciating the view through rain-spattered windows, the softness of the rosy carpeting, and the gleam of the polished brass door of her beautiful elevator. She pressed the down button and stepped inside.

Even before the elevator doors had fully opened, Maureen could see that the lobby, starkly empty only an hour or so earlier, had somehow become a scene of relaxed conviviality. There were couples seated at the few bamboo table-and-wicker chair setups across from the reception desk. Mr. and Mrs. McKenna were seated in tall stools in front of the guest book counter, and more people spilled over into the dining room. George, Sam, Molly, and Gert had moved their chairs indoors and now rocked together in the cocktail bar area. Claire's Uncle Everett sat with another man, along with two schoolteachers who'd booked the McGuire Sisters Suite for the weekend and were due to check out on Sunday. The rest of the cocktail tables, as well as the barstools and a couple of the round dining tables, were filled with guests and familiar faces from the neighborhood including Claire Davis, Paul Jenkins, the Flannagans, and their in-laws. It was a school day, but there were a few youngsters present, and several moms with babies. She wasn't surprised to see the three women from Murder Incorporated seated together at a dining table. The long table usually reserved for buffet-style meals appeared to be laden with food, and almost everybody had plates in front of them or on their laps. Hilda hurried to meet Maureen.

"Isn't this amazing? Here. Have a mimosa." She handed Maureen one of Penelope Josephine's cut glass punch cups.

"Amazing for sure. What happened? Is it somebody's birthday? A holiday I'd forgotten?"

"Mr. Davis's friend arrived early, plunked down a credit card, and told me to wake everybody up and round up the neighbors. He upgraded the room he'd reserved for a suite, and he said he'd played his lucky numbers and hit the Florida Lotto for a lot of money and he wanted to celebrate." She looked around and whispered, "I checked the lottery site. It's true."

"Everybody in Haven must be here," Maureen said, looking around. "How did they all find out so fast?"

"You know how fast news travels in Haven. Quic Shop had it before I started making phone calls. Ted got moving on the breakfast buffet as soon as you two got back from your run. Everyone on the porch had already started coming inside. The rain had turned cold and was slanted so it came across under the porch roof and up to the front door. Ted fired up the hundred-cup coffee urn, and Lennie made a bowl full of mimosas, and the party was on. Gert and Shelly and a couple of the local women are hustling their butts off keeping up with the drinks, and the kitchen is pumping out muffins like crazy."

"All because of Mr. Davis's friend's lucky numbers," Maureen marveled. "Everyone's safe and dry and happy here at the inn. I'll go over right now and thank him." She started across the lobby toward the dining room. "This is a place where everyone feels safe from the storm, and numbers brought them here."

There's safety in numbers, so they say.

She whispered the words *safety* and *numbers* from the newest blue card to herself, looking up when the green door blew open with a loud whoosh, admitting Frank Hubbard.

"What in blazes is going on here, Doherty?"

Chapter 32

"I'm not exactly sure, Frank," Maureen told Frank Hubbard. "It appears that one of the inn's guests has had a stroke of good luck and decided to share it with everyone in Haven. It couldn't have happened at a better time. Want coffee, or a mimosa?" She realized that he was in uniform. "Or are you on duty?"

"I'm on my own time," he said. "I just stopped on my way home to see what's up with Aster. I didn't know there was a party going on." He shaded his eyes with one hand and peered into the dining room. "I don't see her."

"I've had an eye out for her too," Maureen said, "but I haven't seen her, either. I think she's seriously afraid to leave her rooms."

"I've tried to phone her, but she doesn't answer. I can send an officer up there to do a wellness check, but it would be better if you sent one of your people to be sure she's okay." He pointed toward the four rocking-chair comrades. "Send somebody she knows and trusts. If she has reason to actually be afraid for her life, I need to know what it is that she thinks she knows."

"Had Aster told anyone except Peter's ghost that she suspects Elaine?" Maureen asked herself. "Elaine is right here in the room, sitting at a table with Judy and Lynn Ellen. If they did manage to coax Aster to join us, she might take a look into the dining room, see Elaine, and scream or faint or cry or do something else disturbing. Judy Abbott's motives and background are certainly not above reproach either—Lynn Ellen specializes in true crime, and the murders in Haven certainly qualify for that category."

And what about Lynn Ellen? Another dossier to work on?

"I'll ask Molly to knock on her door and try to reason with her," Maureen told Hubbard. "It might be best that we don't insist that she come downstairs with all this commotion going on. We could talk to her in my second-floor office."

"The haunted room. Okay. I wouldn't want to put a damper on your party."

"It's not haunted, and it's not *my* party," Maureen insisted. "But I can't deny that I'm really grateful that this celebration happened to happen here." Smiling broadly, she turned in a circle, taking in the lobby and what she could see of the nearby dining room. "Though I guess it's the only place in Haven besides the Casino that can hold this many people all at once. Excuse me." She walked toward Molly's rocker. Molly was one of those people who didn't see ghosts, so even if Peter happened to be in Aster's room, and she *did* open the door, there'd be no extra ghost-sighting event to deal with.

It took just a brief conversation with Molly to convey the problem. Molly had known Aster for many years, and she let Maureen know that she was willing to do whatever she could to relieve her old friend's fear.

"Text me right away if she agrees to come out of her room," Maureen instructed. "I'll meet you both in Room twenty-seven. Take the elevator so she won't have to see anybody else on the way downstairs. I'm pretty sure all the people from the second-floor suites are already down here spending Mr. Davis's friend's money."

"Speaking of Mr. Davis's friend," she reminded herself, "I need to get over there and thank him for making all this happen."

She made her way past the assorted bamboo tables and white wicker chairs, the cocktail tables and the barstools, shaking hands, greeting old friends, welcoming new faces, heading as straight as she could toward the space where two cocktail tables had been pushed together to accommodate Everett Davis, his generous friend, and their two attractive schoolteacher companions. She remembered greeting the teachers, Sue and Debbie, when they'd checked in together, but Maureen had nearly reached the group when she realized that she didn't know her benefactor's name. Everett Davis raised his hand in greeting. It was too late to go back and look at the credit card or to take a peek at the guest book.

"Hello Sue, Debbie, Mr. Davis." She extended her hand toward the other man. "How do you do, sir. I'm Maureen Doherty. Welcome to Haven House Inn. I can't begin to thank you enough for your generosity to Haven and all of these happy friends and neighbors enjoying your kindness."

The man stood. He was perhaps a few years younger than Everett Davis, with just a hint of gray streaking black hair. Her retail-trained eyes told her that his jeans were an off-the-rack generic brand, and a white shirt open at the throat was of similar origin. He had a good, firm grip.

"Martin Malone," he said. "Pleased to meet you, Ms. Doherty. Nice place you've got here. This Florida weather is a welcome change from New York City." He reached for a vacant chair and pulled it next to his. "Please join us."

"I'd love to, but I can't just now," she said. "I need to keep an eye on things. I imagine this is one of the liveliest events this old inn has seen in a century. Perhaps when the crowd thins out . . ."

"I understand completely," Malone interrupted the thought. "I see that one of Haven's finest has joined us."

"Detective Frank Hubbard," she told him. "He takes a great interest in everything that affects our little city."

"As well he should," Malone said. "I've reserved a suite here for tonight—the woman at the desk said something about Fred Astaire—whatever that means. Anyway, perhaps, as you say, we'll have a chance to chat after the crowd thins out."

"I'll look forward to it," she said. She faced Everett Davis across the table. "I can't thank you enough, Mr. Davis, for introducing Mr. Malone to Haven and to Sue and Debbie, our favorite schoolteachers." There were smiles and good wishes and mimosa toasts all around. "And here's to your lucky numbers," she added. "Thanks for bringing them to Florida from New York."

"Oh, I got them here." He smiled. "They came from a fortune-telling machine I found in a little ice cream parlor on the beach, so I played the Wednesday night Lotto. I found out today I'd won it. Eight million bucks."

She knew without asking who'd given him the numbers.

ZOLTAR KNOWS ALL.

Chapter 33

Maureen had spoken the truth when she'd told Martin Malone that she didn't have time to chat. The unexpectedly busy hotel meant that there were several other important things she didn't have time for. Like finding out what had spooked Aster so badly. Like starting a Reggie-type dossier on Judy Abbott. Like asking Ted if he'd booked one of Key West's haunted hotels for what she was beginning to think of as a pre-wedding honeymoon. Like getting out some rush orders to refill the gift shop shelves.

She moved among the people, stopping to help pour coffee or to grab a chocolate milk for a thirsty youngster. She caught an occasional glimpse of Ted at the buffet table, and they gave each other brief waves or quick salutes. By ten o'clock, the crowd had begun to thin out. The rain had slowed to a soft drizzle, and some of the rocking chairs were back on the porch. She moved close to the now-open green door, accepting thanks from departing guests. That's where she was when the text from Molly arrived.

Aster opened the door. Come up now.

Maureen sprinted for the staircase, taking the stairs two at a time to the second floor. Molly stood just outside the Dawn Wells Suite, one foot propping the door open, motioning with one hand for Maureen to hurry. There was a pleasant smell of baking cookies in the corridor.

"Aster, are you all right? Everyone is worried." Maureen faced the woman through the partially open door. "Please let me in. I want to help you." She gave the door a push, surprised when it swung open easily.

"Maureen, close the door behind you and lock it," Aster croaked in barely a whisper. "Molly can come in too. I know you're not killers. It's Elaine who wants me dead. And I thought she was a friend. She's not. What's going on outside? Your parking lot looks full."

She did as Aster asked, locking the door after she and Molly tumbled together into the room. "A new guest had a stroke of luck and threw a little breakfast party for the whole gang to celebrate," was the brief explanation she offered.

"A little breakfast party for a rainy day," Molly added. "Would you like muffins and coffee? I can have Sam bring some up for you."

I should have thought of that.

"No thanks. Peter and I have already had hot chocolate and shortbread cookies," she said.

Or I should have thought of THAT!

"Peter?" Molly looked around the room. "Like the Peter we all saw in the bookshop window?"

"He'll stay out of sight." Aster took Molly's hand. "Don't worry. It's the living ones we need to worry about. Is Elaine in the building?"

Maureen dodged the question, gazing from the window. "The rain seems to be over."

Molly answered it. "Elaine the mystery writer? I saw her in the dining room having breakfast with her girlfriends. She seems nice. What makes you think she wants to harm you?"

"Because she killed Terry Holiday, and I found out about it, and now she has to kill me so I won't tell anybody." Aster moved to the window and reached for the roll-up shade, pulling it down, blocking the view of the parking lot.

"But now you've told us." Molly backed away from the window. "Are we in danger too?" She faced Maureen. "Are we?"

"No." Maureen hoped that she sounded confident. "Aster, if you have information about Terry Holiday's death, you need to report it to the police. Not just gossip about someone you suspect. That's not fair to anyone."

"Yeah," Molly agreed. "Gossip."

"Well, I'm pretty sure she did it. Didn't you read her awful book?"

"I did," Maureen said. "Is that what you're basing your idea on?"

"Of course. I'm surprised that the police haven't arrested her already. I read some of it to Peter, and he agrees that she describes exactly how she killed that poor man. And I heard her myself shouting that Terry Holiday should be strangled!" Aster pointed an accusing finger toward Maureen. "You were there, Maureen. You must have heard her threaten to strangle him. Just because she doesn't like his books. What an evil woman!"

"Aster, I assure you that Frank Hubbard is totally aware of Elaine's books and that he has the investigation well in hand. You are perfectly safe here, and you may stay as long as you like. Please remember that the mystery books are fiction. Often, well-researched fiction."

"Well, what about Walter's death? He was a ghostwriter, did you know that? I got to know all of the mystery writers, you know. They met in my living room every week. I read their books. He was a wonderful researcher. He had to be to do what he did for other writers. What did he find out about Elaine?" She dropped her voice to a harsh whisper. "Enough so that she had to kill him too?"

Actually, it was a pretty good question. Did Walter do a better job of researching Elaine than Reggie had? It was possible but, she thought, not too likely. After all, the Scotland Yard methods were impressive. It was true that Elaine certainly counted as a suspect, but not by a long shot was she the only suspect. Maureen was about to dig into Judy Abbott's background, and the medical and animal related aspects of her life made the prospect doubly fascinating. She was sure that

Frank Hubbard had not ruled out *any* of the Murder Incorporated members, or anybody else who had reason—real or imagined—to want Terry Holiday dead. It was probable that the same could be said of Robert Taylor.

"I'm positive, Aster, that Officer Hubbard has all of the information you've mentioned about Elaine—and lots more." Maureen spoke calmly, reassuringly, and Aster appeared to relax a bit. "He's a professional police officer and has plenty of experience in investigation. There are for sure other people he's looking into besides Elaine. He won't rush to judgment on anybody until all the facts are in and there is enough conclusive evidence to make an arrest. I promise you can trust him on this."

"Maybe." Aster was hesitant. "You could be right. But I think I'll just stay locked up here until he figures it all out, if that's okay with you."

"You're welcome to stay for as long as you like," Maureen assured her. "I hope, though, that you'll join us for the meeting on Friday. It'll be perfectly safe. Not just one, but two police detectives will be there."

Again, the harsh whisper. "Will *she* be there?"

"Elaine? Yes."

"Two cops?"

"Two cops."

"I'll think about it," Aster promised. "I'll see what Peter thinks about it too."

Chapter 34

Things appeared to be almost back to normal when Maureen returned to the lobby. She thanked Hilda for the extra time she'd put in and once again took her position behind the reception desk.

"I think the party made a good impression on some of the people who'd never been here before," Hilda said. "I had quite a few requests for information, and more than a few promises to come back for a nice long stay here at the inn."

"That would be great, wouldn't it? Maybe the party is the beginning of a happy recovery for Haven." Maureen was hopeful.

"Well, more than one of them said they'd like to come back *after* whoever is killing people gets caught and locked away," Hilda cautioned. "That chicken isn't hatched yet."

"I know."

Once again, "Don't Stop Believin'" plinked merrily from the cocktail lounge. "Is that tune stuck in the rotation somehow?" Maureen asked. "It seems to turn up often."

"Does it?" Hilda queried. "I hadn't noticed it particularly. Maybe Billy Bedoggoned just likes it for some reason." She smiled a knowing smile. "There's no reason he can't have some favorites."

"True," Maureen agreed. "I've been thinking it's a special message for me."

"Maybe it is. Some things in Haven have no simple explanation." Hilda pulled her purse from under the counter. "Well, I'll head home. Thanks for the nice breakfast and the least boring shift I've ever pulled here."

Maureen opened the door to her office and stepped inside, making sure that she'd have a clear view of whatever might be happening in the lobby and a partial glimpse of the dining area. There were still some lingering breakfast/party folks around. The mimosas were no longer being served, but the coffee and muffins continued to be refreshed regularly. This special breakfast event showed signs of running into lunch time. Could Ted and the kitchen staff handle both at the same time? She had no idea. She texted Ted. **DO YOU NEED EXTRA HELP?**

Within seconds, Ted appeared in the doorway. "Are you volunteering?"

She laughed at that. "Only if you're absolutely desperate for amateur cooks."

"I could use a few extra hands for lunch. Can we afford it?"

"We can. Mr. Malone's credit card put us back into the black ink for a while. He spent several thousand dollars on that breakfast, and he's decided to stay here in his suite for a while. I offered to buy some of his sandals for the shop, but he gave me all of his samples and guess what? They're made in Key West. He says he's giving up the shoe business. We can hire a bit of extra help and whatever groceries and other supplies you might need," she assured him. "It couldn't have come at a better time. One more thing. I've decided to buy that Tiki with a camera. Know why? It reminds me of that lady who took our engagement picture. We can leave on Friday with a clear conscience that the inn isn't going to go broke while we're away." She pointed up. "This old roof will be over our heads for a while yet."

"If it hasn't sprung a leak from all this rain," he cautioned.

From the lounge came a plinkity-plink piano rendition of "Raindrops Keep Fallin' on My Head." If Ted noticed the coincidental relationship to the current conversation, he didn't mention it. Maureen knew for sure that the tune she remembered from *Butch Cassidy and the Sundance Kid* had never been of original player piano roll vintage. Maureen was sure that Billy Bedoggoned Bailey, wherever he was, was having a good laugh.

After Ted left, Maureen faced the computer screen and brought up Google.

Judy Abbott, she tapped in. *Books in order.*

As Judy's books appeared, Maureen leaned close to the screen. A good many of her books for young readers featured horses on the covers. They were part of a series called "The Pony Partners." *If I was in my teens instead of my thirties*, she thought, *I'd be reading these*. As an only child, Maureen had had plenty of time for solitary reading, and had read all the classic horse books for kids—from *Black Beauty* to *Misty of Chincoteague*. "I'm sure she couldn't go into weird graphic detail in the animal stories," she told herself. "At least I devoutly hope not."

There was a biography on Judy in the publisher's notes. A child of two teachers, Judy and her siblings—two younger brothers—had all aspired to have careers as teachers also. The boys had excelled in math, and both taught in technical high schools. Judy had never become a teacher, but had collaborated on a number of textbooks on the raising of livestock. Unmarried, she had traveled extensively to other countries, introducing animal husbandry to underdeveloped areas where she'd also developed an interest in poisons derived from plant sources. Most of the accompanying photos, in addition to a formal studio headshot, appeared to have been taken outdoors, some showing the writer on horseback with a woodsy background. Some others showed Judy in a white coat in what appeared to be a medical lab.

It all made sense. *What would Reggie do with it?* she wondered. "I think he'd look at one thing at a time," she answered her own question. "First, about the horses." She looked closely at the various pictures of Judy astride. "Are all these photos of the same horse?"

She examined the photos closely, using a magnifying glass. Yes. They were all pictures of the same animal, a chestnut horse with a blaze of white on his face. On the other hand, the photos on the covers of her horse stories for kids showed different horses on each cover. "The book covers show horses selected by the publisher," she decided, "but the pretty chestnut horse might be Judy's own. I wonder where she keeps it?"

A quick search for "riding stables near me" yielded a dozen likely spots where a person might keep a horse. She knew from checking Judy's address with Google Earth that the woman lived in an apartment building and didn't have a house-with-barn setup, which, she learned, a surprising number of people in the Haven area did, in fact, have.

Reggie would look for identifying images in the photos. Of course!

It only took a few minutes to identify two of the photos with a sign in the distant background spelling out WILLOWTREE REST STABLES. She knew exactly where it was. She'd passed the place hundreds of times on her way to St. Petersburg. "I could hop into my car and drive over there and see if Judy is a customer. I'd be back here in time for a late lunch."

She couldn't resist the temptation to expand the Judy Abbott dossier. Did Robert Taylor have the pretty chestnut horse information? Did Frank Hubbard? The desire to be first with the information overcame her innkeeper instincts, and once again she turned over desk duties to the ever-willing Shelly, climbed into the green Subaru, and headed down Beach Boulevard and away from Haven.

Chapter 35

Walking toward the split-rail fence surrounding the whitewashed wooden building with its metal roof and wide-open front doors brought memories of occasional trail rides with Massachusetts school friends. Even the good horse smell was familiar. *Maybe someday, when I have time, I'll take up horseback riding again.* That thought was immediately followed by *Fat chance I'll ever have time.*

A man approached, wearing a Western outfit so similar to what Reggie had been wearing on his most recent visit that she very nearly giggled aloud. "Howdy," he said. "Welcome to Willowtree Rest."

"Thank you," she said, trying for a casual tone of voice. "Is Judy Abbott around?"

"I think she's inside, rubbing Chief Charlie down after their ride." He peered at her closely. "You a friend of hers?"

"Her writers' group," she said, hoping the reference was sufficiently oblique, and not entirely dishonest. He motioned toward the open double door. She followed his pointing finger and walked along the dirt path toward the barn. She saw Judy in an open stall about halfway down the long room. The woman, wearing jeans and a plaid cotton shirt, brushed the large horse's mane with slow, careful strokes. Maureen had already rehearsed some possible conversation starters.

"Hello, Judy," she began. "I hope I'm not intruding on your private time, but I have an idea I'd like to run by you before our Friday meeting. I took a chance that you might be here with Chief Charlie."

Would Judy wonder how Maureen knew where to find her?

"Sure. What do you have in mind, Maureen?"

Good. The woman didn't express surprise. Maybe all her friends knew this was a favorite hangout for her. "Ever since I announced that the inn would be hosting your writer's critique group meetings, people have been asking about possible writing classes for people who might be thinking about doing some writing of their own experiences." It was a small fib. Only one person had suggested such a class. Gert was thinking about writing a book detailing her days in Las Vegas and her greatly embellished tales of hanging out with Sinatra and the rest of the Rat Pack. But holding writing classes at the inn was a darned good idea, and besides that, it was one more thing that could increase business.

"I thought of you first," Maureen told her, "especially because your horse stories for youngsters are so authentic. The experts always advise to 'write what you know,' and you'd be the perfect person to tell a group how to do just that." She moved closer to the stall and looked into Chief Charlie's warm brown eyes. He looked as though he believed her. "You can charge a fee, of course," Maureen assured her. "The inn can provide space for your classes. What do you say?"

"I'll give it some thought," Judy said. "I could use the extra income, and I enjoy talking and writing about large animals. Did you know I have some medical background on the subject?"

I don't want her to think I've been digging into her background too much.

"That's good to know," Maureen said. "Please consider it. I'm quite sure we can put together a good-sized class for you." She gave Chief Charlie a gentle pat on his muzzle. "I need to get back to work. I'll see you on Friday."

She waved goodbye to the western-clad proprietor of Willowtree Rest Stables on her way back to the Subaru and congratulated herself on establishing some common ground with the woman who had the ability to write disturbingly graphic books for adults along with charming horse stories for children and complex textbooks for students. She wondered if the rest of the Murder Incorporated writers were as multi-talented.

The third woman in the group was Lynn Ellen Crockett who, according to Elaine, wrote true crime and medical romance—mostly of the naughty nurse type. Maureen hadn't yet ordered any of Lynn Ellen's books, but she'd read some of the back-cover copy. Lynn Ellen's appearance, she thought, fit the romance writer image. The woman was pretty, petite, and pleasant. The true crime writer image—not so much—but the back-cover copy of the books Maureen had looked at so far gave the slim blonde some significant street creds. She'd been a TV reporter for an Atlanta station, covering police news. Her research on some historical unsolved crimes had actually put her in harm's way a couple of times when she'd uncovered some long-buried information. Her bio stated that she'd moved to Florida and turned to the medical genre because she was, in fact, a licensed practical nurse and it was "safer," but that she'd never given up her curiosity about true crime and sometimes wove some mystery into her doctor/nurse romance novels.

Maureen had met Lynn Ellen only briefly at that first encounter with the Murder Incorporated critique group meeting at the bookshop. When the whole membership of the group had shouted out their respective preferred methods of disposing of Terry Holiday, what had Lynn Ellen's choice been? She couldn't remember, and wished she'd recorded it.

The "last man standing" of the original group was Paul Jenkins, big guy, big smile, likable, lots of tattoos. Paul's writing credits, in addition to his murder mystery series, included some cowboy romances and some YA Navy Seal adventures. His appearance spoke much more of Navy Seal than of Western romance. Maureen had read some reviews of Paul's mystery series. It occurred to her that in many of the mysteries she'd read over the years, it was often the nice guy like Paul who turned out to be the killer. She shook away the errant thought. That was fiction. Paul was real, and she liked him. Paul's bio revealed that his background was as neither Seal nor cowboy. He'd been an overseas reporter, including duty in some war zones. He'd written one nonfiction book about firefighters. She didn't recall what he'd said about Terry Holiday when the others had shouted their death suggestions, if anything, and she'd not found any bad reviews of the Holiday books on his author pages.

The more she learned about the group in general, the more she looked forward to the Friday meeting. By the time she pulled the Subaru into her parking space behind the inn, she decided that she'd spent quite enough time studying the individuals involved. Maybe she'd even gathered some information that could be helpful to Frank Hubbard's investigations of the deaths of Terry Holiday and Walter Griffith. She hoped so. But her curiosity about Murder Incorporated hadn't yet been satisfied. In fact, in some respects, it had grown. What had researcher Walter discovered that had made him a target?

She entered the inn via the side door, bypassing the porch sitters and heading straight to the reception desk, where Shelly looked up from a copy of *People*. Not a good sign.

"Where did everybody go?" Maureen looked around the long room, which had so recently bustled with activity. "What happened?"

"Once the free breakfast ran out, most everybody left," Shelly reported. "They all said 'thank you' and didn't leave a crumb. A few even asked for doggie bags. There are some people here for lunch already, though." She pointed to the dining room. "The lucky shoe salesman and the researcher seem to have hit it off."

Maureen turned, following Shelly's pointing finger. Martin Malone and Carleton Fretham sat by themselves at one of the small tables, their heads close together, apparently in deep conversation. She took a second look at Carleton. "For goodness' sake, Shelly, look at that. I've never seen Mr. Fretham without his glasses before."

Shelly smiled. "I asked. He got contacts. He said he's got a new lady friend who likes the way he looks without the Coke-bottle lenses. He's trying to get used to them."

"Good for him. A lady friend, huh?" She stood on her toes, craning her neck to better view Malone and Fretham. *Oh, to be the proverbial fly on the wall for that conversation,* Maureen thought, *or to have one of those recording bugs that fits under the table in the old spy movies.* She looked a little closer. There was no need to hide a mic under the table. There was a compact little recording device right there in plain sight between the two men—one of the professional researcher's regular bag of tricks, no doubt. *I wonder if he has the necessary doo-dads to make ghosts like Peter appear, as poor Aster is suspected of doing,* the thought process continued. *And speaking of bags of tricks, how about that ice cream store Zoltar, who really does seem to know all?*

It was time for lunch, as Shelly had reminded her. There was no reason that she couldn't seat herself at one of the tables where two of the moms with toddlers she'd seen at breakfast had settled down with their sleepy children strapped into high chairs. If she seated herself right next to one of the kids, she'd have her back to Carleton and might be able to overhear a word or two from the men. She introduced herself again to the moms, and asked how they'd heard about the morning's special breakfast event.

Each of the mommies credited Quic Shop for the invitation—no surprise there. They'd each enjoyed the experience and said that the muffins would bring them back regularly, even when they had to pay for them. That was good news. Maureen made a mental note to send flyers around featuring the breakfast buffets, especially when the giant blueberry muffins were featured. She didn't encourage further conversation, and a companionable silence ensued—probably because nobody wanted to wake the sleeping babies—enabling some unencumbered listening for Maureen.

I'm getting better at this eavesdropping thing all the time.

Carleton was in mid-sentence. ". . . publisher would be interested in your story. I can make that happen for you." So the ghostwriter was making a pitch for the job, she realized, and a rich client like Malone was surely an ideal subject. She leaned back in her chair, straining to hear the recent millionaire's answer. He was seated across from Carleton, so his words would be harder to hear.

"No kidding? You really think anybody would care about what's happened to me?" The man sounded doubtful. His voice was softer than the writer's, and he tended to lose volume at the end of his sentences. This was not going to be easy.

There was no problem in hearing Carleton's precisely pronounced words. She remembered hearing him speak at the Murder Incorporated meeting. He'd probably given lectures on ghostwriting before. "I know people in the publishing business," he said. "The big guys. I have almost daily contact with top New York agents. Trust me. Yours is the perfect 'rags-to-riches' story. I wouldn't be a bit surprised if we have an NYT bestseller on our hands here."

Maureen noticed the present tense. *He's making it sound as though it's already a done deal. Clever.* She waited for Malone's response.

"I'm just a shoe salesman who got lucky. Not much of a story except . . ." His voice trailed off. This wasn't going to be easy. One of the kids woke up and started to cry. Mom fished calmly in her large bag and pulled out a bottle. Maureen thought about Ted's comments about "our kids." Would she be good at being a mother? Baby stopped crying, but the moms began a low-pitched conversation about a sale on towels at Dillard's. A waitress appeared to take the lunch orders. She gave up on the eavesdropping and ordered the crabmeat salad sandwich and sweet tea.

Chapter 36

The men finished with their lunches before she did, and the two went in opposite directions—Carleton took the green exit door to the porch, and Malone headed toward the elevator. There seemed to be no point in following either one. She'd leave the "suspect tailing" up to Frank Hubbard, after giving herself a mental pat on the back for her recent morning's successful tracking of Judy Abbott. Satisfied that she'd done quite enough amateur sleuthing for the moment, she once again relieved Shelly at the desk, determined to get back to business—such as it was.

Shelly had reported no new business—no guests coming or going, one way or the other. Dull, dull, boring. She stared at the phone, willing it to ring. That didn't work, so she picked up Shelly's discarded *People* magazine. The cover promised the latest news about the two battling royal princes. Diana would be appalled. The bell over the door dinged. She looked up from an article about Taylor Swift's latest concert and was surprised to see the very woman she'd just thought about. Judy Abbott, still in plaid shirt and jeans, held forward a paperback book—one of those with a pretty girl-on-a-horse cover. "Hi, Maureen," she said. "I just got a shipment from the publisher of advance copies of the newest 'Pony Partners' book. You were so complimentary about them, I thought you might like to have a signed copy." She looked shy, hesitant, almost embarrassed.

"Why, thank you, Judy. I've never outgrown my love for horse stories." Her words were sincere, and at the same time, she felt some regret about the way she'd been prowling about in Judy's past—looking for . . . for what, exactly? She reached for the book. *Allison's Appaloosa.*

"I hope you'll like it."

"I'm positive I'll love it—and I'll give it a good review, too."

"Thanks, Maureen. Authors love those good four- and five-star reviews," Judy said.

"We're still serving lunch, Judy. Can I invite you to stay and have a bite?" Maureen hoped the woman would accept the offer. "I've already eaten lunch, and I can recommend the crabmeat salad, but I can always use a cup of coffee and maybe a cookie or two."

"Well . . ." Judy seemed hesitant. "If it's no trouble—I mean, I did skip breakfast . . ."

"I insist." Maureen had already buzzed Gert's phone. "Wait a sec, and I'll get someone to cover for me here."

Gert arrived promptly. She'd been on the porch on her accustomed rocker and announced that she was happy to get away from one of George's old war stories. Maureen introduced the two, told Gert she'd be in the dining room if needed, and led Judy to the corner table Malone and Carleton had recently vacated. Once seated, she searched for a topic of conversation that didn't involve prying into Judy's life. She'd done quite enough of that and wasn't proud of it.

"All of the mystery writers are thrilled that we're going to be meeting in this beautiful room," Judy said. "Aster's living room is lovely, of course, but since we can't meet there for now, we all really appreciate your letting us meet here."

"It's my pleasure," Maureen said, meaning it. "The group meeting planned for Friday should be especially interesting to everyone involved."

"It is to me," Judy said. "We write about crime and murder and all, and we try to get the details right, but nothing beats actually talking to detectives and police officers and getting the real skinny on all of it. We're all excited about it. Thanks for thinking of it."

Maureen wondered what Judy would say if she knew that the idea had come from a fashion-conscious, long-dead movie starlet who shared her third-floor suite. She dodged the thanks by pointing out the largest table in the room. "I think that one will be big enough to seat everybody involved. If not, I'm quite sure Penelope Josephine Gray had table-extenders in the warehouse."

"I've heard the story about how you inherited the inn from that lady you'd never even met. Did you ever think of writing a book about it?" Judy asked.

"It's a tempting idea. She left a wealth of material here at the inn. I've been too busy running the place to take time writing about it."

"You could get a ghostwriter. A lot of people do," Judy said. "Even some famous writers."

"I know," Maureen agreed, wondering at the same time when she'd get a pitch from Carleton Fretham offering that very idea. A waitress took Judy's order—she'd taken the advice about the crabmeat salad sandwich. Maureen stuck with her coffee and shortbread cookies plan. There was a brief silence, but not an awkward one, as they ate.

Maureen began a new conversation, hesitantly, because the subject was a sad one. "Walter will be missed by all of the group," she said. "I'd met him only briefly, but I liked him immediately."

"Yes." Judy nodded. "He was that kind of person. It's hard to believe he's gone. In that terrible way." Her eyes grew misty. "Who would do such a thing?"

"The police are working diligently, I'm sure," Maureen said.

"All of us are hoping they'll solve it soon. It's affected our group so personally."

"All of Haven is hoping they'll solve it." Maureen was forceful. "It's affected the entire city."

"I hadn't thought about it that broadly," Judy admitted. "Of course. Two murders in a row. It must have impacted your business. Everybody's business. Oh dear, how awful for the city."

"I'm hoping getting everyone together will be helpful. You writers think of such original and imaginative ways to describe all the aspects of murders, and the police have to depend on the cold hard facts alone," she mused. "It could be that blending the two will provide some answers that neither of you have found so far."

"Wow! This will make a great true crime book!" Judy's eyes sparkled with excitement. "I can hardly wait to get started. Thanks for the inspiration!"

By mentioning Walter, Maureen had meant to steer the conversation in the direction of whether or not Judy had assisted him with information on horses for his popular cowboy series. Had they worked closely together? Somehow, it had all veered off into a topic for an entirely new book having nothing to do with four-legged characters, only the two-legged killing variety.

Read the words to find your way.

Chapter 37

Maureen nibbled around the edges of her shortbread cookie and at the same time, nibbled around the edges of the conversation she wanted to have with Judy Abbott. She tried again. Picking up the copy of the Pony Partners book, she tapped the cover picture. "Your knowledge about so many kinds of horses must have been helpful to Walter when he was writing his cowboy books. I know that you all try to be as accurate as possible, whatever the subject is that you're writing about."

"Oh, yes. Walter was a stickler about having details right—even in those cowboy stories of his. So in his ghostwriting business, you can only imagine how much research he had to do on every single subject he got involved with. And being a ghostwriter means you don't talk about what you're working on. After all, the guy who's paying wants all the credit. He wrote about a lot of businesses, you know? Like if he did one for a florist, he'd wind up with a file cabinet full of books and magazines and brochures about flowers and an apartment full of houseplants. Same thing with a retired railroad engineer. And a Canadian hockey player. His mind was so full of details about so many things, I don't know how he kept it all straight." Judy's smile was wistful. "He was a wonder. We all loved him."

Feeling bolder, Maureen pushed harder. "Were he and Elaine dating?"

"You know what? I don't know." She looked away, over toward the bar, where the angelfish swam silently, and paused for a long moment. "When they showed up together, with her all decked out like some kind of showgirl, none of us knew what to think. Next thing we knew, he was gone. I don't know what to expect at the funeral. Will Elaine show up in black mourning clothes? You know, with the veil and all? It would be just like her. Always the drama queen."

The animosity in Judy's voice was unmistakable, and took Maureen by surprise. Whenever she'd spoken with Elaine about the varied members of the Murders Incorporated group, there'd been no indication of any conflict within the group. On the contrary, the woman had always displayed good humor. What was going on here? Professional competition? Was one of them more successful than the other? Another thought popped into mind. Were they both interested in the same man? Was it a case of garden-variety jealousy?

Garden variety? Like the body in Aster's garden?

Judy pushed her empty plate away. "This was delicious. Thank you, Maureen. I need to get back to work now. Deadlines, you know. I'm almost at the end of *Pam's Palomino*. I'll see you at the Friday meeting."

Maureen signed the check, then stood and walked with the writer to the front door, then resumed her post at the reception desk. "Thanks, Gert," she said. "You aways seem to be there whenever I need you. I hope you know how much I appreciate you—and the others. I could never manage this place without you all."

The reply was a smiling, offhand "Oh, we all know that for sure."

Maureen returned the smile. "Did anything interesting happen while I was at lunch?"

"Business-wise, no. Nobody coming. Nobody going. But there was a message from Frank Hubbard. He said not to bother you at lunch, but he'd like you to call him about a picture he got from one of the bus stop kids."

"Thanks. I'll call him right now." She stepped into the office, leaving the door ajar. "Hello, Frank? You called?"

"Yeah. Hello, Doherty. I'm sending you a screenshot of a photo one of the bus stop kids took on the day Holiday turned up dead. There's a man in the background. I've blown it up. It's a little bit grainy, so you can't make out his face very well, and his hat is shading his eyes. He's wearing one of those bright-color shirts like you sell in that fancy shop on your porch. See if it could be one of your customers."

"Okay. Send it."

"Well?" He sounded impatient.

"Jeez, Frank. Give me a minute." The picture showed a couple of young boys mugging for the camera as one tried to take a football from the other. The man was in the background. "Okay. Yes. That's a Tommy Bahama shirt. I sell them, but so do half a dozen other shops in Haven."

"What about the hat?"

"That's a nice Cuban Panama black fedora hat," she told him. "Good quality and not too expensive." She felt her heart begin to race. "I've only sold one like it." She stalled, trying to deny the reality of what was on the screen. "Most men like the white or tan Panama hats." She knew she was babbling. "That one was a special order."

"So you recognize it?"

She recognized it. She recognized the shirt and the hat and the man. She was just a little bit disappointed to realize that without his glasses, he didn't really look like Superman at all.

"It's Carleton Fretham." She blurted the words. "Oh my God, Frank. That's him. The ghostwriter. He . . . he lives here. In the Arthur Godfrey Suite. I'm sure he had a good reason for being there that day."

"I hope so," Hubbard said. "Maybe he was just in the wrong place at the wrong time." Within minutes, the Crown Vic arrived in the driveway next to the Tiki hut.

Maureen met Hubbard on the porch. "I'm not sure Carleton's home. He's on the second floor. Follow me." She led him toward the staircase.

"Let me go ahead of you, Doherty. He may be armed."

Surprised, she dropped back, following his lead to the head of the stairs.

"What's the room number?" he asked.

"It says Arthur Godfrey on the door," she explained. "Right there." She pointed.

"I like numbers better," he said. Once outside the neatly lettered door, he knocked on it. Once. Twice. "Police. Open up," he commanded. There was no reply from inside. "Is there another exit in there?" he asked.

"No doors. Just a couple of windows."

Once again, he knocked—louder—on the door and repeated the demand. "Police. Open the door." Silence. "Fretham. Police." He spoke in a normal tone of voice. There was no answering voice. No sound at all. "He hasn't checked out, has he?"

"No. He was planning to be at that meeting tomorrow," she explained.

"I'll bet he was. Lotta nerve. He must be pretty sure of himself. Has he mentioned any plans to be out of town for any reason?"

"He said something about taking a trip up to the University of Maryland. They have a collection of four thousand Arthur Godfrey tapes," she recalled.

"Godfrey again," he mumbled. "Fretham wouldn't have time to do that if he's going to the meeting. Okay. Let's keep it quiet about me wanting to talk to him. I'll post a plainclothes man here to watch for him to show up."

The guest list for the meeting was getting shorter. Poor Walter wouldn't be there, of course, and now it appeared that Carleton might be missing too. It looked as though there'd be no need for Penelope Josephine's table-extender.

Chapter 38

Friday morning dawned with a pretty pink sky—no red sun. "Just another day in paradise," Maureen quoted the old Florida publicity tagline to Finn, as they stepped out of the side door into pleasantly cool weather. The humidity was low, and a soft breeze stirred the palm fronds above their heads. Her comment about "paradise" had a slightly sarcastic edge to it, although Finn's confirming "woof" sounded as positive as ever. Her thoughts about this looked-forward-to Friday were mixed. The trip to the Keys, with its long-awaited "honeymoon" aspect, brought heart-pounding anticipation, while the scheduled meeting between cops, writers, and possible suspects meant confusion and maybe even fear.

She'd begun her pre-run stretches when Ted joined her next to the tallest Tiki. "Good morning, my beautiful bride-to-be." His embrace was warm and welcome and lasted so long that Finn pushed his wet nose between them and gave a demanding "yip." They moved apart, and Ted picked up the leash Maureen had dropped onto the sand.

"We'd better get going. Finn's getting impatient, and we each have a busy day ahead." They completed their stretches, with exercise motions smooth and perfectly coordinated, and began the jog toward the shell line. "Have you heard any more about what happened to Fretham?" he wanted to know. During their late date at the bar the previous night, they'd discussed Hubbard's unsuccessful attempt to contact the ghostwriter.

"Just questions. No answers," she said. "I guess someone on the second floor heard Hubbard knocking and announcing 'police,' and reported it at Quic Shop. Now *everyone* wants to know what happened to Fretham."

"Have you told anyone about the photo?"

"Nope. That's police business. Not my job."

"I hope Carleton hasn't done anything—well—anything bad." Ted and Finn moved ahead of her.

"Me too," she said, took a deep breath, and adjusted her pace to his. "He can be a little off-putting because he's so intense, but he can be quite likable sometimes—so willing to share his knowledge." She remembered the colorful drink brochure he'd given to her. "I'm wondering if he'll show up at the meeting this afternoon. He may just be off researching something. If he's really involved in a topic, he might not be answering his phone. He may not even know Hubbard is looking for him."

"I've thought of that." Ted gave a short laugh. "He told me once that he got so preoccupied studying about General Custer that he forgot to go to his own mother's birthday party."

"It can't be easy, being a ghostwriter," Maureen said. "I mean putting your heart and soul into it like Carleton apparently does, and never getting the credit for producing the finished product. No book tours. Never seeing your name on the bestseller lists—not even being able to talk about it."

"I wonder if it was like that for Walter too," Ted wondered.

"I'll bet it was."

Feet pounding on the hard-packed sand, the two raced toward the distant sign, the dog keeping pace with them. Maureen was first to reach up and tap the sign with her hand. "I win," she yelled, then, embarrassed, looked around to see if anyone besides Ted had heard her gleeful shout of victory. They were, as usual, alone beneath the sign. "Sometimes I think of that nice woman who took our picture when you proposed," she said. "It was such a lucky chance that she happened to be here at just the right moment."

"I know. I've thought of her too—but we're lucky anyway. Lucky that we found each other. Lucky that we're going to be together forever." That statement prompted a long, sweet kiss. "And tonight," he whispered, "we'll be in Key West, and we'll finally be *really* alone together."

"Woof?" Finn asked.

"It's true," Maureen said, and patted the golden. "*You* won't even be with us. Isn't it amazing?"

"We'd better turn around and head back," Ted said. "I need to get breakfast service started pretty soon. The sooner we get past this day, the sooner we get to Key West."

"My mother always says 'never wish time away,'" Maureen warned as they reversed direction and headed for home. Once the Casino was in sight, Ted handed her Finn's leash and pulled ahead.

"I can't let you beat me twice in one day," he announced.

"Maybe I'll let you win," she countered.

Laughing, the two arrived at the sprawling white building within a minute of each other, with Ted tagging the pillar of the porch first. "I win," he mouthed silently. Their cool-down routine was accomplished efficiently, without conversation, and holding hands loosely, they strolled along the sidewalk edging the broad boulevard.

"The bookstore looks so forlorn, doesn't it?" Maureen said, as they approached the building. "The window display hasn't been changed, and Erle Stanley is nowhere to be seen."

"That droopy crime scene tape doesn't help the impression any, either." Ted pointed to the offending yellow plastic festooning the border of Aster's flower garden.

"I'm glad Aster and her cat are safe at the inn and that she doesn't have to look at the shop the way it is now." Maureen faced away from the building, toward the beach side of the street. "But she's still too terrified to come out of her rooms."

"Do you suppose she'll come to the meeting? She'll be among friends."

"Along with two cops," Maureen pointed out. "I've told her all that. I think she might do it. I'll be very careful not to seat her beside Elaine."

"What's up with that? Elaine's the good-looking one, right? Is it a jealousy thing?"

"She's quite attractive, no doubt, but Aster has it in her head that Elaine wants to kill her because of something she knows. And there seems to be a bone of contention between Elaine and Judy too."

"Woof?" Finn asked.

"Not that kind of bone," she told him.

"Wow. Do you know what it is about Elaine that has Aster upset?"

Maureen shrugged. "It's the same stuff everyone knows. Aster has read Elaine's creepy book—the one where she goes into detail about strangling somebody—and she's decided that it proves that Elaine killed Terry Holiday. That's all."

"That doesn't make sense." They'd reached the Tiki hut, and Ted turned toward the side door. "Maybe if Frank would talk to her, tell her he's looked into all that, she'd feel better about it."

"I'm hoping so. We'll see who shows up at the meeting. Maybe we'll all get some answers."

"Woof." Finn sounded doubtful.

Chapter 39

A few early lunch customers had filed into the dining room, some glancing with curiosity at the RESERVED sign Maureen had placed on the large round table at the rear of the room. There hadn't been any occasion for advance reservations at Haven House lately, for either tables or beds, and to make matters worse, the planned-for beach wedding had been cancelled—along with the wedding guests' reservations for suites at the inn. "They didn't exactly say it was because of the murders," Hilda had reported. "They just said they hoped to find another beach site that suited them better." That meant lost business not just for the inn, but for the kitchen too. Ted had planned on catering the whole event, from appetizers to the wedding cake.

Well, at least one full table in the dining room will give the illusion that we're still in business, Maureen thought. *I'm not anywhere near ready to give up on this place.* She'd made use of Penelope Josephine's collection of elegant Victorian sterling silver place card holders to determine who'd sit where and next to whom. She'd been surprised to learn that Gert had once taken a calligraphy course, and the woman had hand-lettered each card with the person's full name in gracefully embellished cursive.

The two police officers would face each other across the table. Lynn Ellen would be seated at Hubbard's right, Elaine to his left. Robert Taylor would be flanked by Aster on the left—perhaps she'd feel more comfortable with the policeman beside her—and Maureen would sit at his right. She'd placed Paul Jenkins between Aster and Elaine so they wouldn't face each other—Carleton, if he showed up, would sit between Lynn Ellen and Judy, and Walter was supposed to have been beside Maureen. It had worked out to a perfect boy-girl seating arrangement. Penelope Josephine would have been proud.

She decided to leave Walter's place card where they'd originally planned. "It'll be like the 'missing man formation' in aviation, where they leave a space where a plane should be—or like the 'riderless horse' in a parade for a fallen comrade—with the boots reversed in the stirrups." *The Missing Man.* It just seemed right that way.

Two of the mystery writers were the first to arrive. Maureen greeted Judy and Lynn Ellen warmly, pleased with their compliments on the table setting.

"We'll have the ghostwriter sitting between us," Judy said. "There's no chance that we'll run out of things to talk about."

"That's for sure." Lynn Ellen laughed. "He knows a little bit about a lot of things, and he loves sharing information with anyone who'll listen."

Paul Jenkins arrived shortly after the women. Circling the table, he stood behind his designated chair. "I guess that's what we're all here for. Sharing information, right, Maureen?"

"That's right, but we'll be sharing lunch first." She pointed to the blackboard over the bar. "The Friday specials are all tried and true."

"And on the house," Paul added with a grin.

Frank Hubbard had used the side door. "I parked out back, Doherty," he said. "I wouldn't want the cruiser to scare any prospective customers away. I see that the vacancy sign is still on." He lowered his voice. "Is the Yankee here yet?"

"Not yet," Maureen told him. "Be nice, okay?"

"I'm always nice. By the way, your friend Carleton phoned me late last night. He heard somewhere that I was looking for him. We got that picture thing straightened out. He was at a meeting with Aster at the bookstore that day. I talked to her. She vouched for him." He peered at the place cards, moving behind the chairs one at a time. "Good. You remembered that I like to have my back to the wall."

"That's just the way it worked out," she admitted, pleased that Carleton had contacted Hubbard.

"My plainclothes guy is still in the lobby," he said.

"Yes. We've noticed. Everyone has noticed. His clothes are much too plain. He looks like a cop. The department should buy him something nice from my shop."

Robert Taylor was next to enter the lobby. Maureen was surprised to see that his wife, Janie, was with him. She welcomed the couple. Taylor was quick to explain Janie's presence. "I hope it's all right that I brought my wife along. She'll be recording the proceedings."

"So will I," Hubbard announced, glowering in Taylor's direction, slamming down his well-used Sony voice recorder in front of his place card.

Maureen motioned for Lennie to bring another chair, relieved that the table was one of only three that could seat ten people without an extension. "It's no problem, Detective Taylor," she said. "It's nice to see you again, Mrs. Taylor." *Too bad Janie won't have a place card, though.*

Unbidden, the player piano started up. The old tune from the 1920s was one in the regular rotation. "Side by Side," it plinked. Eight pairs of eyes looked toward the dining room entrance as Elaine Cremonis, in skin-tight black jeans and a very short white lace crop top, strolled in, arm in arm, with Carleton Fretham, sans glasses.

Somewhere, Billy Bedoggoned Bailey is laughing his butt off.

Lennie hastily unplugged the piano. Carleton and Elaine took their pre-designated seats as though nothing unusual had just occurred. Shelly, efficiently as usual, beginning with Janie Taylor and moving from left to right, took the lunch orders.

Considering the varied personalities involved, Maureen thought, the meal went very well. There wasn't a great deal of conversation going on, and most of what Maureen heard from her tablemates consisted of complimentary remarks about the food. Both police detectives remained stoically silent for the most part, other than the occasional "please pass the salt," while the writers mostly chatted among themselves. Carleton, who appeared to be in professional-researcher form rather than his frequent imparting-information mode, seemed to be listening to everyone else.

Once the dishes had been cleared away, Maureen, struggling to remember Robert's Rules of Order and wishing she'd thought to bring a gavel, stood. "I call this meeting to order," she said. She began the introduction with the two detectives. Hubbard first. "Alphabetical order," she reasoned. "I can't go wrong with that." Frank Hubbard stood, gave his full name and rank, and sat down. Robert Taylor was somewhat more relaxed. "I'm Captain Robert Taylor of the Peabody, Massachusetts Police Department, in charge of criminal investigations. I am not here in Haven on official business of any kind. I've been invited to sit in on this meeting."

Maureen began to introduce the others, starting with Lynn Ellen. "Please tell us a little about yourself, especially about the murder mysteries you write," she encouraged. "We're hoping that perhaps something in your experience as an author will trigger a thought, a clue, an idea to help solve the very real mysteries we're encountering now here in Haven."

Frank Hubbard's eye-roll was hard to miss. Robert Taylor simply nodded. Lynn Ellen, quite undaunted by the detectives, reported that she specializes in writing about true crimes, quite often of the historic variety. "Sometimes," she said, "we can learn a lot from the past. Actually, there are some similarities to this case in a nonfiction book called *The Orchid Thief* by Susan Orlean. It even happened in Florida. Wow. There are so many cool ways murders can happen in gardens," she enthused.

"Poison plants, sharp shears, a handy shovel. When this case gets solved, you can bet I'll get a book out of it."

"I've done some research on the poison plants," Carleton offered. "Not that that's of much help in this case. Sorry." He turned to speak to the writer sitting beside him. "I think you know more about poison than I do, Judy."

Maureen remembered the passages about the agony of the poisoning victims she'd read about in *Sipping Death* and wondered once again if Judy's books had ever inspired real murder. Judy admitted to writing about poison, but claimed no special knowledge of strangling. "That would be Elaine's specialty," she said. "She's the queen of the garrote, the noose, the bare hands. Of course, poor Walter was shot, and I've written about gunshot murders, but nothing that would be useful in this case, I'm quite sure. Paul knows about guns. At least the cowboy kind. Right, Paul?"

"A little," he agreed good-naturedly. "Remember, I'm writing cowboy romances. My heroes spend more time in the sack than they do in the saddle. But I do know how to break down a rifle into small easy-to-stash sections in case my hero has to bug out of a situation in a hurry."

Judy spoke up. "Remember, we're a critique group. We've all read and heard every word of each other's books." She waved a hand, encompassing all at the table. "Usually more than once. Like over and over and over." That remark was met with smiles and affirmative head-nods from all of the writers.

"Judy is right," Elaine said. "Every single one of us knows how to poison, strangle, chop, dismember, shoot, smother, stab, behead, run over, or otherwise kill somebody—anybody."

"Behead?" Lynn Ellen asked in a small voice.

Elaine grinned, poking Carleton in the arm. "*Missing Your Smile*. My latest. It will release next fall. It's available for pre-order now, though." There were a few words of congratulation to Elaine from the writers. Both detectives frowned. Carleton offered Elaine a high-five.

Judy continued with a rundown of the murder mysteries she'd written. "I'm partial to poisons, because that's what I know the most about," she said, "but I've done my share of hit-and-run, smothering, and stabbing." Smile and wink. "I really like stabbing."

Aster giggled out loud. Everyone at the table turned to look at her. "Sorry," she said. "I really loved Judy's *Sharp Insights*. The one where the killer stabs all her ex-husbands and boyfriends to death and leaves a lipstick kiss imprint on their foreheads. So funny."

Funny?

"I agree, Aster, I liked that one too." Carleton gave a short laugh. "Murder can be funny, and often it is in books."

"I know. Some of you definitely have a funny bone. I've read them all, and Walter had some funny ones. Especially the baby animal series. He was so fond of God's littlest creatures." Another smile from the bookshop owner. "This is a good meeting, Maureen."

There was a respectful hum of agreement from the group. "It was nice of you to include Walter's place at the table, Maureen," Paul said. "We all miss him a lot. Seeing that empty chair is sad, but it holds good memories of the man for all of us."

"The missing man." Carleton spoke the words Maureen had thought about when she'd left the card in place.

"Exactly," Paul said. "In my *Lasso the Lady*, when the sheriff gets murdered, there's a riderless horse in the funeral procession. If they have a riderless horse for Walter, they'll use those old cowboy boots of his. He always wore them whenever he did a book signing of his Western stories."

"The missing man," Carleton said again. "Did you know that when Abraham Lincoln died, his horse, Old Bob, riderless with boots reversed in the stirrups, led the mourners to the grave."

"That's interesting," Robert Young said. "You seem to have a wealth of information, Mr. Fretham."

"I know a little bit about a lot of things." Carleton gave a modest lift of one shoulder.

"That'd because he's a ghostwriter," Elaine said. "He has to do so much research on so many subjects, I don't know how he keeps track of it all." She aimed a warm look in Carleton's direction. "He's very smart."

Once again, the term *smarty-pants* occurred to Maureen.

Chapter 40

"Do you think your meeting turned up anything the police can use in their investigation?" Ted asked. Maureen sat in the wicker chair beside Ted's desk in the corner of the kitchen he called his "office."

"It's hard to say. Police officers seem to have a special ability to keep a poker face no matter what's going on around them," she said. "I learned a few new things."

"Such as?"

"For one thing, it had never occurred to me before that all of them, including Aster, share a knowledge of everything each of them has written about murder," she told him, "and it's not from a casual reading. It's from seeing and hearing the same words over and over at the critique group meetings."

"You're right. That means that Walter may have picked up on something one of the others said or wrote."

"I think so. He may have heard or seen something that got him shot," Maureen said.

"That's a lot of information to process. Cops don't have a lot of time to read murder mysteries." Ted's words were thoughtful. "But Aster does. Is she back upstairs, safely locked in her room?"

"She's much more relaxed. She may have even given up her obsession with Elaine. I saw them chatting together over coffee after the meeting, and she stopped on the porch to visit with Sam and George."

"That sounds encouraging." Ted frowned. "But I hope she hasn't put herself in danger."

"I was so pleased to hear her laughing and talking that I didn't think about that," she mused. "If knowing too much is what got Walter killed, it could happen again, couldn't it?"

"Before we leave this evening, I'll remind all of the staff to keep an eye on her," he promised. "The cop in the lobby adds an extra layer of security, too; I'm sure Hubbard has already tipped him off to watch over Aster."

"I'll remind him before we leave."

"Good. We can take our mini-vacation worry-free. Bags packed. Boarding passes ready. Everything is good to go. Right?"

With only the tiniest bit of hesitation, she answered, "Right."

Shortly after noon, with the promised phone call made to Frank Hubbard, and following the Clearwater Airport's advice to arrive an hour before flight time, Maureen and Ted climbed into the inn's van with George at the wheel and waved goodbye to the assembled group of well-wishers on the Haven House Inn front porch, along with Finn in Molly's arms with her hand helping him to wave one paw. George dropped them off at the entrance to the terminal with a promise to pick them up on Sunday morning. They joined the curving line, took off their shoes, offered driver's licenses, made sure that their carry-on bags fit the required measurements, then lingered over celebratory glasses of wine at the airside bar.

"It won't seem real until we're on the plane," Maureen said.

"It's real," Ted assured her. "Key West, here we come."

Maureen was assigned the window seat. "You'll like seeing the Keys from the air while we're approaching," Ted promised, "and after we land, you're going to love the sunset celebration at Mallory Square. There are magicians, and street performers dancing on stilts. Sometimes they even have trained cats that jump through hoops. It's amazing. I can hardly wait to share it with you." He reached for her hand. "I can hardly wait to share everything with you for the rest of our lives."

The one hour and fifteen minute flight was a pleasant one. As Ted had promised, the view of the Keys, stretched out over azure water along the famed Seven Mile Bridge, was stunning. "Amazing," Maureen breathed. "Someday, when we have more time, let's drive along that bridge, and stop on every Key."

"We can do that," he promised. "We'll have time to do that, plenty of time, years of time together." He squeezed her hand. "The rest of our lives."

The thought came unbidden. *We don't know how much time we have. No one does. Walter didn't know. Neither did Terry Holiday.* "We'll make every minute count," she promised. "Every single minute."

The Key West International Airport was small, but efficient. Within fifteen minutes of landing, they were on their way via shuttle bus, to the motel. It wasn't on the beach, but it was in a pleasant cul-de-sac. The MaryAnna was not a traditional motel, but a cluster of small cabins nestled among old growth palm trees and vibrant, hot pink, almost-red bougainvillea bushes. Maureen was pleased to realize that it was not among the island hostels thought to be haunted. Ted signed the register and picked up a key—not unlike the vintage room keys at Haven House—an old-fashioned metal key attached to a green plastic fob marked *MaryAnna* and a numeral 4.

"May I carry you across the threshold?" They approached the white cabin.

"Absolutely," she agreed. Putting both bags on a white-painted rocking chair, on a tiny porch surrounded with a neat picket fence, he unlocked the door; and lifting her easily, they entered the almost-a-honeymoon cottage. He kicked the door shut and deposited her ever so gently onto a king-sized bed.

"We're in easy walking distance of Mallory Square," he said. "And it's nearly time for the sun to set." He made no move to leave her side.

She stretched both arms toward him. "The sun will set again tomorrow night," she said.

Their carry-on bags were still on the rocking chair in the morning, undisturbed, each with a slight glaze of morning dew on the leather surfaces.

They made good use of their remaining vacation time. The Saturday evening sunset ceremony was all that they'd expected it to be and more. They visited Duval Street, and as Ted had suggested back in Haven, there was, indeed, a Zoltar machine in Key West. They found it in Ripley's Believe It or Not! Odditorium. Maureen was hesitant to slide the bills into the slot, but Ted laughingly insisted on it. She heard the by-now familiar words as the turbaned mannequin moved plastic hands over the crystal ball and intoned, "Zoltar knows all."

Maureen had tossed the blue Zoltar card into her purse with a promise to read it later. "It's all just silly nonsense, you know," she'd told Ted. "It's just for fun."

It had been Ted's first Zoltar experience. "I'll read mine now," he said. "Want to hear it?"

She shouldn't have been surprised when he read the words aloud. They were as familiar to her as they'd been when she'd first seen them in the red-covered astrology book. "Make sure your relationship is full of affection, great conversation, emotional connection, and shared dreams and projects," he said. "Truth and sensitivity are the foundations of love. Zoltar knows all."

"Interesting," she said, trying to mask her feelings.

"Read yours now," he insisted. "We're going to share everything. Remember?"

She remembered, and reluctantly pulled the card from the purse, focusing on the printed message. She couldn't disguise her amazement as she read aloud. "Make sure your relationship is full of affection, great conversation, emotional connection, and shared dreams and projects. Truth and sensitivity are the foundations of love. Zoltar knows all."

"That is so weird!" Ted exclaimed. "Imagine that. Of course they must print hundreds of cards with the same messages—but to have the machine spit out two in a row—that's just weird."

It's much weirder than you know!

"That proves it," Ted said, pulling her close. "We are absolutely meant for each other."

"Zoltar knows all," she said, meaning it.

Chapter 41

Maureen and Ted were welcomed back to Haven House on Sunday morning with the not unexpected "wink-wink-nod-nod" silly grins from the closest friends, along with a few knowing smirks from some others. Finn had accompanied George to the airport, and even after arriving at home had not stopped his excited, loving, tail-wagging, happy woofing welcome. Ted had taken him for a walk, hoping that would calm him down.

Once back in her own suite, Maureen tossed her bag onto the chair, opened her purse, and tucked the Key West Zoltar card into a desk drawer. Lorna, shimmering splendidly in a strapless white satin mini from the gift shop window, already seated on the couch, patted the cushion beside her. "Come on. Spill. Tell me everything. Don't leave anything out."

"Everything?" Maureen laughed. "I don't think so."

"Come on. I'm a ghost. Been dead for years. I deserve a little vicarious thrill once in a while." She leaned so far forward, she nearly shimmered off the couch. "How was it?"

"It... all... everything was wonderful," Maureen stammered.

"Better than you expected?"

"I wasn't . . . I hadn't . . . I mean . . . yes."

"I believe it. I can tell by looking at you. All glowie and everything. I love Key West. Tell me what you did—besides *that*, I mean." A shimmery wink. "Did you eat conch chowder? Did you watch the sunset? Do they still have the trained cats?" Bogie had stepped down from the tower and strolled through Lorna at the mention of the word *cats*.

Maureen laughed. "Yes, yes, and yes. Someday we're going to go back and spend more time—and drive across that Seven Mile Bridge."

"Was the motel haunted?"

"Nope. At least I don't think so. The MaryAnna. We'd stay there again. A perfect place for a honeymoon."

"A *real* honeymoon, you mean. When's the wedding?"

"We haven't set a date yet, but it'll be a beach wedding. Soon."

"I'd offer to be your maid of honor," Lorna said, "but bridesmaid's dresses are always so ugly."

"I appreciate the offer anyway," Maureen said. "I think I might ask Aster to be my matron of honor. She's been so glum lately. It might cheer her up."

"She wouldn't mind wearing a bridesmaid's dress one bit. But she's still scared. So are some of the writers." She gave a knowing look. "I kind of sat in on the meeting you all had before you left."

"Did you? I'm wondering if the information they shared was helpful at all to the cops."

"It should have been," Lorna insisted. "Like what the cowboy writer said about breaking down a gun so it will fit in a small space. That was interesting. Who'd think of that? Putting a big, long gun into a purse or a backpack."

"A backpack? A backpack. Somebody recently said something about a backpack." Maureen struggled to remember, then snapped her fingers. "Got it."

"What? Who?" Lorna prompted.

"It was one of the photos from the bus stop kids. One of the first ones that turned up. A neatly dressed man wearing a face mask. They thought he might be a teacher. *He* had a backpack."

"Do you think either of the cops picked up on that like you just did?"

"I don't think Detective Taylor knew about it," Maureen speculated. "I'm sure Frank Hubbard will remember it, though."

"Are you going to call him?"

Maureen hesitated. "I don't know. He hasn't been too happy to hear from me lately."

"But what if he *doesn't* remember it," she insisted. "What if it's important? What if the teacher saw something? *Did* something?"

"Well, maybe I could call him. I could ask if I could have a look at that photo." She smiled. "I could tell him I have a feeling about it. He'll like that."

"Do you have a feeling about it?"

"You know something? I think I do." She reached for her phone.

"You have a feeling about that photo?" Hubbard's voice was gruff, but he sounded pleased at the same time. "Why didn't you say so before this?"

"I just now made the connection," she told him. "It might be something. It might be nothing. Can you send the photo over to me?"

"I'll dig it up, Doherty. Wait for it."

She waited. It didn't take long. She recognized the low curb where some kids sat, messing with their phones, waiting for the school bus, just in front of the thickly wooded area behind Aster's garden. The photo seemed larger than she'd remembered it. The photographer had focused on a boy in the foreground holding a beer can. Hubbard must have blown it up to get a closer look at the figure in the background. The curved brim of the bucket hat was pulled low enough to shade the top half of the person's face, and a small sprig of green—a flower or a leaf of some sort—was tucked into the hat band. A bit of dark hair showed over the ears. The lower half of the face was covered with a plain white face mask —the same kind everyone used to wear back in the Covid days. Everybody in

Florida has a bucket hat. Maureen had two or three of them herself. What about the sprig of greenery?

Lorna remained beside her, peering over her shoulder. "Is that helpful?"

"Not really," Maureen said. "At least nothing above his neck so far, anyway."

"The clothes look kind of ordinary," Lorna said. "A loose plain plaid shirt. Tight black jeans. Flared ankles. No designer labels on any of it, I'll bet."

"I can't make out a brand name on the backpack, either," Maureen said. "But look at the feet. Those shoes look like boots of some kind. See the heels?"

"Cowboy boots, maybe?" Lorna asked. "Like Reggie's?"

"Could be," Maureen agreed. "And like Walter's."

"Maybe that man is somebody who writes about cowboys and horses too, like Paul and Judy and Walter."

Or somebody who writes about everything—like a ghostwriter.

Chapter 42

The germ of an idea had taken root in Maureen's mind, and it was an idea she didn't like. The guy in the picture clearly wasn't Paul, he of the tattoos and bulging muscles. This man was average height, slim, and had dark hair. The eyes, shaded by the bucket hat, could be the plain, non-Superman variety she'd already noted. She'd been so relieved when Frank Hubbard had explained that Carleton's appearance in Aster's garden on the day of Terry Holiday's death had been explained to his satisfaction, and that she wasn't harboring a murderer under her roof after all. Was it possible that Hubbard had been wrong about that, or that Aster had been confused about the time she'd sworn Carleton was with her at the shop? Was it also possible that Carleton Fretham had been present at the scene of Walter's death too?

"I hope, hope, hope I'm wrong about all this," she murmured, almost forgetting that Lorna was still close beside her, peering over her shoulder at the glowing computer screen.

"All what? Do you recognize the teacher—or whoever this is?" She pointed to the person who, in Maureen's mind, looked more like the ghostwriter every minute.

"I'm afraid maybe I do," she admitted. "And it's somebody I've learned to admire and respect."

"You mean a friend of yours could have offed a couple of writers?"

"Not exactly a friend," Maureen explained. "But I sure would hate to think he's an evil person. He's been very kind to me."

"Are you going to tell the cop?" Lorna wanted to know. "You don't sound real sure about this."

"You're right. I'm nowhere near sure."

"Maybe you'd better sleep on it," she suggested. "You've got a lot on your plate right now. Just engaged and planning a wedding and running a hotel and just back from a honeymoon. No wonder you're confused. Why don't you spend the rest of the day sorting things out? You keep everything so organized around here. Why not write all your ideas down and sort them out like you and Ted do with the menus?"

Sorting things out. It was a worthwhile idea. "The plaid shirt," Maureen said aloud. "It's sort of like the kind Judy wears."

"So you think the picture could be Judy?" Lorna moved closer, so that her head was between Maureen and the computer screen. "I don't think so."

"No. It's not Judy. She's shorter and more curvy. That plaid shirt is loose, though. It's hard to tell the body shape of the teacher—if this guy is a teacher."

"Or if this teacher is a guy," Lorna corrected. "Cover up his head with something and see what you think about just the body."

Maureen reached for the screen, covering the masked face with one hand. "I see what you mean. Now the teacher—if this is a teacher—looks kind of like anybody—or nobody."

"Right," Lorna declared. "This is what you'd get from central casting if you wanted a 'background actor.' It could be a man or a woman. A non-speaking part. It's an 'extra' or an atmosphere actor. They only appear in the background; sometimes the scene is even out of focus." She patted perfectly styled hair. "I was *never* an extra."

"You said a man or a woman." Maureen tapped the screen. "Do you think this could be a woman?"

"It definitely could be a woman. Who do you have in mind?"

"Elaine," Maureen stated. "I think it might be Elaine because of the shiny tight black jeans. She might be wearing a shirt like Judy's and boots like Walter's or Paul's just to confuse whoever might see her."

"So, are you going to tell the cop?" Lorna demanded once again.

"Maybe I'd better sleep on it," Maureen said. "It's a crazy idea, isn't it? Maybe I'm thinking it's Elaine because Aster thinks she's guilty. Or because she wrote that book about strangling people. Like you said, it could be *anybody*."

"Even the friend you like and admire and hate to think is an evil person?"

Deep sigh. "Yes. Even Carleton. But whoever it is could have a rifle in that backpack, and could have taken it into the woods and shot Walter with it and then disassembled it again and walked away looking as innocent as an extra in a movie."

"I hope you're going to be careful, Maureen." Lorna stood, looking down at her. "I hope you're not going to discover whatever it was that Walter found out. Whatever it was that got him killed. I like you a lot, you know, but I don't want you to join me here on the other side for a long, long, time. Tell the cop."

"I'll tell him," she said. "I'll tell him as soon as I figure out a couple of things. I don't have enough yet." Again, she studied the picture, tapping the screen, making the image of the person's head larger, but less distinct. "Lorna, do you know anything about plants?" She pointed to a spot of green on the hat.

"Plants? Not me. Just the expensive flowers that come in bouquets or corsages. Roses. Orchids." She sighed. "I always loved it when men gave me orchids. Green leaves? Not me. Why don't you ask Aster about it? She's the gardener."

"Of course. That's what I'll do. I'll call her right now. Thanks, Lorna."

She tapped in the number for the house phone in the Dawn Wells Suite, knowing that Aster no longer answered her cell phone.

"Is that you, Maureen?" Aster's voice was hushed. "I haven't given this number to anybody."

"It's me, Aster," Maureen told her. "I really need your help with something. Could you take the elevator up here to the third floor? It would only take a minute." No reply. She tried again. "There's no one here except me," she said. "And Finn, of course. I'd really appreciate it."

"Wait a sec. I'll ask Peter." There was a muffled sound, as if Aster had put her hand over the phone. Did Maureen actually hear *two* indistinct voices? And was one of them male?

Maybe.

She waited. "All right, Maureen," Aster said. "Peter says it's okay. We'll be right up."

Did Aster say WE?

Lorna's suggestion had been a good one. As soon as Aster arrived, she was able to identify the green leaf on a twig easily. "I never hope to see this in *my* garden," she said. "It's more apt to grow in the woods. It's poison sumac. Why anyone would wear it on their hat, though, is beyond me. That stuff can give you a terrible rash."

"I don't get why it's on a hat either," Maureen agreed, "but look, as long as you're here, will you take a look at the person wearing the hat? Does he—or she—seem familiar to you at all?"

Aster pulled a pair of glasses from the deep front pocket of a white apron—similar to the ones the workers in Ted's kitchen wore—and perched them on her nose.

"Sure. I'll take a look. Peter told me to help you in every way I can, didn't you, Peter? He's worried about business getting so bad you might have to close the inn. Then what would become of all the gang? Gert and Molly and George and Sam?" She peered more closely at the picture. Maureen looked around the room. Did Aster think Peter was here?

"It looks a little bit like a lot of folks we know, doesn't it?" Aster asked. "Look. That's one of Judy's plaid shirts she wears when she rides Chief Charlie. I guess the poison sumac would be Judy's too. She's so into poison. And there's Elaine's shiny black pants. They're made out of that spandex cloth she wears every chance she gets. There's Paul's old US Navy Boonie hat he used to wear when he signed the Navy Seal books. Oh, hey. There's dear Walter's genuine Cracker Western riding boots he was so proud of, and even Lynn Ellen's Naughty Nurse Nancy face mask. Quite a clever costume, don't you think so? It's the whole Murder Incorporated critique group."

Maureen did think so, and wished she'd figured it out herself. *I'll just bet smarty-pants Fretham would have spotted it all right away too,* she thought. *I'll ask him some day when all this is over.* "Now just to figure out who that is wearing the costume," she said aloud. "Who do you think it is, Aster?"

"Same as always. It's Elaine." She backed away from the screen. "She's a professional costume designer. Didn't you know that? Frank Hubbard almost had me convinced that it isn't her. I even sat next to her. I spoke to her at that party the rich man threw. She could have killed me right then. I even shook her hand at that meeting you made us all go to. I need to get back into my suite and lock the door. Goodbye, Maureen. Goodbye, Finn." She pulled open the door. "Come on, Peter." That was when Maureen saw the man. It was definitely Peter, and there was not a camera or a mirror in sight. Out the door went Aster. Peter gave Maureen a broad wink and shimmered away beside his wife.

Maureen decided that she had enough information to share with Frank Hubbard after all, excluding the new part about Peter's ghost. She called him. "This may sound kind of nuts," she began.

"Why does that not surprise me, Doherty? But go ahead. Lay it on me. I'm ready for any help I can get. Did you learn something new from that picture?"

"I did, with a little help from Aster Patterson."

"Aster again, huh? I don't suppose she's told you how she faked that ghost thing in her shop window, did she?"

"No, sir. We didn't discuss that at all."

"I didn't think so," he grumbled. "Does she still think the lady writer who knows how to strangle people killed Terry Holiday?"

"Kind of. Can you bring that picture up on your screen now? Aster has an interesting interpretation of it."

"I've got it. I'm looking at it right now. What's your feeling about it?"

She actually *did* have a feeling about it and told him so. Frank Hubbard was silent while she repeated as closely as she could what Aster had said about the person in the hazy shot. "It's one of the Murder Incorporated group for sure," she said. "Maybe Aster is right. Maybe it is Elaine."

Even as she spoke, she regretted the words—and the thought. Carleton and Elaine had looked so happy together—so right together. It would be terrible if one of them turned out to be a killer.

Chapter 43

Once the conversation with Hubbard came to a close—as unsatisfying as the conversation had been—she struggled to get her mind off of ghosts and back onto business. As Lorna had so recently pointed out, she had a lot on her plate right now. She took the stairs down to the lobby, said hello to Shelly, and opened her office door. She reached across the desk for the old-fashioned spindle with the spike on it that Penelope Josephine had used for bills and the like. Maureen still used it for gift shop-related merchandise records, keeping them an easily identified distance from the other inn-related expenses. Ted had warned her that she might impale her hand someday in her haste to sort things out, but it had never happened, and besides, she liked the look of the old-time gadget on the desk.

She pulled the stack of slips from the spike, matching them with the business credit card statements, realizing that a quick inventory of back stock was in order. Sales had been better than expected on several items. She could go to the stockroom at the rear of the shop and take a quick inventory and at the same time, select something special to wear for her late date with Ted.

She passed through the lobby. In the next room, the player piano plinked one of the popular old tunes in the regular rotation—an upbeat version of "Smoke Gets in Your Eyes."

There were only a few guests on the porch as she made her way to the shop entrance. She paused to admire the window display, recognizing the satin outfit Lorna had worn the night before. She slipped the key into the lock and stepped inside, pulling the door closed behind her. The CLOSED sign remained in place. Evening hours were the best for the shop during a slow time like the one they were experiencing. "When Haven gets back to normal after the killer gets caught," she told herself, "I'll need extra help to keep up with it all."

Bypassing the counter and pushing the dressing room door open, she proceeded through the narrow corridor to the stockroom—such as it was. Someday she planned to add to the back of the place, but for now she made do with plain pipe racks of hanging garments, each one with a protective plastic cover, the old pink table from Penelope's storage locker that served as the marking table where price tags were affixed by hand to each garment. There was one straight-backed chair for a worker to sit in, and if there were two working, the other one made do with a sturdy, partially open wooden carton where cleaning materials, ironing spray starch, fabric deodorizers, and the like were stored. "Not pretty, but all functional," she told herself, and approached the hanging rack. She noted stock numbers and codes of things to reorder on her phone. She pulled the strapless white satin mini she'd admired on Lorna earlier from the rack. "This one, with one of the wide cubic zirconia chokers, will be perfect for my date with Ted." She put the dress aside, realizing that although the diamond choker Lorna had worn with it had most likely come from Tiffany's, the general effect would be fine. She sat on the wooden box, and emailed orders to one of her favorite Boston wholesalers, confident that the desired merchandise would arrive in a timely fashion. Once again, she was grateful to the liberal-spending habit of Martin Malone, whose frequent use of his credit card had continued unabated since his arrival at the inn.

She stood, carefully putting the plastic-wrapped satin dress over one arm. The man's voice came from close behind her.

"Leaving so soon? I'd like to see you try the dress on."

Without turning, she knew that Carleton Fretham was in the room with her.

"Sit down," he commanded. She obeyed, resuming her place on the box. He moved around her, placing the long rifle on the table between them. He stared at her, the raw light from the bare bulb overhead reflecting in his thick glasses.

"What do you want? How did you get in here?" she demanded.

He held a ring full of keys in the air, jingling them. "Master keys. You shouldn't be so careless with them. That ancient safe in your office is so easy to crack, a child could do it."

"What do you want?" she asked again. "I have no money here."

"I already grabbed the few bucks that was in the register out front." He grinned. "You're even poorer than I am, aren't you? It doesn't matter. I'll be long gone when they find you. New name. New address. New personality. I can be anyone I want to be. You've seen me do it. Doctor, lawyer, Indian chief . . . anyone I want to be." He stroked the gun barrel. He wore latex gloves. "I've added a silencer since I shot Walter with it. I didn't need a gun when I killed Holiday—that no-talent scum. He didn't deserve to live in the first place."

Fretham was always awfully pleased with himself. She tried flattery. "The book you wrote for him—*How to Make Your City Famous and Attract Big Spenders*—was a wonderful piece of work. I'm putting your ideas to use myself. You must be proud of it."

"It may be the best thing I've ever written." He didn't look happy about it. "It's already on a few major bookstore chains' bestseller lists. I won't be surprised if it shows up on the *Times* nonfiction list before long." He shook his head. "Don't you realize what all that meant in the book world?" He didn't wait for an answer. "It meant that Terry Holiday would be doing a national book tour. It meant that the dumb SOB would be signing *my* book with his stupid fake name. It meant that the moron would be able to take credit for *my* months of research. *My* talent. *My* brain. I couldn't very well let that happen, could I? Could I?"

Maureen didn't—couldn't—answer the question. Fortunately, he didn't press the point, but continued talking. "He'd started to hang around when we all met at Aster's place. Usually he'd just be in the bookshop, pretending to be a customer, but sometimes he'd be out in the garden right behind her house. He used to actually press his ugly nose against the living room picture window, trying to hear what we were saying. I tried to get Aster to pull down the shades, but she was sorry for the guy." He looked away from her for a moment, and she took the opportunity to glance quickly around the room again, hoping to see something, anything, that might help her to get away from him. Behind the glasses, the brown eyes focused on her once again. His right hand fondled the wooden stock of the rifle that lay between them. "Oh, don't worry about fingerprints on this baby. Wiped her clean. Anyway, when my agent approached me with the assignment, I could hardly believe that the little twit had come up with enough money to hire a ghost—but he had. So I took it. It wasn't as though I had to meet with him or interview him or anything. I just had to do the work and take the money."

Carleton's voice droned on—still talking about himself.

"It was so easy." The broad grin, so incongruous within the situation, was terrifying. Maureen looked down, tempted to close her eyes. "I just walked up to him. 'Hi, Terry,' I said. 'How're you doing?' The poor slob was thrilled that I—a *real* writer—would speak to him, call him by name. I could tell he was excited. He was practically dancing. 'Hi, Carleton,' he said. I'd already made the noose. It was laying there on a cement garden bench. He saw me pick it up. He saw me walk toward him. It didn't matter. He was so happy." Again, the awful grin. "He didn't even catch on to what was happening until I pulled it tight. 'Goodbye, Terry,' I said, and I swear he tried to smile at me."

Maureen tried to inch the wooden box backwards. It squeaked. His hand tightened on the gunstock. "I hope you're not thinking of running away, Maureen." His voice was calm, quiet, almost polite. "I don't want to have to shoot you in the back. These bullets make a tiny hole going in, but the exit wound can be quite messy."

She thought about the pointed spike on the spindle on her office desk. If only it were here on the marking table. She could stab his hand with it. *Wishful thinking.* "There was a picture of you. You wore the Hawaiian shirt from my shop. Aster Patterson testified that you were at the bookshop with her."

"So easy. I was with her. I killed Holiday, made sure the flowers covered him up pretty well, and went right into the shop, and we had a nice long chat about the publishing business." He grinned. "So easy."

There was a long silence. Maureen didn't want to say anything that might upset him. Carleton looked nervous enough already, and his hand was too close to that trigger. She thought about what he'd said about that small bullet hole. But one thing Carleton liked talking about was himself. *He loves showing off all the things he knows,* she thought. *He's so sure he's smarter than everybody else.* Smarty-pants.

She decided to take a conversational risk.

"I saw another picture," she said. "There was someone at the edge of the woods. Someone with a backpack. I thought it could have been Elaine. Was it you?"

He made a scoffing noise. "Elaine? Why? Because of the sleazy pants?"

She nodded. "Well, yeah."

"I'm disappointed in you, Maureen. I really am. I didn't think the dumb cop would figure it out, but I thought you'd get it." Again, the awful grin. "Walter finally got it."

"Is that why Walter had to die?" She knew it was a bold question, but she also knew how much he liked to brag. *Keep him talking.* "Was it because he found out what you'd done? How you'd killed Terry Holiday?"

"He found out because I told him what I'd done. How I'd done it. I thought that of all people, he'd understand." He looked away from her for a second—staring into space—then snapped his attention back to her. Back to the gun lying between them. "He was a ghostwriter. He knew exactly what it's like to work your heart out on a project. Get every detail right and then have some no-talent slug get all the credit for it. I was sure he'd know that I'd done the right thing—sure he'd understand."

"And he didn't?" *Keep him talking. Someone will come. Just keep him talking about himself.*

"Oh, he understood. How could he not?" The man sounded absolutely crestfallen. His voice broke as though he was near tears.

"What did he say?" She pressed for more information.

"Walter said that what I had done was wrong. He said it with a straight face. He said it was against the law. Can you believe that? The stupid *law*!" Carleton struck the table hard with his open palm. "As if that dumb bastard Holiday hadn't violated all that was right and holy by putting his worthless name on *my* book. Walter said he could help me." He changed his tone then, tilting his head from side to side, speaking in a high falsetto singsong voice. "I can help you, Carleton. This is a terrible thing to have on your conscience. I'll go with you when you confess to the police. I can make them understand why you feel the way you do." He stared at Maureen for a long, silent moment, then spoke in his normal voice. "I knew right then that I had to kill him. Soon. Before he could tell anyone else."

Stall. Keep him talking.

"You had a plan then?"

"Oh, yes. A beautiful plan. He needed to know—you see, don't you, that we—all of our little writing community—could not tolerate his betrayal. His disloyalty."

"All of you?" That question slipped out. *All of them?*

He nodded, waved gloved hands in the air, letting go of the gun for that instant. "I dressed the part. I made up a costume out of thrift store clothes." An evil smirk. "Damn clever, if I do say so myself."

Maureen understood. "Judy's shirt," she recited. "Elaine's pants. Lynn Ellen's face mask, Paul's hat, even Walter's boots."

His look was almost admiring. "You *are* quite bright. It was a brilliant idea. Anyway, when he told me he'd help me, naturally, I agreed that I'd listen to what he had to say. Oh, I was so sincere. So grateful. So willing to do the right thing."

"But how did you get him to go into the woods?" *Keep him talking. Ask questions.* She shifted her position on the box ever so slightly.

"That was easy. Walter was such a do-gooder. He used to go over there every morning to feed the damned squirrels. He'd bring a big bag of dried corncobs for them. He invited me to go with him and we'd talk, make arrangements for me to make things right. He told me I could bring some peanuts. In the shell. I told him that was what was in the backpack. Then while he was busy making squirrel noises, handing out the corn, I snapped my buddy here together." He fondled the gun again. "And shot him." Carleton rubbed his chin with one hand, looking thoughtful. "Then I shot a couple of those damned squirrels, just because I knew he loved the little rodents. I don't think he ever figured out what the costume meant, though, like you did. Too bad. That would have made it perfect."

"A perfect crime? Frank Hubbard says there is no such thing."

"Hubbard!" He scoffed. "He hasn't figured out the first one yet, let alone Walter's, and he won't get—well, yours—right, either. Sorry, Maureen." He turned his head slightly, looking down at the gun. Fondly. *He's in love with the damned thing.* With one hand, she felt the open side of the wooden box. Her fingers touched metal. A metal can. Round and cool to the touch. It had a cap on it. She moved her hand again. Another can. This one was uncovered, the spray button exposed. It must be something she'd used lately. *Think! What is it?*

Think, she told herself, trying to remember. *I used some furniture polish on the mirror frame,* she recalled, *and I used some disinfectant spray in the bathroom. Both of them have missing caps, and both of them have plenty of alcohol in them.* She grabbed the closest can, aimed at his face, and pressed the button.

He screamed. Squealed, actually, tearing the dripping glasses away. He dug at his eyes with both gloved hands. She dropped the can, grabbed the discarded glasses, and ran for the entrance to the shop. She heard him stumbling, bumping onto the wall, trying to reach her. She burst onto the porch. He followed.

"Get him," she called. George and Sam didn't need to know anything further. They got him. Actually, they sat on him, while Maureen called 911.

Chapter 44

All of the rockers on the porch were abandoned at once while the occupants crowded around the chaotic scene.

"She blinded me," Carleton yelled. "I can't see! The woman is crazy. Someone help me. Get my glasses away from her!"

Eyes turned in Maureen's direction. She slipped the glasses into her pocket. "The police are on the way." She tried to keep her voice steady, her manner calm. "He had a gun."

George and Sam had not lessened their hold on the man. In fact, Sam had put a large hand on the back of the man's neck, pressing the side of his face onto the floor. "Calm down, Carleton," he ordered. "You heard the lady. The police are coming."

"I want my lawyer," Carleton squeaked. "She's a crazy woman. Give me my glasses."

The green door swung open. Ted pushed his way through the gathering onlookers. Putting one protective arm around Maureen's shoulders, he stretched the other arm in front of him with a warning hand facing the crowd. "Back off," he growled.

Sirens howling, lights flashing, two police vehicles pulled up onto the sidewalk in front of the inn. Frank Hubbard climbed out of the first one, slowly, deliberately, followed by another man in plainclothes. A uniformed officer left the second car in a hurry, bounding up the stairs, gun drawn, looking back toward Hubbard as if seeking direction. A second uniform followed.

Haven's top cop took his time. On the top step, he looked down at the struggling Fretham, then faced Maureen. "What's going on here, Doherty? You reported a man with a gun."

"It's Carleton Fretham. He broke into the stockroom. He had a rifle." She was surprised that she sounded so normal. "He was going to kill me." Ted's arm tightened. A low groan escaped him.

"She's a crazy woman," Fretham insisted. "Give me my glasses. She threw acid in my face. Tried to blind me."

Hubbard paused for a long moment. He pointed to Fretham. "Cuff that one."

"You have the right to remain silent . . ." One of the uniformed officers droned the familiar Miranda warning, while the other assisted Carleton to his feet and fastened his hands, still gloved, behind him.

"You say he had a gun?" Hubbard asked.

"A rifle. It's on the marking table in the gift shop stockroom." Maureen pointed to the still-open gift shop door. "The stockroom door is open too."

Hubbard gave a head-jerk, signaling to the man who'd accompanied him to approach the shop. "Take an evidence bag with you," he said. "Use gloves." He looked on, without further comment, until the two cops, with the still-complaining Carleton between them, left the porch, placed their prisoner into the vehicle, and drove away.

"All right then, everybody. The show is over. Move along." Hubbard waved a hand at the onlookers. "Nothing more to see here." He approached Maureen. "You'll come with me now, Doherty. I'll need a statement."

"I'll come with her," Ted announced. It was not a request.

"Okay." Hubbard turned and walked down the stairs, followed by the man with a long narrow evidence bag. Ted motioned to Sam. "Tell Joyce to take over. I'll call as soon as I can," and taking Maureen's hand, followed.

Hubbard's cruiser had just pulled into a space next to the Haven police station marked CHIEF. Maureen recognized the

Lexus a few spaces away. Nora Nathan, the attorney who specialized in criminal cases for Jackson, Nathan and Peters, had apparently already arrived to defend Carleton Fretham.

Maureen and Ted followed Hubbard inside. The plain-clothes officer was right behind them, carrying the evidence bag. Fretham's whining voice could be heard from the nearby single barred cell that served as a place to hold prisoners temporarily while their immediate fate was being determined. "Talk to my lawyer," he demanded. "She'll tell you. I've done nothing wrong. Anyone in my position would do the same. Arrest Maureen Doherty. She attacked me for no reason." Hubbard took a seat behind a tall desk. Maureen and Ted remained standing, Ted's arm once again across her shoulders.

Maureen recognized Nora, who sat in the cell facing Fretham. She recalled that she'd once needed the capable woman's legal expertise herself. "Please don't say anything more, Mr. Fretham," Nora said. "Anything you say here can be used against you. Anything at all."

"She's lying if she says I killed those men." His voice grew louder. "And she's a thief too. She stole my glasses and tried to blind me."

Hubbard addressed Maureen. "Do you have the man's property?"

"Property?"

"His glasses." He held out his right hand.

"Oh, yes." She reached into her pocket. "Here they are."

He examined the glasses, turning them over. "He's claiming you threw something in his face. What was it?"

"A spray disinfectant. I knew he couldn't follow me if he couldn't see," she explained.

He held the glasses by one of the long temple pieces. "I see. These are the glasses you took from Mr. Fretham?"

"Yes, they are."

"I'm going to turn them over to his attorney so that he can read the necessary paperwork."

"That's fair," she agreed, then added, "she'll need to clean them."

"Of course." He reached inside a desk drawer, producing an open package of tissues. He handed glasses and tissues to the closest uniform, pointing toward the cell. "Give these to Nora."

Carleton's voice again. Loud. Complaining. "You'd better make her stop lying. No matter what she says I told her. I'm an innocent man. She's a lying crook."

Nora said, "Please don't talk anymore, Mr. Fretham. You don't need to tell them anything right now." She spoke louder. "Let me handle this from here on."

"Okay. But remember, she lies."

Nora used the kind of voice one might use to quiet a troubled child. "Just relax, Mr. Fretham. You don't have to say anything. I'm here for you. Look, here are your glasses."

He reached for the glasses and put them on without a *thank you*. "She's going to say I confessed to murder, don't you understand? She lies. *And* steals."

"If he keeps talking," Ted whispered close to Maureen's ear, "he'll convict himself right here and now. He sure loves to brag about himself. Look at Hubbard's face."

He was right. Hubbard leaned forward in his chair, not speaking, his expression rapt.

Carleton raised his voice, sounding whiny. Petulant. "Maybe I need a better lawyer."

Nora didn't respond. Maureen could imagine what thoughts the very capable attorney might be having. Hubbard spoke. "Do you wish to dismiss counsel, Mr. Fretham?"

Fretham sighed a long, obviously fake sigh. "No. She'll do. There's not much choice in a small town like this, is there?"

Nora's response was low, unintelligible. Hubbard turned his attention to Maureen. "Okay, Doherty, let's get your statement. Is it all right with you if Ted here listens?"

"Yes."

"I'm recording. Okay?"

"Yes," she said, and proceeded to repeat to him, as accurately as she could, the chilling conversation that had taken place in the stockroom. He nodded occasionally as she spoke, but made no comment until she'd finished.

"He admitted to both killings?" he asked. "He said he strangled Terry Holiday with the cord and then shot Walter Griffith with the gun we found inside your gift shop, is that correct?"

"That's correct." She shuddered slightly, realizing once again how close she'd come to being Carleton's third victim.

Chapter 45

Maureen and Ted were together in the cocktail lounge when the breaking news of Carleton Fretham's arrest for the murders of Walter Griffith and Terry Holiday flashed on the TV set behind the bar.

"I think you were right when you told me if Carleton kept talking, he'd convict himself," Maureen said. "I'm sure Nora did the best she could, invoking his fifth amendment rights against self-incrimination, but he just can't help bragging about himself. He still must think he's smarter than everybody else."

"He was smart enough to wipe his gun clean of fingerprints, but not smart enough to know the bullet that killed Walter could be easily traced to that gun," Ted said.

"They're saying over at Quic Shop that he admitted to Hubbard that he'd killed Terry Holiday too, just the same way he admitted it to me. Bragging about how cleverly he'd planned it." She shook her head. "He even offered to help Frank write a book about his favorite murder cases."

Hilda rushed into the lounge. "Are you watching the news? The killer is caught!"

Maureen gave her a hug. "What a relief for Haven. For all of us."

"That's what I came in to tell you. I just got a call. That big beach wedding is back on again, along with reservations for the wedding party and guests. They want a sit-down dinner too, and wedding cake and all the fixins."

The player piano interrupted "I Love You Truly" with a jazzy rendition of "Happy Days Are Here Again." Hilda gave a subtle wink with a whispered, "Billy Bedoggoned knows. I'd better get back to the desk. There may be more reservations coming."

Ted pointed upward. "It looks like this old roof is going to be over our heads for a while after all."

"It's a good thing. There's a leak starting around the window in my suite. Now we'll be able to get it fixed," she said.

"You can start taking reservations for those Wednesday night bingo parties."

"Aster will be able to go home and open the bookshop."

"The mystery writers will be able to have their meetings there."

"The regular customers will fill the dining room every day."

Maureen grew silent, watching the angelfish, swimming in their lazy circles, seemingly content with their undersea castles and make-believe treasure chests and regular meals of nutritionally balanced, shrimp-flavored, veterinarian-approved tropical fish food. "Normalcy will be nice," she observed.

An excited Hilda dashed back into the lounge. "A reporter from *Dog Fancier* magazine just called. He's coming with a photographer to do a feature article on Yappy Hour."

"I'll be sure to tell Finn," Maureen promised. "He'll love having his picture in a magazine."

"We're going to be awfully busy," Ted said. "That's a good thing, isn't it?"

"Things seem to work out for the best, don't they?" She focused on the fishes again. "We're lucky that way."

"Lucky that we found each other." He pulled her close.

"Lucky that Penelope Josephine left the inn to me, even if we don't have the full story of why." She leaned in to receive his soft kiss.

"You'll have time now to dig into that trunk for answers and write that book you've been talking about." He smiled.

"I'm lucky I'll have writer friends to help me. I'm so glad that none of them were guilty." She returned the smile.

"We were lucky that Martin Malone showed up with that winning Lotto ticket just in time to keep us afloat for a while."

That wasn't ordinary luck. That was Zoltar. She didn't speak the thought out loud.

"I have a big beach wedding to plan. Let's make it Hawaiian-themed, like a rehearsal for our own beach wedding." Enthusiasm rang in his voice.

"With Tiki torches and Hawaiian wedding clothes and a coconut-rum wedding cake and ginger flower leis for everybody," she added.

"I guess this means that we might not have time for our own wedding for a while." He frowned.

"I know. But it will be worth waiting for." She reached up and touched his face.

"It will be perfect." His smile returned.

"Yes. And we'll go back to the MaryAnna motel for our honeymoon."

"This time we'll drive across the Seven Mile Bridge."

"We'll stop at some of the Keys along the way. Key Largo, Islamorada. Marathon, Bahia Honda," she recited happily.

"We'll go back to that place on Duval Street that has the Zoltar machine again," he promised, "and learn what our future will be like."

"We'll certainly do that," she agreed, already knowing exactly what words would be printed on the blue card.

Make sure your relationship is full of affection,
good conversation, emotional connection
and shared dreams and projects. Truth and
sensitivity are the foundations of love.
Zoltar Knows All.

RECIPES

Joyce's Triple Coconut Rum Cake

Serves 8 (generous slices)

For the coconut cake
2 cups of all-purpose flour
2 ½ teaspoons of baking powder
1 teaspoon of salt
1 cup of shredded coconut
1 cup of softened butter
1 ½ cups of sugar
1 teaspoon of coconut extract
2 large eggs
1 cup of coconut milk
¼ cup of coconut rum

Preheat the oven to 350 degrees F. Spray three 6-inch cake pans (or two 8-inch cake pans) with cooking spray and line with parchment paper. Whisk together the flour, baking powder, salt, and shredded coconut. In another bowl, cream the butter and sugar together with an electric mixer on medium speed until it gets fluffy. Then add the coconut extract and the two eggs. Mix until completely mixed. Add half of the flour mixture and half of the coconut milk. Mix well. Repeat with the second half of the flour and coconut milk.

Divide the batter between the pans evenly and bake them for 20 minutes or until the centers are set and a toothpick inserted comes out clean. Let cakes cool in the pans for 10 minutes, then transfer them to a wire rack to cool completely. When they are cool, brush the top of each one with coconut rum.

For the coconut frosting
1 cup of butter, softened
1 teaspoon of coconut extract
2 tablespoons of cream or milk
3 cups of powdered sugar
2 cups of toasted coconut

In the bowl of a standard mixer, cream the butter until it is smooth and there are no lumps. Add the coconut extract, the cream, and half of the powdered sugar. Mix this on low speed until combined, then medium-high speed until the powdered sugar is all mixed in. Repeat with remaining powdered sugar.

Place one cake layer on a plate stand and top with frosting and a layer of toasted coconut. Repeat with the other two layers.

Overnight Strawberry Cream Cheese-Stuffed French Toast Casserole

Serves 9 (generous slices)

16 ounces French bread, crusts removed and cut into cubes
8 ounces of cream cheese, cubed
4 cups of fresh strawberries, sliced
10 large eggs
2 cups milk
⅓ cup sugar
½ teaspoon vanilla extract
pinch of salt
powdered sugar for garnish

Lay half of the bread cubes over the bottom of a 9-by-13-inch pan. Place the cream cheese cubes on top of the bread cubes, then layer the sliced strawberries over the cream cheese and cover with the bread cubes that are left. Combine the eggs, milk, sugar, vanilla, and salt in a medium-sized bowl and mix well. Then pour the egg mixture all over the bread, pressing down to make sure the bread absorbs the liquid. Cover it and put in the refrigerator overnight. Take the pan out in the morning and leave it out while you preheat the oven to 375 degrees F. Uncover and bake for 30 to 40 minutes. Dust with powdered sugar before serving.

(Ted always uses fresh strawberries, but Joyce says that strawberry preserves work nicely too. She uses a 13-ounce jar of Bonne Maman strawberry preserves.)

Haven House 500-Degree Prime Rib Roast

Serves 8

Select a bone-in prime rib roast—about five pounds. Have the roast at room temperature. Set oven at 500 degrees F. When it reaches 500, put the roast in and leave it there for five minutes per pound. (So for the five pound roast, you'll leave it in the oven for 25 minutes. If it weighs more or less, just multiply the weight by 5.) Then—and this is important—TURN THE OVEN OFF and LEAVE IT CLOSED for two hours. (Ted uses some tape to close it to be sure no one else opens it by mistake.) Then take it out. It will be perfect!

Note: This works well for less expensive cuts of beef too!

Trader Vic's Original Mai Tai

Makes one drink

¾ ounce fresh lime juice
½ ounce orange curaçao (Ted uses Pierre Ferrand)
¼ ounce orgeat—an almond flavored syrup
(Lennie says you can get away with using amaretto)
¼ ounce rich demerara simple syrup (with 2-1 ratio water to sugar)
2 ounces aged, blended rum

Combine all ingredients with 12 ounces of crushed ice and some cubes in a shaker. Shake until chilled and pour, ice and all, into a double old-fashioned glass. Garnish with spent lime shell and mint sprig so it looks like a little island with a palm tree on it on the surface of your drink.

Notes: Fresh lime juice is critical. Don't squeeze too hard. Get just the juice, not the pith. Trader Vic did not use the cute umbrellas. He didn't like them. (But Maureen does. It's up to you.) Ted uses Appleton Estate Reserve Blend Rum, but any good blended molasses-based rum is okay.

Joyce's Creamy Coconut Pie

Serves 6 or 8

Dough for a single crust pie
Joyce makes hers from scratch, but you can use a 9-inch pre-made one.
1 ½ cups whole milk
1 cup sugar
¾ cup sweetened shredded coconut
3 large eggs, lightly beaten
3 tablespoons all-purpose flour
1 tablespoon melted butter
¼ teaspoon pure vanilla extract

Preheat oven to 350 degrees F. Using a 9-inch pie pan, trim crust to ½ inch beyond the rim and flute the edge. In a large bowl, combine milk, sugar, coconut, lightly beaten eggs, flour, and vanilla. Pour the mixture into the crust. Bake it until a knife inserted into the center comes out clean—45 to 60 minutes. Cool it to room temperature on a wire rack. Before serving, top it with homemade whipped heavy cream or Cool Whip. Sprinkle toasted coconut on top. Enjoy!

Haven House Hawiian Chicken

Serves 6

⅓ cup ketchup
⅓ cup soy sauce
⅓ cup packed brown sugar
2 tablespoons rice vinegar
1 tablespoon Worcestershire sauce
1 tablespoon sesame oil
1 ½ tablespoon minced garlic
1 ½ tablespoons fresh ginger, peeled and minced
3 pounds of skinless, boneless chicken thighs

Combine ketchup, soy sauce, rice vinegar, Worcestershire, sesame oil, garlic, and ginger in medium-sized bowl, mixing well for marinade. Put ¼ cup of the marinade into a small bowl and refrigerate for later use. Add the chicken to the remaining marinade, tossing to coat each piece evenly. Cover and refrigerate for 2 to 8 hours.

Preheat grill to medium. Put chicken on the grill, basting with the reserved marinade. Grill until done, about 15 minutes. Serve hot. Makes 9 servings.

Acknowledgments

Here's a somewhat overdue acknowledgment of my adopted home state of Florida. It's been an inspiration during my previous years as a travel writer—and currently as the locale of my fictional city of Haven!

My earliest impressions of Florida—on vacations dating back to the 1950s—and on actually moving here in the 1970s—centered on how *new* everything seemed to be. Rows of pretty pastel houses with spacious lawns, fruit trees, and graceful palms. Downtowns with sparkling tall buildings, plenty of shops and malls, and sprawling parking lots. Once in a while, we'd notice another new building going up, and we couldn't even recall what had been there the week before!

I'm from New England, where things don't change quickly, and a new building or a new neighborhood is something to be speculated upon and awaited with curiosity. We New Englanders are comfortable with our crooked streets, our varied architecture, the names of our famous men and women, places and things known the world over. In short—our history.

When Dan and I moved to our present home in Seminole, Florida, we were invited to join the Seminole Historical Society. An historical society for a city that was founded in 1975? I realized then that I'd become something of a "history snob." After all, kids on school trips in Boston visited Paul Revere's house. In Salem, we could walk around in the rooms where the witch trials were held in 1692 or even visit the jail where the poor souls were imprisoned. What kind of history could our new home offer?

It didn't take long to find out what a rich and varied history Florida has to offer. Writing the Haunted Haven series has given me the opportunity to weave bits and pieces of it into my stories. Within a few miles of our home, we can visit Jungle Prada, once the site of a Tocobaga Indian village from 1000 CE until 1600 CE. There's a nine-hundred-foot-long Indian mound there, composed of whelk and conch shells. In 1528, Conquistador Pánfilo de Narváez landed there and began an eight-year journey from Florida to the Pacific Ocean. Our Historical Museum highlights ancient archaeological treasures from tools and weapons and breastplates to bones of exotic animals. (Florida was once home to an armadillo the size of a Volkswagen!)

St. Augustine is home to America's oldest wooden schoolhouse—circa 1716. We've had our share of famous pirates, too. A favorite is José Gaspar, whose thirty-eight-year career of piracy includes attacking and robbing over four hundred ships in the Gulf waters, including the 11.75 million dollars in gold bullion that the US had paid Napoleon for the Louisiana Purchase. (His memory is kept alive by a raucous three-day celebration held in Tampa every February called "Gasparilla.")

Florida has its share of ghost stories too, and I've fit some of them into the plots of the Haunted Haven books. Lorna and Reggie like to go dancing in the haunted hallways of the 1887 Mediterranean Revival Casa Monica Hotel in St. Augustine, where ghosts in 1920 clothing waltz late into the night. There are at least six haunted hotels in Key West. Tampa has a wonderful haunted movie theater.

As I continue to research and write this series, I'm learning more and more appreciation for Florida's rich history. I look forward to sharing some of it as we follow Maureen and Ted's adventures. Finn and Lorna's too!